MOST OF ALL

"I better go up and change for dinner," she said, with a hint of laughter.

"From the way the food smells, my illustrious maid has outdone herself."

"You've outdone yourself too, Bradley."

"I have?"

"Inside here," she whispered, and glanced down at her heart.

Bradley was so touched he eased close to Elandra. Feeling the heat between them blazing, she longed to move closer, too, to move right to his soul. Instead she willed her desire away by running up the steps. From the bottom of the stairwell Bradley watched her until she was out of sight. God knows he wanted to make love to that woman more than anything on this earth. It was all he could think about lately—when he woke up, when he laid down at night, when he worked, when he did anything and everything. As certain as he was of his own existence, Bradley knew they were meant to be together. Their lovemaking would no doubt be *the* unforgettable moments of their lifetimes. They were magical already. Above all, they were in love. *Deeply, passionately*. Yet he had to be patient. He wanted Elandra to know that he truly loved her. Whatever it took, he would do.

ENJOY THESE SPECIAL
ARABESQUE HOLIDAY ROMANCES

HOLIDAY CHEER   (0-7860-0210-7, $4.99)
by Rochelle Alers, Angela Benson,
and Shirley Hailstock

A MOTHER'S LOVE   (0-7860-0269-7, $4.99)
by Francine Craft, Bette Ford,
and Mildred Riley

SPIRIT OF THE SEASON   (0-7860-0077-5, $4.99)
by Donna Hill, Francis Ray,
and Margie Walker

A VALENTINE KISS   (0-7860-0237-9, $4.99)
by Carla Fredd, Brenda Jackson,
and Felicia Mason

Available wherever paperbacks are sold, or order direct from the Publisher. Send cover price plus 50¢ per copy for mailing and handling to Penguin USA, P.O. Box 999, c/o Dept. 17109, Bergenfield, NJ 07621. Residents of New York and Tennessee must include sales tax. DO NOT SEND CASH.

MOST
OF ALL

Louré Bussey

Pinnacle Books
Kensington Publishing Corp.

http://www.pinnaclebooks.com

PINNACLE BOOKS are published by

Kensington Publishing Corp.
850 Third Avenue
New York, NY 10022

First Printing: November, 1997
10 9 8 7 6 5 4 3 2 1

Printed in the United States of America

One

Money is the master of some people. Sex is it for others. But love is everything to those who follow their hearts. Elandra was one who followed her heart and tried to live the right way. She liked people and went out of her way to show it. Yet she never listened to her heart when it came to men. Never listened to its voice screaming inside her *this isn't the one!* Never even understood she had another master too—loneliness. Always somewhere around, it moaned that no price was too high for someone to love her.

She didn't realize how much she was paying. Dan broke big promises and lied so much he forgot the truth, standing her up on special dates, like her birthday. He didn't compliment her about anything, ignored her wants, dismissed her dreams, made her second to his work, and nothing before his family, and overall took her for granted. But love has no sense, especially when gazes are so smoldering they whisper of wickedly sweet pleasure to come, and being in his arms melts you into silk, and kisses beckon a river of desire to flow down inside you, so that you are alive in a way that makes you ache to feel like that twenty-four hours of the day. Elandra was always weak for his seduction. The closeness and tenderness with someone was what she cherished. Heightening such moments were the most sensuous words and much grander promises, which eventually turned out to be words, syllables, letters and nothing more.

Elandra was surprising Dan at the office tonight. The past three months he was always working overtime and triple-time, trying to prevent his realty company from closing. He'd started Dan Tager Realty nine years ago, and business was great for the first six. It was the last three that were a struggle. Dan could barely pay for his extravagant office in the lavish Glazer Building.

Elandra stopped at the Chinese restaurant, and ordered his favorites for them both, General Tso's chicken with broccoli. Strawberry daiquiris came from the corner bar and grill. Riding the empty elevator to the 39th floor, the steaming food drowned out the usual ice-like air oozing from the vents. The meal and her unexpected presence were sure to surprise. However, there was an even greater one to share. The real surprise, the one the doctor had told her about earlier in the day, would put the biggest jolt into this night.

Six weeks pregnant. It was as exciting as it was frightening. Elandra speculated that Dan might not be ecstatic the instant he heard the news. After all, with business not at its peak, thoughts of supporting a child might be stressful. Even so, after a few moments of it sinking in, she was certain the amazement of creating a new life would make him feel like magic existed between them. That's what had happened to her. Hours later, Elandra was still floating. She couldn't believe it. Elandra Pat Lloyd was having a baby. A baby of her own.

She was bursting to tell her sister Crystal. Elandra had called her as soon as she stepped out of the doctor's office. Unfortunately, Crystal wasn't home, so Elandra had left a message on the answering machine. In fact, Crystal hadn't been home in a while. Elandra had been phoning her for nearly two weeks, leaving messages. None of the calls were returned. It made her wish they didn't live so far apart, Crystal in Nassau, Bahamas and Elandra in New York City.

Possibly her sister was too busy working, or had taken a much needed vacation, Elandra reasoned. It was better than giving in to those little creepings of worry that were thriving in the back of her mind.

After she stepped off the elevator, a smile spread Elandra's full lips. Such a surprise she had for Dan. The glow highlighted the sparkle in her wide, exotic eyes. As she sauntered down the long hall, any connoisseur of beauty would have just sat aside and watched the young woman. Staggeringly gorgeous, Elandra was. Satiny brown skin and thick, healthy hair were complemented by a body that boasted a small waist, shapely legs, a generous bosom and a high, apple-shaped bottom. In the two and a half years she'd dated Dan, and years before, men had always told Elandra she was beautiful, and followed her long distances simply to stare at her, asking her out on elaborate dates and offering her vacations to foreign lands she never could afford on her own. That being as it may, she never accepted any offer, never did anything to hurt Dan. He was embedded in her heart so deeply Elandra would sooner cut off a limb than betray him. Every day she prayed he would ask to marry her. Every night as her head hit the pillow, she tried on his last name. And although getting pregnant was purely accidental, she hoped it would prompt him to stop dragging his feet and ask the big question.

Odd sounds coming from the direction of Dan's office dimmed the smile on Elandra's face. Trying to identify what the noise was, she slowed her pace, stopped completely, then sped up. Her pump heels thumped hard in the lush, beige carpet. Two lines crept between her brows. The closer she was to Dan's office, the louder the sounds became. Clearer they became, too. So recognizable her heart beat rapidly. A full, overbearing sensation grew in her stomach. *No,* she told herself, *it's not that.* For those weren't just any sounds; they were moans— Dan's and someone else's.

The hammering in Elandra's heart spread to her ears and head. Her steps grew brisker. Hysteria assailed. She could hardly breathe, hardly think. Sweat moistened her forehead. Elandra felt desperate, helpless, on the verge of stumbling off a cliff. *Dan wouldn't do something like that to me. No, he doesn't treat me great all the time. What man does? But women problems were never our concern. I've been working too much at that secretarial pool. It's too hectic. I need a vacation. It's making me start to imagine things.*

Finally reaching the office, Elandra's wet palm turned the knob and faintly opened the door. What she saw made it evident imagination wasn't her problem. Dan and a woman were on the desk, locked together, kissing, fondling, stripping off each other's clothes, not even seeing her, their passion was so ignited. Far worse, it wasn't merely any woman he was with. Red hair tousled, overdone makeup all smudged, it was Joyce Washington, the colleague she had introduced Dan to at her company's Christmas party. Joyce was Elandra's boss.

"I don't believe this," Elandra gasped, drawing their eyes to her.

Straightaway they sprang up, clumsily gathering their clothes, putting them in front of them. "Elandra," Dan said, "I . . ."

Elandra's eyes shifted everywhere, filling with water. Her hand stuck to her chest.

"Oh my God, tell me this is not happening."

"I'm so embarrassed," Joyce prattled with a silly smile. "This is something we never expected."

Elandra just looked at her in strained silence, before going further into the room. It seemed like she moved without budging a foot. A haze of astonishment was pushing her, lifting her.

"I just don't believe it. How . . . Why . . . I . . ."

"I'm sorry," Dan said. He was breathing hard and rubbing his hand repeatedly over the curls in his hair. "I didn't want you to find out like this."

"Me either," Joyce added, buttoning her blouse. "We didn't want this to happen." She wiggled her broad hips into a too-small mini skirt, then tussled with a side zipper. "We didn't want to fall for each other, but it just happened."

Everything was unbelievable. Repeatedly Elandra questioned if she was really seeing what she was seeing, or was she still sleeping and dreaming? There Dan was, his cat-like eyes narrowed, his angular cheeks sunken deep, and the soft lips she loved to kiss constantly tucking themselves in and out because he had been caught in the act with another woman. There he was, standing half dressed right beside Joyce, after giving her, *Elandra's loving*.

No one liked Joyce around the office. Her I'll run you over, kill you and keep going attitude was such that few people talked to her outside of work issues. On top of that, she looked like a hooker, nothing like the executive that she was. Worse, her behavior matched her appearance. She was always flirting, always forcing herself on some man, taken and married men being her specialty. Many employees in the highly conservative accounting firm often drew conclusions as to how she had reached such a prominent status in the company. Rumor had it she had been around and around and around—while lying down.

"I would have done anything for you not to find out this way," Dan droned.

Joyce nodded. "That's true. He was always trying to figure out a nice way of telling you." She tossed a lock of hair from her eye. "But I guess there is no nice way."

Shaking her head, Elandra closed her eyes and opened them. Their babbling and this entire nightmare was making her dizzy. She gripped the side of the desk to get some equilibrium. "I don't . . . understand." She glanced at Joyce, but her eyes lingered on Dan.

His lingered back, and were still lingering on Elandra when he asked Joyce, "Will you leave Elandra and I alone for a moment?"

"Alone?" Joyce echoed, and looked like she didn't want to go anywhere. Fiercely blue eye-shadowed eyes were jumping from face to face, noting how intensely Dan and Elandra were looking at each other.

Elandra was trembling. His image was distorted by the water bubbling in her eyes.

"Yes, alone," Dan responded. "We have to end things the right way."

Joyce looked relieved. A subtle smile even tilted up her thin, red lips. She brushed past Elandra and went into the hall. Dan stepped toward the door and closed it behind her.

He turned back around to Elandra. She wiped her eyes clear and shook her head at him. "Here I am going to surprise you with dinner, but I'm the one who gets surprised." A strange laugh escaped, but stopped abruptly.

"I never meant to hurt you, Elandra."

"But you did." She wiped her eyes clear. "You sure weren't being sweet to me by sleeping with my boss."

One hand on his side, he rubbed back his hair with the other. "Things happen. At the Christmas party I gave her a business card. She wanted to buy a house and contacted me about three months ago."

Looking down, Elandra shook her head again. "So she was what you were working on, when I thought you were really working?"

"Look, she and I are more compatible. She's much more ambitious than you are."

Her head snapped up. "Ambitious? Ambitious, you say? So why did you lie and tell me you loved the way I was?" She took a step closer to him. Dodging winds of Joyce's acrid perfume, gazing into his eyes, Elandra didn't want to cry. She wanted to be strong. Nevertheless, without even feeling the water in her eyes, it ran down her cheeks.

"You made me think I was the most special person in the world. When I told you how my mother raised my sister and I, to be simple and be quiet, you told me you thought that was so sweet and old-fashioned and that was the kind of woman that you liked. How can you do something like that if you don't mean it? You were probably laughing at me. How can you build someone up, then break them down?"

"You were what I needed at the time, but now I need something else. You think I like hurting you?"

"I don't know what to think about you anymore." She wiped one cheek, then the other. "I saw things in you that I knew weren't right. But like a fool I ignored them. Ignored them because you did have that certain *sick* something that drove me crazy. You made me feel so desired. But most of all you told me you loved me." She knocked her chest. *"Me!"*

"Elandra, feelings change. We don't plan that they do. They just do."

"Wish I would have known that before—" She stopped herself. What did her beautiful surprise matter now?

"Before what? What were you going to say?"

"Nothing. You just go on with your ambitious woman. You're right. She's better for you."

"This is right for both of us, Elandra. You can find someone more like you, and I can be with someone more suited to me. I need someone ambitious, and bright, and outgoing, who is going places, doing things, someone who can be—I mean, someone who is helpful."

"Helpful?" She raised a brow. "That's an odd word in this discussion. Do you mean someone who can help you?"

Dan looked uncomfortable.

"I didn't say that."

"Yes, you did. Thought I wasn't smart enough to get it."

He was more uncomfortable.

"You were going to say that Joyce can help you. And I know what you mean—financially. She can help you get out of debt. Everyone knows how much money she has, because she loves to brag about it. On top of her executive salary, she's been lucky in the stock market. But no, she hasn't told you that, has she?"

Cat eyes darted around the room nervously, then found their way back to her. Dan took a few steps closer. "Keep your voice down before she hears you." He was whispering.

"I don't care if she hears me!"

"Come on. Stop it." He was taken aback by her feistiness.

"No, you stop lying! Your business is going down the tubes and you want someone to help you out. And I can't. Well, that should make me feel better, knowing *you want her money as much as her*, but somehow it doesn't. I'll never get over what I saw here. I can never erase that picture from my mind. You and *that slut!*"

"Jealousy doesn't look good on you, Elandra. I've never seen you act like this."

"You're right. You haven't ever seen me like this. Because I've never caught the man I loved with my boss!"

She took a deep breath.

"But I'm tired of people walking on me. I'm tired of being Ms. Nice. What did it get me? A broken heart. More than once, too. But you're not worth it! You're a weak, pathetic excuse for a man! You're making her think you love her too, but you only love yourself, Dan. I knew that long ago, but I didn't want to face it. You're a nothing and Joyce is a damn fool, but she'll learn that soon enough."

With that, Elandra stormed out the door, slamming it behind her. She met Joyce's self-satisfied smirk in the hall. They stood face to face.

"I hope this doesn't cause problems at work, Elandra. I can always recommend you to one of the other managers if you feel awkward around me. I know it would be hard for me to work with someone who took my man. I can't imagine how you must feel. But I know how much you need the job. I'll help you out."

Normally Elandra wasn't the type to unleash her rage. Her upbringing didn't encourage that. When other drivers cut her car off on the highway, she usually didn't react too much, other than to avoid an accident. When someone jumped in front of her in the post office or bank line, there was no commotion. Even when a known thief among her secretarial pool stole $100 out of her desk after Elandra had cashed her paycheck, she didn't drag her by the heels and beat her senseless; Elandra went in the bathroom and cried. And then there was the time a male co-worker grabbed her bottom. She was *mad,* rolled her eyes, but she didn't slap him or report him to superiors. However, there was just something about Joyce standing there so self-satisfied that raised Elandra's hand from her side and made it into a giant fist, which soon slammed her boss hard in the face. A scream filled the hall as Joyce grabbed her eye. Hearing her, Dan rushed into the hall. Elandra hurried on her way.

Wrapped in peach-scented bed covers that warm April night, Elandra reached for the night table phone and dialed Crystal's number for the seventh time since arriving home. Again she heard the machine, and once more she left a message. If her sister didn't call her soon, what was she going to do? Who was she going to talk to? How would she relieve this bottomless ache? Who was going to assure her that everything would soon be all right? Crystal had always been there for Elandra, as Elandra had been there for her. It was a bond few shared.

They had grown up poor, the maid's daughters, living with their mother in the servants' quarters on a wealthy family's estate. Elandra's father had died in a car accident when the girls were four and two. There were vague, positive memories of him. On the other hand, Elandra would always remember her mother as a good woman, a woman who loved God and church, a woman who would do anything for anyone, a woman who took good care of her children, a woman who worked so hard her heart just stopped. But Elandra embraced something else with her mother's memory—her mother was a broken woman.

Throughout the girls' lives, Helen Lloyd stressed that her daughters should always behave well and always know their place. According to her, their riches would be in heaven.

"If God intended for you to have it, you would have

had it already," she explained to her girls. "Don't set yourself up for disappointment and heartbreak and looking like a fool. Down here on the earth, *we* are here simply to serve God, not to enjoy life. Our joy is going to come later, when we go home."

It took a while for the words to beat all the hopes, and crazy dreams out of Elandra, but somehow they did without her even being aware of it. Anything that was too hard, she gave up. Anything that seemed too grand, she didn't even aim for. Along with it, she didn't feel she was worth fighting for when treated unfairly.

Her mother's attitudes even affected her love life. Helen never dated after her husband died, so she couldn't impart to Elandra that she should be treated like a queen or not treated at all. Helen had claimed she didn't get "those feelings" anymore. Quite the opposite, Elandra did have "those feelings." She wanted to be held on to like wind on a humid night, and kissed like her mouth was his last breath, and looked at like she was the sun when for centuries there had been only rain. More than that, she craved a companion to talk to, to laugh with, to be connected to, to appreciate her, to grow with, to give her heart and soul to and have him reach inside and touch hers, so that they always had a piece of each other with them.

Her choices were wrong. Every relationship ended with her heart broken. This time seemed worst of all, as if she was shoved in the ground, with dirt poured over her, to suffocate her with pain. Right then Elandra could see them on the desk. The image made her head pound, and for some odd reason she was cold and the bottom of her stomach hurt. She ran to the bathroom, thinking something might be wrong with the baby. Fortunately it was merely a queasy stomach.

Moments later, Elandra felt better. She gripped the sides of the sink and leaned over it as a mixture of cold and hot water ran. She splashed her face, patted it with the towel, but for some reason couldn't move from where she stood. She was frozen by her mind, standing there alone . . . but Dan and Joyce were right with her. What could she do to make them go away? *God tell me how to make the pain stop. Please. . . .*

The next morning Elandra stepped through the plush halls of the accounting firm Myerson & Myerson. A smile lit up her face as she greeted colleagues and they greeted her. Her small amount of makeup was impeccable, and her red fitted suit hid no curves as she swayed gracefully to her work station. God knows, she hadn't wanted to get up and come in this morning. Nonetheless, what options did she have? Vacation wasn't scheduled until July. Plus, sick days were all used up during those days of fooling around with Dan. Adding to her woes, she lived from paycheck to paycheck. She couldn't afford not to come in. The firm looked rich, but paid poor.

Elandra saw something upsetting as she approached her desk. She had imagined that it would happen, but not until seeing it did she believe how real it could be. Her desk had nothing on top of it. She searched the drawers. Nothing inside it, either.

"That's right, you're history." A voice blew over her shoulders and crawled down the back of her neck.

Slowly Elandra turned around and just stared for a moment. With hands on hips, wearing dark shades, Joyce stood tall, breathing fire.

"Leave, right now," she added. "And don't you ever show your pathetic face around here again!"

"You just can't fire me like that."

"I did it. You attacked me. You physically attacked your employer, but the word is that you're just resigning. You're lucky I didn't bring you up on charges at the police station, but Dan talked me out of it. If it wasn't for him, you would be behind bars."

Not able to stand any more, Elandra rushed down the corridors out into the reception area and couldn't wait for the elevator. Friends were watching, asking what was wrong. There was no answer. She had to get away from there as soon as possible. Catching her eye were the stairs.

Hurrying down them, a thousand thoughts raced. How was she going to survive without a job? How long would it take to find another one? How was she going to support this baby? And where was Crystal? Didn't she know how much she needed her? Couldn't she feel it? They had always been able to feel when each other was in trouble. Why hadn't she called? Why had any of this happened? And why, why, *why* didn't Dan love her anymore?

Like the confusion in her mind, her balance was off, too. One step too many and too fast, and it was a fall Elandra would never forget. Over and over and over she tumbled. When she stopped, the world was black.

Two

"You're only thirty-one years old. You can have more babies."

Dr. Sarah Wesley tried to sound like all was not lost. Yet when Elandra turned away from the wall she was facing and met the doctor's dark eyes, she saw pity.

"Doctor, you don't have to sit here and baby me. I can handle it. I just lost my child and I have to deal with it. I've been dealing with a lot lately. It makes you strong." Speaking the last word, a tear rolled down her cheeks.

What stunning eyes to look so sad, Sarah Wesley thought. Eyes slanted up at the outer corners and flanked with the longest lashes she had ever seen. Eyes like a doll she'd had once. Sarah's thick fingers grabbed a tissue from the box on the nightstand. Carefully she dabbed it across the damp streaks on Elandra's face. "You shouldn't have to go through this alone. I'll go outside and get the baby's father."

"Father?" The words would have pushed Elandra straight out of bed if she hadn't been so sore and weak. "Who told you about him?"

"You listed the child's father, and his address and phone number, on the forms when you were admitted."

"But I didn't mean for you to call him!" Her frustration and panic were heaving her entire body, making the weakness and soreness worse. "Tell him to go!" Merely the thought of seeing him was draining her last bit of energy. "Please!"

"Oh, I'm sorry, dear. There must have been a mix-up. But he's here and anxious to come in."

"I don't—"

Before Elandra could vent her protest further, Dan's thin frame was entering the room. His face was pale, haggard-looking, the cat's eyes shrunken and rather scary that way, not at all breathtaking like they had once looked to her. Of most concern to her now, there was pity on his face, too. That she couldn't stand.

Appearing a bit out of place, Dan sat in the chair by the bed as the doctor left. He leaned forward, locking his hands together, letting them hang between his spread-out legs. "How are you?"

She turned her head back toward the wall. She didn't want to look at him.

"I was a lot better before you came in."

"Elandra, don't be this way. Why didn't you tell me about the baby?"

"Why?" Her head rolled over the pillow. She gawked at him. "Why? Do you really have to ask?"

"I would have wanted to know. That's not fair, to keep my child from me. I would have wanted to raise it."

"Liar. You wouldn't have cared."

"How can you say that? You didn't give me a chance to care."

"I didn't have to. You didn't care about me." Her body was shaking again. *Why did he have to come here? I can't stop seeing them like that. I want to forget it all. Why did it have to happen to me? What did I ever do in my life that was so terrible I deserved all this?*

"I had deep feelings for you, Elandra."

"You did, huh? If you did, who cares now? You go to hell, you hear me! Go to hell!"

Her tone was shocking. Never had Dan heard her curse or raise her voice. Usually when she was extremely hurt, she handled it by just crying until she was cried out. Dan had imagined she wouldn't take everything well, but he hadn't anticipated this type of reaction.

Dan wasn't basking in hurting Elandra. At the same time, he had to do what he had to do. He refused to lose his business. He cringed at living like those losers who begged him for quarters every day as he entered the Glazer Building. He would rather die than trade his Armani suits for dirty khakis. And if it meant losing this gorgeous woman, that's what had to be. Money was always his master. Joyce and his master had a good relationship.

"The baby is gone," she went on. "Far and away."

"You can have more."

"But I can't have that one! Why can't anyone understand that?"

She began to cry and rock. Dan looked so upset by her emotion, he reached over and held her. For a moment she accepted the comfort, too, burying her head into the curve of his shoulders and neck, letting his unique, herb-blended cologne melt her with warmth and an ache to be touched more. Deft fingertips on her chin encouraged more weakness. In the haze of the moment, Dan was cupping her cheeks. Closer and closer he moved his face to hers. Lips were an inch apart.

That's when the picture flashed across her mind. The desk, Joyce, what they were doing. She recalled the stairs, but most unforgettable, she touched her now-empty stomach.

"No!" she yelled, shoving him back. "I'm not desperate anymore."

"I was just trying to make you feel better."

"You were just trying to see how much power you still had. Your ego is something, much bigger than your intelligence."

"Elan—"

"Leave!" She pointed to the door. "Go on back to Joyce."

"I can't leave you like this. You just lost our child."

"You heard what the hell I said!"

He looked shocked by her tone again. "You have so much anger. You used to handle things with such sophistication."

"I used to be a fool, that's why. But in the last twenty-four hours my life has turned upside down. So how am I supposed to stay the same after all this? Tell me how? Lost my so-called man, lost my job, now lost everything when I lost my baby."

"I can ask Joyce to give you your job back."

"Don't do me any favors."

"No, really."

"Don't do me any favors! I won't be here anyway."

"What do you mean?"

"I'm leaving New York for a while. Other than the baby, that's all I've thought about."

"Because of me?"

"Because I need to find the one who really loves me." Her eyes darted around tensely. "I need her and I can feel she needs me, too."

The plane's air conditioner was on full blast. Goosebumps along Elandra's arms urged her to put on the red blazer she had slung over the chair. Afterwards she fastened her seat belt and reclined in the blue velvet cushions. Closing her eyes, she wanted to forget all that had happened, and concentrate only on Crystal. Positive thoughts. She pictured everything.

Elandra had sent an overnight letter detailing her arrival. That way when she landed in Nassau, Crystal would be at the gate waiting. Bright eyes and a piano smile would greet Elandra. Crystal would explain that she had been out of town. Thereafter they would catch up on all the events in each other's lives.

Except deep inside, Elandra knew that all she envisioned was impossible. A kind imagination, it was. The reason being, Crystal wouldn't dare just take off somewhere without letting Elandra know. Something was wrong. Elandra could hear it whispering in the air.

Riding in the limousine to her sister's home, it was as if Nassau was more breathtaking than the last time she visited. Crystal had moved there the previous summer, after accepting a desk clerk's position in a major hotel chain. Elandra had helped her get settled in the long-distance move.

As the driver pointed out specific sights, Elandra was amazed by the picturesque landscapes. Underneath the explosion of afternoon sun, mile after mile of the most exotic trees and pink sand beaches made her feel like she was floating through paradise. More captivating, the various fine architecture of the hotels and houses made the atmosphere more dreamy.

When finally the driver pulled off the road to the address of Crystal's home, Elandra gaped at a lavish condominium, certain he made a mistake. Sure enough, Crystal had written to her about relocating since last year. Nevertheless, this address she'd sent couldn't be the correct one. The vast land surrounding the home, and the elaborate, contemporary structure of it, all indicated a fortune Crystal couldn't possibly have. Not on a desk clerk's salary.

"There must be some mistake," Elandra informed the driver. "You must have taken me to the wrong address."

He shook a shining, bald head before speaking with an unmistakable Caribbean accent. "No mistake, ma'am. This is the address you told me to come to."

In awe, Elandra surveyed the place. It was huge, with three floors. What's more, the immense, luxurious flower garden had to require a gardener's upkeep. How could a desk clerk afford to pay a gardener?

Elandra was stumped. She took a deep breath and rubbed her fingers back through a bundle of brown hair. "If it is the address, then I must have written it down wrong."

"What is the party's name, ma'am?"

"Crystal Lloyd."

"I'll check things out for you."

Elandra trailed the glossy head as he walked over to the mailbox, then bent over to read something on it. Shortly after, he waved for Elandra to join him. Frowning beneath the harsh sun, she rushed out of the car, over to the box, and peered closely. *Crystal Lloyd* was inscribed there.

After paying and thanking the driver, Elandra instructed him to pick up her luggage, which was coming in on a later flight. A giant smile showed he was grateful for the business. In seconds he drove off.

For a minute, Elandra shuffled over the porch, trying to find some sign that Crystal was there. Noticing a few neglected plants and molded bread scattered about for the birds, she felt disheartened. It all compelled her to knock and ring the bell, praying Crystal would miraculously open the door. Moments later, realizing that she wouldn't, Elandra opened her purse and removed the spare key, which Crystal had sent her months ago. Unlocking the door, she almost felt like she was entering a stranger's home. How could her sister afford such a place? Crystal had never mentioned coming into lots of money.

The door opened, drawing her inside easily with the scent of peach potpourri. It was Crystal's favorite fragrance for the house. That was a sign it was her home; though it was more than the lush sweetness that overwhelmed Elandra. Stepping slowly and further inside, the interior decorating tugged Elandra's mouth open in astonishment. It made her clutch her chest. For she couldn't believe what she was seeing. Had Crystal won the lottery and didn't tell her? Piece after piece screamed of riches, from the super plush couches to the antique ornaments. Even so, one question puzzled her more than how Crystal afforded the expensive house and furnishings. Where *was* Crystal? Elandra searched through the house, but she wasn't there.

Fortunately, when the hospitals, police station and even the morgue were checked, there was no one with Crystal's name or fitting her description. Therefore, the first stop in tracking her down was The Hotel Mandarain where she worked. As soon as Elandra strolled up to the desk, one of her sister's colleagues remembered her from last year. Back then, Crystal had excitedly given Elandra a tour of her new job, introducing her to everyone.

"You're Crystal's sister," the young woman greeted her. She had an infectious, gap-toothed smile, which somehow made Elandra hopeful that Crystal was somewhere nearby. "I'm Daisy, remember?"

"Yes. How are you?" Elandra responded. "How are things here at the hotel?"

"Business is booming," she said, laughter breaking

through her accent. "Tourism is always good to Nassau. But tell me, how is your sister?"

Any hope Elandra felt slipped away with that question. "My sister? I was going to ask you about her."

"Me?" Daisy tapped her chest. "I haven't seen Crystal in about a month. I thought you were coming to tell me something about her. The boss is furious. She left one evening, and never came back or called."

A chill ran over Elandra. Her fingers rubbed back through her hair as she thought. Her eyes darted everywhere before returning to the woman. "The last time you saw her, what did she say to you?"

"Oh, I remember good, because my boss asked me the same thing. You know, he became tired of waiting for Crystal to come back or call, and hired someone else"

Oh God, Crystal doesn't have a job, either.

"She was with that girl, Trina."

"Trina?"

"Yeah, she's a pretty wild one. She used to come in here with rich American men. That's how she and Crystal met. Always checking in, you know." She winked. "And out."

"Really?" Elandra didn't like the way this was sounding.

"Yeah. Trina rents this boat and I hear she lives there, too. Crystal was leaving after doing her shift and Trina was with her. Said they were going to the boat."

"Where is it? How can I get there?"

Dressed in white cotton shorts and a matching halter top, Elandra stood on the pier, examining several yachts lined along it. If Trina rented big, expensive boats, then she probably rented expensive condos, too,

Elandra thought to herself. That had to be it. Trina rented the condo and Crystal was living with her.

The yacht she was searching for was white with a red line bordering the top. Etched in script on the side were the small words, *Fun Ship*. Nevertheless, the sole one Elandra saw fitting that description had a different name. It was called *Dreamer*. Much the opposite, the word was written in large, plain lettering. Elandra stepped toward it anyway. Possibly Daisy had mixed up the name.

No one was standing on the deck, so Elandra took the liberty to go inside. She found herself in what had to be the main quarters. There she was surrounded by tasteful decor and coziness, but not a person in sight.

"Trina?" she called.

No answer.

"Trina, I'm Crystal's sister. I'm looking for her."

Still no answer.

"Crystal, if you're here, let me know. *Please*. I'm going crazy trying to find out what's going on with you."

Silence again.

Feeling her frustration reaching its peak, Elandra plopped down on a deeply cushioned couch. Her heels elevated somewhat as her bottom sank deep into the back. Over and over she rubbed back her hair, and afterwards buried her face in her palms. What was she going to do? Go to the police again?

At the sound of footsteps, approaching the room she was in, Elandra raised her face from her hands. It was Crystal, it had to be Crystal, she thought. Relief and excitement swelled in her heart, that is until she saw legs swinging in first from a doorway—hairy and muscular. No, they weren't Crystal's legs, but whoever they were, God had blessed him. So much so her eyes couldn't help traveling upward where a white towel covered him from mid-thigh to waist. Elandra gazed higher, where a flat stomach flaunted rich brown abs, set below the broadest shoulders and arms resembling thick brown melons stacked on top of one another. Entrancing as all that was, there was more when she looked up to the top of him. Eyes she had never seen before in the world, but eyes she could have easily dreamed, were staring down into hers. As unusually beautiful as they were, they were warm and passionate, too. It was the rest of his expression which was cold.

"Who are you?" he asked, in a clearly American accent. He didn't sound pleased.

Her hands mashed into the bulky pillows on the sofa as she supported her weight to stand. "I'm Elandra."

"Yes?" He tensed his forehead. "What do you want?"

"I was looking for Crystal."

He shook his head. "Never heard of her."

"No, you had to." Panic rose in her. "She was last seen coming here with Trina."

"Trina?" For a second he looked off, as if recognizing the name. "I know who she is." His eyes narrowed. "Yes, I know who she is."

Elandra was so relieved, she laughed. "I'm so glad you do. Where is she? I think my sister is with her. I came all the way from New York to see her. When is she coming back?"

He didn't join in her amusement or enthusiasm. "She isn't. I know her by name. She was the girl who used to rent this boat."

"Used to?"

"I bought it. Trina doesn't rent it anymore."

Elandra lowered her head as she sought answers. She raised her face back to him.

"Well maybe she used to rent this one, but now she rents *Fun Ship*."

"This was *Fun Ship*. I changed the name."

"When did you buy it?"

An aggravated scowl screamed *None of your business,* but instead she heard, "Three weeks ago."

"Well do you know anything about Trina?" A feeling of helplessness was overcoming her. What if she never found Crystal? "How am I going to find my sister?"

"I don't know." The coldness on the rest of his face now seeped into his eyes. She was annoying him, but didn't care. She was desperate.

"Look miss, I can't help you." A step was made toward the door. He was going to throw her out.

Elandra jumped in front of him. "But you can. What did the people you bought the boat from say about the *Fun Ship*? You have to know something. Where does Trina live?"

"You know what I know."

"What?"

"You heard me. You know what I know."

"What do I know?"

"Look, stop playing games with me! You know who I am, and I know what you are, and I'm not buying."

A frown, along with clear resentment bloomed across her face. It was some nerve implying that she . . . "How dare you—"

"You think I don't know why the *Fun Ship* was called what it was? They had those wild parties on this boat."

"So, anyone can have a party."

"So nothing! This Trina person and the rest of your crew were probably selling some fun."

"My crew?"

"Did they move on without you? Aw, don't fret. You can still make it on your own." Narrowed eyes slinked up and down her body. "I know plenty of guys in the market for your type. But no woman's ever going to rob me again. All of you just want to take and take and take and drive a man insane!" His eyes grew wild, three times their size.

He pushed open the yacht's door and Elandra suddenly had invisible wings. She had promised herself no one would reduce her to tears again. Yet this man had insulted her beyond what she could withstand. And mean as he was, he was crazy, too. Elandra wasn't hanging around to see what happened next. She ran and ran, never looking back.

Bradley Davenport watched her from the yacht's door. It was like a rabid dog was chasing her. A blur in the wind, everything seemed to move out of her way. Finally, on a remote area of the pier, she stopped running and walked slowly with her head hung. The sight didn't make him feel good. What if all she wanted from him was to find those women and nothing more? When was he going to stop letting what happened rule his life?

Three

"I'm coming. I'm coming," Elandra yelled, rushing to the door.

Somebody was ringing the bell incessantly. When she opened the door, standing there, shocking the hell out of her, was the guy from the yacht. Exactly like the other day, he wasn't smiling. With that serious expression, he just stood there, looking much cooler than he should have been in that cream-colored suit. Elandra wished he was hot and bothered, and perspiring profusely. She wanted the sun to burn him up.

"Hello," he said, leaning toward the doorway, resting one hand on the side of it.

Elandra rolled her eyes. "You must have the wrong address."

"No, I'm at the right address. It wasn't even too hard to find you, either. I gave a few islanders a description of you and they knew exactly who you were and where you lived."

"Guess I'm popular." Folding her arms, she shifted her weight to one side. "But you already know that, right?"

"Look," he said, lowering his gaze uneasily, then meeting hers, "I want to apologize. That's why I've been trying to find out where you lived."

"Apologize to me?" She pointed to herself.

"I was wrong. I admit it. I was having a bad day, too

much work to do and remembering some bad things that happened to me. Then, here you come and I took everything out on you. I'm sorry."

Back in the old days, Elandra could have easily accepted his apology. Probably even the other day she would have accepted it, when she was feeling distraught and powerless about finding Crystal. Yet after this guy humiliated her like that, her fortitude was rekindled. Elandra liked the toughness she'd displayed with Dan before she left New York. She was in control. She also loved the toughness she'd shown the police the other day. She fought with them about finding Crystal and now they had three detectives searching for her. She would be firm with this character, too. He would never make her run like a maniac or cry like that again. She was almost hit by a tour bus.

"Your apology is not accepted here, mister . . ."

"It's Bradley Davenport. But you can call me Bradley."

"I'd rather not call you at all."

A hint of a smile tilted his lips. "Okay, that's fine. I just wanted to let you know that I'm sorry. I had no right to call you a pro."

Hands on hips, she leaned right in his face. "You certainly didn't."

He didn't move back. Actually he smiled some more, and let his eyes linger on hers a while. Feeling awkward so close to him, and with him looking at her like that, Elandra moved back. On the contrary, he remained where he was.

"You know," he went on, "I'm right about one thing. The young lady who used the yacht before me, was a . . . well, I'll say a very friendly lady. She had a reputation."

"That doesn't mean my sister was one. And that doesn't mean I'm one for looking for her."

"I don't believe you are."

"I'm not!" Her loosely tied kimono opened with her insistence. Except Elandra didn't know it until his eyes dropped, stopped and stared while he was swallowing something in his throat. It made her look down at herself to see what was so interesting to him. Cleavage was spilling out of her nightgown. Straightaway she tied her belt tight. When her eyes raised, he was staring into her face.

She didn't want to stare back. She looked around his shoulders toward the car behind him. "Well, if that's all you want to tell me, then you should be on your way."

He nodded. "Right."

Designer shoes scraped across the cement to the edge of the porch. As he was about to take the first step down, Bradley turned back around. Oddly enough, there was that warmth in his eyes, the warmth that was there when Elandra first laid eyes on him. This time it was throughout his expression. "Hope you find your sister."

"Don't worry, I will."

No sooner than she had assured him, Elandra closed the door. Even so, she couldn't stop herself from peeking out the front window inside the house. She observed the cool, sophisticated sway of his walk, and how the jacket of his suit molded to his shoulders so perfectly.

Before long he was closing the door of a black Jaguar parked in the driveway. Still watching him, Elandra was curious. What did he do to have such a nice car and a yacht? Did he really not know Trina and Crystal? Did everyone live like kings in Nassau? And what had happened to him which made him so mad remembering it that day? What was his story? But why did she care? She didn't want to. She wouldn't. There were more important things to think about.

* * *

Out in the car, Bradley didn't start the engine right away. He was too busy being amused. So she refused to accept his apology. That shouldn't have surprised him, considering the way she was leering. Easily Elandra could have taken him for a few rounds. As he gazed back up at the house, he recreated her image in the doorway. Slowly the smile drained from his lips. Suddenly he looked hungry, but not for food.

It hadn't gone without Bradley's notice how beautiful Elandra was when he saw her on the yacht. No man could ignore eyes like those, lips like those, skin that beckoned to be touched like that. And Bradley would have to be an imbecile not to memorize the curves on that body. On the yacht, however, he was too busy protecting himself to appreciate her attractiveness. Today he understood what he missed.

Too bad, he thought, and started the engine. Women. He was finished with them, at least romantically. Not even one like that could make him change his mind. And all the wondering and questions that had begun circling his mind about her had to stop. He didn't need to know any more than he already knew. Nothing was worth the trouble he had been through. Nothing was worth the endless ache. It would all turn out the same. Hence, he was going to stay centered. Work was all he wanted to care about.

In front of the mirror, Elandra zipped up a peach silk mini-dress, perused her profile, turned to one side and the other, then examined how the clinging fabric fit in the back. A smile spread across her lips, seeing a weight loss in the right places. Inspecting further, she scrutinized her face and ran lithe fingers through yards of hair. Burgundy lipstick brought out a full, succulent mouth. Salmon eye shadow accentuated the unique upward slope of her eyes and the shimmer in vibrant, brown skin. The hair was simply loose and carefree.

The club Midnight Express is where Elandra was headed. Daisy had volunteered to accompany her there because she knew it was a place that Trina and Crystal frequented. Daisy knew of all their retreats because Crystal always recited Trina's and her adventures at the desk during work. Together Elandra and Daisy believed that maybe Crystal was merely living somewhere other than the condominium, perhaps somewhere with Trina. If so, she would possibly turn up at the club, and if she didn't turn up, someone who knew her would. That being the case, perchance the friend would know her whereabouts. Daisy knew the people they socialized with there, because many times they picked Crystal up at the hotel. What's more, she offered to escort Elandra to even more of their recreational haunts if this place turned out futile.

Midnight Express was first on the list, and hopefully the last. If extreme luck was with Elandra, she would walk in and see her sister. If she wasn't so fortunate, at least Daisy could introduce her to people Trina and Crystal knew. Someone had to know something. Elandra couldn't sit around and just wait, especially for the police. Their investigation hadn't discovered anything yet.

A Caribbean tune Elandra had never heard before was finishing as they entered the club. A pause in the music dramatized their entrance. Men's and women's eyes shot up over to the admission door—except the fellows' eyes wouldn't leave. Elandra was accustomed to attention. She ignored it, accepting it as part of being a woman. Daisy adored it, chortling out, "An old married gal like me still has it."

"Girl, you never lost it," Elandra teased. Snickering like school girls, they ventured further inside.

Maneuvering through the crammed establishment, guys lightly grabbed Elandra's arm, whispered in her ear, blew beer breath on the side of her face, and tried to ease their hands into hers, attempting to lead her to the dance floor. Tactfully she handled each situation. A man was the last thing she desired after what Dan had done. Her interest was getting Daisy to a table. There they could scan the crowd for Crystal, or at least Daisy could point out all Crystal and Trina's friends.

The music commenced again, bringing with it the heart and soul which Elandra always felt in music. It brought life to the atmosphere. A fine lyric, melody, harmony, and rhythm was her great love. This song was an American one, "Kissing You," by Faith. Elandra adored the tune. She remembered it from the *Waiting To Exhale* soundtrack. Over and over and over, she'd played it when it first hit the airwaves. She and Dan were supposedly in love back then.

Listening to it, memories began floating around her like a warm blanket on a cold night. In spite of it, she refused to sit and ponder about the good old days that were no more. Shaking off the images, Elandra focused her attention on Daisy. Sitting across from her at their table, she was searching through the crowd. Finally her gaze met Elandra's.

"I don't see Crystal or Trina, but there is this guy who knows them over there." She pointed.

Elandra's line of vision followed her finger until she spotted a guy wearing a white shirt and black pants. Elandra pointed, too. "Him? The one in the white and black?"

Daisy peered closer at the tall, slender man, with his hair tied in a ponytail. She glanced back at Elandra, nodding. "Yes, that's him. I'm sure it is. His name is Irving."

Not wasting a moment, Elandra hurried up from the

table, wiggled through the pack, eventually reached Irving. He smelled good, like fresh starched shirts sprinkled with a mild cologne. Irving eyed Elandra up and down, obviously happy to see such a gorgeous woman interested in his company.

"Anything you want, you can have it, pretty lady," were his first words. A strong accent preceded a boyish smile.

Elandra smiled back. "Well, I do want something."

"Name it. I can serve it to you like you never been served before." His tongue rolled over his lips.

Returning a dry laugh, she wanted to tell him not to waste his tongue. *I'm immune to the opposite sex now. The rest of these women can have them.* "I'm looking for my sister. Someone told me you know her. They say she hangs out in here with you sometimes. So I was thinking, maybe you might know where she is?"

"What's her name?" His hand eased onto her pinky.

"Crystal." She eased it off.

"Crystal?" Irving thought for a moment and curled up his thick lips. "Yeah, I know her. Pretty just like you. You two do look like sisters."

"Have you seen her lately?"

He moved closer, his adoration of her attractiveness evident. "No, haven't seen her in a while. But I would like to see you. Can I get to know you better?" Eyes snaked along her body. "I can make you feel so good. I have what you need."

"You sure aren't shy, are you?"

He was clearly enjoying this. "No. Not with you. I might not ever see you again, so I have to make my move. We can have such a good time."

"Well, I'm sorry. I'm not in Nassau for romance or whatever it is you have in mind. I'm looking for my missing sister. Thanks for all your help."

Elandra turned to walk away. As she did, Irving

grabbed her arm. Her head curved around. Once again, there was that slithering tongue.

"You sure I can't do anything for you? I'm good." He raised his brows, as if surprised.

"And I'm not interested."

By the time Elandra reached the table, she hoped Daisy would have at least spotted one other person Crystal and Trina knew. No such luck. Quite unexpectedly, Daisy was bouncing up and down and looking quite strange in her expression, a half-empty glass sat near her on the table. Her eyebrows were raised, too, and wouldn't come down. She appeared to be in a perpetual state of surprise.

"Did you have a good time?" she asked Elandra. *No, but you sure did,* Elandra thought. Daisy did a bounce to the right, a bigger bounce to the left.

"Not really," she then replied.

Elandra studied her for a minute, then slid down in a chair. She put her elbows on the table, her chin in her palms. "That guy hasn't seen them."

"Aw. Better luck next time. We're going to find them or my name isn't . . ." She looked like she didn't know. "Or my name isn't . . ."

Yet instead of finishing her sentence, Daisy laid her head on the table.

"I'm so tired. My husband says I can't . . . I can't drink worth a poop. I'm so tired. I . . ."

"But you have to look some more," Elandra insisted to the back of Daisy's head.

There was no answer, solely quiet from her, interrupted only a second after by a snore. Elandra swore she heard a cow's mooing, a moose's grunting, and a dog's howling all in one. So mighty the noise was, Elandra peeped around to see who was listening and watching. Luckily the music was so loud and so much activity was taking place, no one seemed to notice. Hence,

Elandra put Daisy's arm around her shoulder and tried
to escort her out. Luckily two of the club's hosts saw
her struggling with her buddy. They intercepted and
soon Daisy was put in a cab and sent off home. Elandra
settled back at the table. She wanted to search the
crowd. Maybe, just maybe, Crystal would show up.

A half hour later, Elandra was getting tired, too.
Tired of men trying to pick her up when she didn't
trust any of them. Mostly though, she was tired of looking for Crystal when she was nowhere in sight. The
condo was about a block away from the club. She began
strolling home.

The night air was warm, but with just enough breeze
in it to let you know you were in paradise. Elandra
knew she could easily get used to living in a tropical
place like this, with all its trees, beaches and the easy
pace of life. She would have done anything to have
been enjoying this island on a vacation, rather than
searching for a sister she couldn't find. It was taking
too long to find Crystal. Where in the world was she?
Fighting the horrible thoughts that were sneaking in
her head, Elandra repeatedly told herself that Crystal
was all right. She would find her. They would be re-
united again.

In trying to think positively, Elandra observed the
scenery in this downtown area of Nassau. A row of restaurants and boutiques stood across the street. The
stores were closed, but people were constantly tracking
in and out of the eateries. When a pregnant woman
and a man entered one arm and arm, it made Elandra
wonder if she would have been showing by now.

Water was welling in her eyes when she saw a shadow
to the side of her. Whirling around, Elandra was un-
pleasantly surprised to see Irving again. One big wipe
took the water away. She stopped. His lips spread con-
tentedly, he rushed toward her.

"Can I help you?" Elandra asked. She wasn't in the mood for his little Casanova routine right now.

"No, I can help you, pretty lady. I can make you feel things you never felt before. I can really ram you right."

"You can what?"

"Ram you right. I mean it. I promise you won't regret it."

She rolled her eyes. "Didn't I tell you before that I wasn't interested?"

"I never take no for an answer." He lifted her hand, brushing her knuckles across his lip. "I can never take no from you."

"You're going to take no tonight!" She snatched her hand back. "I told you I'm looking for my sister. I have no interest in you or any other man down here, for that matter!"

Fumbling with his ponytail, Irving grinned mischievously. "You're not a . . . you don't like ladies, do you?"

"Yes, I like ladies, but not in the way that you think. Just because I don't want you, I have to be gay? Please. Get out of my face."

She started making fast, high steps to flee from him. He stood there for a moment watching her, then raced up behind. Sticky hands clamped firmly around Elandra's waist. At once she tried to throw them off. It didn't work, because this Irving character was strong. Before she knew anything he had forced her around, locking her within his arms.

"Get off of me, damn it!" she yelled, struggling from his grip.

"Let me kiss you." He bent his head. Steadily he was aiming to get his mouth close enough to hers. "Just one taste of these lips and you'll be hooked." He wiggled his tongue.

Elandra was sickened. As hard as she resisted, she couldn't get free. She couldn't even get her knee toward his groin. He was too tall. Alarm gripped her. Confusion about what to do made her feel a growing hysteria. Luckily though, there was rescue in sight. All halted with four words. "Let her go, Irving!" a familiar voice demanded.

Without delay Irving did as asked and released Elandra. Gathering her breath, she quickly turned to the shadows to see who her rescuer was. She knew who it sounded like. Although she just knew it couldn't be him. Emerging from beyond a street light, that's when she saw someone whose presence didn't please her, either. Bradley Davenport was approaching them.

"How long were you watching this man pawing me before you decided to do something?" she lashed out.

Lips parted, lips that Elandra couldn't help noticing were moist and wide. Yet before the words came out, Irving was apologizing to Bradley.

"I'm sorry, Mr. Davenport. I didn't know this was your friend. I was just trying to get to know her. She's so pretty. Could you blame me?" Irving chuckled. Bradley didn't join in his amusement.

Elandra's head rolled from face to face. *Why is he calling him Mr. Davenport?*

"You apologize to the lady," Bradley demanded. "She was the one you were harassing, not me."

Like a soldier obeying a commanding officer, Irving gazed intently at Elandra.

"Miss, I am so sorry. I was quite taken by your pretty face and body. It will never happen again. Forgive me."

"Never!" Elandra blasted.

"Please," Irving begged. He was dividing his caution between her and Bradley.

"Never," she repeated. "You're an animal! You deserve to be locked in a cage."

"You're cold," Bradley remarked.

Elandra cared less about his opinions, as long as her

words served her well. They did too. A strong wind they were, whisking Irving far and away, urging her close to Bradley. "You didn't answer my question. How long were you standing there, letting this man practically rape me?"

"Not long. He wouldn't rape you."

"How do you know what he would have done?"

"Because he's not like that."

"That's what you think. And how long were you there?"

Bradley dug his hands deep in his pants pockets. Warm brown depths searched deep in hers. "For your information, I had just come out of the restaurant across the street with some business partners of mine when I saw you two. I hurried right over. I know Irving has an eye for the ladies and he looked like he was harassing you. But he's harmless."

"Harmless my foot! How do you know him anyway? Why did he call you mister?"

"I'm his employer. I didn't ask him to call me that. He just does. I would prefer being called Bradley."

"His employer?"

"Yes, his employer."

She speculated for a moment. The Italian suit he was wearing now had to cost a fortune. The shoes, chain, ring, watch, all screamed extreme wealth, too. On top of that, the Jaguar and yacht had to cost several years of her salary. "You're a drug dealer, aren't you? Admit it? You're not fooling me."

Surprise and insult stretched his eyes. "I am?"

"Yes, you are. That's why Irving was so terrified of you."

"He's so terrified of me because I'm his boss and he doesn't want to lose his job. The man has a wife and five kids."

"Liar!"

"He does have a wife and five kids."

"No, not about that. About why he's terrified. You sell drugs. You probably even had something to do with Crystal's disappearance. You know where she is, don't you?"

"Believe me, if I knew where she was, I would surely tell you. Then you could go back to where you came from—fast!"

"Oh really?"

"Yes, really? You need to go back there and relax. You are just too uptight!"

"You weren't the sweetest thing in the world to me either, the other day on the boat."

"I told you I was having a hard day with my work, and thinking about something that happened."

"Well, I'm having a hard day, too, finding my sister! And life hasn't been that easy for me either lately! So excuse me if I seem a little unpleasant to you." Then she was studying him. He was suddenly looking like a wounded kid. "What happened anyway? You were going on and on about women driving you nuts. Did one dump you or something?"

His lip twitched. "No, nobody dumped me." A hint of anger coated his voice. "Did somebody dump you?"

The question raced her heart. "No—no, nobody dumped me. I don't have men problems."

"I don't see anybody on your arm now."

"No one's on yours either."

"Because that's the way I want it."

"I want it that way, too! I don't want a man and I don't need one." She eyed him up and down. "Especially you."

His eyes widened. "Where did that come from? Who said that I wanted you either?"

"On the yacht, you were implying that I was offering you something. Well, I wasn't. I'm not that hard up!"

Elandra strutted off, leaving him standing there watching her. The highly competitive sort, he was itching to get her back for that last remark by yelling something clever. Except what he saw left him speechless. Words were the last thing on his mind. From side to side, the roundest buttocks moved and moved and moved, somehow calling Bradley to step with them. Step he did. Distant enough for her not to see him, but close enough to enjoy the view. Of most concern to him, he was close enough to see her arrive on the doorstep safely.

Four

Sunlight splashed over the hot pink bikini against coppery limbs. To the males in the vicinity, the beautiful American appeared as delectable as the ice cream children licked so insatiably. Flocks of admirers attempted to make Elandra's acquaintance as she strolled along the shore. To their disappointment, she was no more eager to know them than she was the devil in hell. After what Dan did, how could she dare trust a man again? On top of that, there were others before who had shattered her heart. Never again. Romantic love was one taste in life she vowed to live without.

Settling down on a nearly deserted section of the beach, Elandra felt the area private enough to spread out her blanket and really kick back. After all, she had come to the sand and surf to relax and think. Since arriving in Nassau, she had been running without stopping to analyze where she was running to. Perhaps there was something she hadn't thought of in finding Crystal. Quiet time would allow room in her mind for that something.

Within seconds, Elandra adjusted the blanket, until she was lounging restfully on her back. So reposed she was, she simply closed her eyes and surrendered to the warmth of sun on her face. It roamed delicately across her features and caressed down her neck and below. It was easy for the mental racing to disappear. When it did a dream seeped into the slumber that soon came, taking all else away.

The fingers ran along Elandra's jawline and up across the swell of her lips. Faintly the two middle ones parted them, drifted away, replacing themselves with his mouth. His lips and hers barely brushed. Softly pressing and lingering, they were intent to savor the feeling. It was more than lips making her insides come alive. It was breath near breath. Cheek near cheek. Chest near chest. Heart and soul, she bonded with him. They touched each other in places no one ever touched them before. It was the magic people wait their entire lives for. It felt so good and right, throughout every fiber of her being, Elandra knew it was meant to be. Not soon enough, their hunger to express more overpowered them. Elandra welcomed all of his love.

When her lids fluttered open, she realized it had happened again. The wonderful dream she was having lately, had once again invited itself into her sleep, this time in the afternoon sun. Not that she was complaining. Ever since she left New York, Elandra wasn't dreaming and sleeping at all. Quite the contrary, she was always awake worrying. If she wasn't wondering where Crystal was, she was thinking about the miscarriage, or recreating the scene with Dan and Joyce. This dream rescued her from all that suffering. It was a blessing. Strange as it was, though, she couldn't see all of the mystery man's face. Merely his lips, cheeks and below were seen. But who cared what he looked like? He was a fantasy and she would enjoy him. He was completely safe. Fantasies couldn't break you into pieces the way a real man could.

Closing her eyes Elandra hoped to dream of Mr. Wonderful again. She loved the way his mouth and hands felt. She loved the closeness of his hard body against her soft one. She loved the way he smelled, like

woods and herbs and something uniquely his own. She
loved the way beholding him stirred her desire to make
love. It was only something hitting her leg which
stopped her from willing him in her sleep again. Raising up on her elbows, she squinted to get the sun out
of her eyes and see what that was. A ball was near her
ankle and had most likely hit her leg. Sniggering, loud
boys were running about. There was no harm done.
That is, until she saw the unexpected sight. Of all the
people in the world to inhabit the beach now, there *he*
was.

Elandra propped up some more on her elbows, taking in hard, hairy legs, the abs, the chest as wide as a
river, and arms a woman could lose herself in. It was
all enclosed in rich brown skin, which she could see
was slippery from sweat. Bradley Davenport looked like
fresh cherry cheesecake in the middle of a famine beneath the afternoon sun. As he played with those boys,
Elandra's head was stuck in his direction. It was only
pulled away when Bradley caught sight of her. Straightaway she yanked her attention elsewhere, where an
enormous wave was galloping and farther to where a
yacht sailed. She wouldn't give him the satisfaction of
seeing her stare. Wrong assumptions could be made.
Like she was attracted to him. That definitely wasn't
the case, Elandra assured herself. She reasoned he had
captured her attention because he was playing with
those boys. She didn't figure him the type to take time
with kids.

Minutes later, Elandra was daring to doze off and
have that dream once again. The boisterous boys were
being ignored. She was almost there, too, into dream-
land. Though it was too good to be true, too peaceful,
too calm with the ocean water clapping, quelling the
noise of Bradley's pack. Comparable to the ocean rising
to suddenly rage and drown her, what seemed like an

avalanche of sand came flinging across her face, her shoulders and neck, down farther—dousing all over her body.

Her mouth stretched open, her nostrils breathed fire. Elandra sat up, flinging bits of sand off her nose, tongue, lips, stomach, arms, legs, neck. "Yuck! Who did that?"

Snickering came from a boy who retrieved a ball next to her foot. It was obvious the ball had bounced near her again, this time somehow splattering her with sand.

"Go further down, boys," Bradley instructed them, and waved his hand toward another area of the beach. "We don't want any more accidents."

Seconds later, Bradley was making tracks in the sand toward Elandra. Watching him, she was seething and planning to tell him off but good. How could he have let this happen? Was it on purpose? Except when he bent down beside her, with blinding sunshine narrowing his eyes, she couldn't get enough of what she was seeing, regardless of pretending that she could. The rays brought something out in Bradley's eyes. There was a sensuality, a warmth Elandra could feel reaching into her own as he stared at her.

"I apologize for the boys," he said. "They didn't mean to get sand all over you." His eyes dropped to her breasts, hips, legs. A finger quivered to help her wipe off, but he restrained the urge. He gazed back up. "They're just kids, you know?"

"Kids, my foot!" Elandra was concentrating on her leg, dusting off sand. "Can't you keep them under control? Who are they anyway? Are they all your tribe?"

He laughed, making her aware for the first time that he had dimples—tiny cute ones. She gazed at them for a second, then whisked grains off her arm.

"No, they're not my tribe, as you say. I'm a Big Brother volunteer."

"Liar. No, you're not."

"Yes, I am."

"Really?"

"Yes. I love it, too. Love it with a passion. My dad wasn't there for me, but I feel I'm better than him. That should be all the more reason I'm there for someone else."

The divulgence made Elandra look up at him. If that was truly his heart talking, she was very impressed. Eyes met eyes. They lingered for a moment before she began wiping her stomach.

"I was a kid in that program," she revealed. "I used to have a Big Sister. She made an impact on my life."

Bradley nodded, while striving to keep his attention up. "It's a great organization." Try as he might though, it trailed everywhere she wiped. When Elandra reached her inner thigh, he was constantly swallowing. The sight made him so uncomfortable he had to shift his weight and sit completely down.

"My Big Sister was real good to me," Elandra went on. "Took me all kinds of places, and she told me I could be anything in this world that I wanted to." Halfway smiling, her eyes wandered off. Bradley watched her, watched those unusual eyes filling with something that made her look vulnerable. "But she was just trying to be nice." She gazed back at him.

"No, she was giving you hope and if you have that, you have everything."

The words made them look at each other in silence. Everything was beginning to feel too strange to Elandra. She diverted her concern to her back. Somehow a few bits of sand from her shoulders had slid there. She was reaching around, but was having a hard time getting to the middle.

Bradley inched closer. "Wait a minute. Let me help you."

He raised his hands and she swerved around. Sure enough, a few bits of sand were scattered about her back in the most hard-to-get places. Carefully and slowly then, he began to rub the grains away, rubbing with hands feeling like silk. More than once her eyes fluttered closed. It felt so good.

"By the way, how're things going with your sister?" he asked. He was gently kneading her back. "Any luck finding her?"

The hands felt so good to her. Soft moans were escaping without her even realizing it.

"Mmm . . . I'm still searching. Mmm . . ."

Feeding off the sweet sounds Bradley was pleased with himself. This was really a massage and he was expert at it. He was getting to her—to Ms. Uptight. He thought that was something.

"I can recommend an excellent private investigator to help you," he volunteered. "He did some work for me."

Elandra parted her lips to respond, but before the words hit the air, she heard a snap in back of her. Instantly her breasts felt loose and dangling. Her eyes flew open. She swung around, scowling at him. "What did you do?" She fingered around her back. The bikini was unsnapped. *Fast,* she hooked it back.

"I was massaging—I mean getting the sand off around that area of your bikini and it just opened."

"It didn't just open. You opened it!"

"I wouldn't do something like that." Beads of sweat popped along his forehead. "Not unless you wanted me to."

"Do I look like I *want* you to unhook my bikini top?" She was rolling her eyes.

"Do I look like I *want* to unhook your bikini top?"

"Yes."

"Keep dreaming."

"You were trying to seduce me."

"If I was trying, believe me, you would be seduced!"
She snickered. "You're not my type."

"You're not mine either."

"I haven't seen you with any type since I've been here."

"I could say the same for you."

"I'm looking for my sister. What's your excuse?"

"I'm a businessman. And right now, women aren't my business."

"What's the matter? Having problems?"

"Are you?"

"I don't have men problems." She stretched her neck high. "If I want one I can get one."

"But do you have what it takes to keep one? You wouldn't know what to do with a man if the instructions bit you across your head."

Her mouth flew open. *He has some nerve!*

"And you couldn't even rise to the occasion if a buck-naked woman were lying right next to you."

"You're right, if that woman was you." With that, he saluted her, then sprang to his feet. She saw little dimples pinching his cheeks as he walked off.

Elandra started twice to yell something at him. Too distracted she was, though, to think of the ultimate insult. Such broad shoulders were swaying like he owned the earth. It made her so curious about him. Who was he, really? Whoever he was, he made it impossible to lie back down and resume her dream. She watched him and watched him so much that even strolling along the shore, heading back to the condo, she was watching him then—watching him in her mind.

A black Jaguar rolled onto the grounds of 822 Topika Manor. A sprawling estate, it boasted an eight-bedroom mansion, myriads of palm trees and exotic flowers, a horse stable, pool, tennis court and statued waterfalls. The coupe parked in a section where nine other cars stood. Some antiques, some the finest modern-day models, the cars were trailed by a white, red and black minibus. When it slowed and came to a standstill, the driver opened the door and twelve noisy boys spilled out. Bradley observed them running about, peeking inside the cars, chasing each other, running around the back to the pool, and the tennis court, some simply slouching on the grass.

"Help yourself to anything, guys," he yelled, knowing they weren't listening to his invitation. There was just too much fun to be bothered with a 36-year-old man who they'd beat to death playing volleyball at the beach. Glad they were enjoying themselves, Bradley smiled and headed in the house.

He was wondering how they had so much energy after an active day at the beach when he noticed a stack of mail on the table. The house was so immaculate, obviously the maid had been there and put the letters in the usual place in the dining room. Sorting through them, he saw nothing out of the ordinary until he reached a certain envelope. The handwriting was so familiar Bradley just looked at it for several seconds. It had no return address. A strange feeling began to crawl over him, settling uncomfortably in his stomach.

Heartbeat growing, Bradley's fingers toyed with the envelope until it was open. He removed a letter and unfolded it. Seeing who it was from made him completely still. Moreover, it blocked out all sound. He couldn't hear anything other than what was going on inside him—the pounding. A racing heart was now blaring in his head and ears. The letter read:

Dear Bradley,
   I know you're surprised to hear from me. I also know

you probably still hate me for what I did to you. But back then I wasn't the person I am now. Now I am the person you thought I was, the beautiful woman inside and out that you fell in love with.

Back then, I was selfish, materialistic and vain. I made horrible choices I know. Every day I realize that more and more. All I do now is think about you. Such an extraordinary man you are. I think about what I gave up, hurting you as cruelly as I did. I know I was a fool. They say you never miss the water until your well runs dry. It took a while, but I now understand what that means.

My mother hasn't been doing well lately. Her heart is acting up again. I will be visiting her soon. Perhaps we can get together then. Perhaps you'll give me another chance to make it up to you. Think about it. I still love you. Never stopped.

> *With all my love,*
> *Kim*

The instant Bradley finished reading, the paper was crumpled and tossed in the trash. Why did she have to contact him again? Just when he was getting over what happened, here she came. No way in the world. He would never set himself up to be tortured again.

Not wanting to think of Kim anymore, Bradley gazed out the window to check on the boys. Most of them were doing the same things they'd been doing when he came inside. Certain they would be fine, he headed upstairs to the shower. He was tired. Kim's letter somehow enhanced it.

A T-shirt, jeans and briefs came off briskly, before stepping underneath the warm stream. Letting his head fall back, the water poured over his skin. Bradley closed his eyes and tried not to think about Kim. Unfortunately, it was impossible to do. They'd shared many showers right where he was standing at that moment. So clearly Bradley could see her—tall, slim hips, and legs. Most captivating, were her delicate features, beset with hair cropped so short and close, you couldn't miss any of the face's beauty.

After Bradley stepped out of the shower, he toweled off the wet beads and relaxed on the bed. Closing his eyes again, he expected to be haunted by visions of Kim once again. Oddly enough, though, it wasn't her who invaded his fantasy. Captivating his mind, desire for him breathing from her every pore, was Elandra. She wanted him—bad. Why was he fantasizing about a woman he hardly knew and didn't like, Bradley asked himself. He couldn't answer. He could only surrender to the vision in his mind—*Elandra*. Everywhere he turned there she was.

On the front porch of the condo, Elandra scraped her sandals against the concrete, trying to get the last trace of beach sand off the bottoms. The carpet in the house was light beige and she cringed at tracking anything on it. A neatness fanatic, Crystal had left it immaculate. That's how it would be when she returned home.

The sand was removed. Elandra unzipped her purse, then fumbled around assorted articles for the keys. Finding them in a special compartment, she unlocked the door swiftly. Exhaustion was seizing her bones. She was going to bolt to the bed.

Peach potpourri summoned her further inside after she shut the door. Elandra inhaled the sweetness, took off her sandals and headed straight to the bedroom. The enormous water bed appeared like heaven. Sprawling across it on her stomach, her body's fatigue shrieked that it had been a long day. Making it much longer had been running into Bradley and his brat pack. Yes, he had insulted her very well today. Even so, whatever his mouth said, she saw his eyes saying something different. Or was it imagination? Worse, was it wishful thinking? Perhaps being spurned by Dan made her want to be extremely desired by another man. But why him? Was it because they had been thrown together a lot lately?

Against her will, the pondering about Bradley progressed. So easy it was to recreate all that took place on the beach, every terrible and interesting bit of it. Most unforgettable was what he said about being a mentor to those boys. Did he really mean that, or was it meant to impress? Surprising, too, was his asking about Crystal. Turning over on her back, Elandra remembered all that was too intriguing to forget. It was only lulled by what she began wondering and imagining. Thoughts and visions of Bradley, which made her feel unlike herself—unlike who she had been lately. They made her feel soft and feminine, like she did when having that dream. Why was she thinking about him? The last thing she needed or wanted was a man, especially that one. Too bad the mind didn't understand that. Images were running so wild and rampant, she almost didn't hear the telephone. It was snatched up on the third ring.

"Hello?"

She listened.

"Yes, this is Elandra Lloyd."

She listened.

"You need me to come down there? Is Crystal there?" She sprang up. Her heart was racing so hard, it was shaking her entire body. "Have you found her?"

She listened.

"You found . . . a body?"

Five

Everything that was in Elandra's line of vision, anything that occurred on the way to the morgue, was not perceived. All was a blur because of the hysteria in her head. Deep down she was sure Crystal wasn't dead. As close as they were, Elandra was certain she would feel it if she were. On the other hand, logic knew it could be a possibility. Reality was what it was. There was a dead body of a young woman and she could be Crystal.

"Are you ready?" A plump, bald attendant approached Elandra from an adjoining room. His expression was blank.

Elandra flung some hair off her forehead and took a deep breath. "How do you ever get ready for something like this?"

"Oh, you'll have the strength," he said matter-of-factly. Afterwards he strode over to a table. She followed.

Aiming her eyes at the white sheet covering a human form, Elandra couldn't believe this was really happening. She was about to view a deceased person, which could be Crystal.

"I would give anything not to be here, doing this."

"You can do it."

Watching the chalky gloves peel the sheet down, Elandra unconsciously held her breath. When the body was finally exposed, she took one look at it and bolted out the door. The attendant caught up to her in the hallway. Elandra was backed against the wall. Tears slid down her cheeks.

"Is it your sister?" Two lines dented between his brows. "Oh, I'm so sorry if she is."

Elandra closed her eyes tight and opened them. A stream of water rolled down to her chin. "No, she's not my sister. Thank God for that. But she's someone to somebody."

The High Life Casino was next on Daisy's list of places where Trina and Crystal might turn up, or at least where someone who knew them could be hanging around. Dressing for the evening, Elandra was very anxious, too. Squirming into her lavender silk jumpsuit and beige pumps, she was determined to find her sister or else drastic measures needed to be taken. The private investigator Bradley mentioned was an idea. Unfortunately she didn't have the funds to pay one.

Elandra was putting on a silver hoop earring when the phone rang. It was Daisy. She couldn't accompany Elandra because her husband was sick. It didn't matter. Elandra was still going. Fortunately for her, too, Daisy gave her the name of a guy who worked at the blackjack table. A friend of Crystal and Trina, he might know their whereabouts. His name was Peppy.

The casino was decorated in a burst of color. Red, yellow, green, black and white, all splashed over tables, walls, furnishings and embellishments, awakened the senses the instant you stepped in the room. Grandiose chandeliers dangled from various points, spotlighting the action at the tables below and complementing thick red carpet.

The High Life was packed with tourists and islanders attempting to make that million-dollar dream come true. Elandra knew better than to have that wish. Her mother told them never to aim too high. In that case, you would never be disappointed. All Elandra wanted at that moment was simple—just to see her sister's face.

Maneuvering through the crowd, she eventually spotted the blackjack table. A light-complexioned black guy with bleached blond hair was dealing the cards out. Perfectly, he fit Daisy's description of Peppy.

"How are you?" Elandra asked, easing up to the side of him.

Dealing, he glanced at her, then looked at her again. Elandra was smiling. He didn't return the sentiment. Instead dark eyes searched her face, then wound down her body.

A patron's winning hand called his attention back to the table, but he was answering Elandra, "I'm fine. What can I do for you?"

"My name is Elandra."

"And you're not from here."

"I'm from New York."

"Mine is Peppy."

"I know."

That made him peer over at her. She was still smiling. Through tiny eyes, he scrutinized her lips for a second, then focused back on the cards, chips and people. "How do you know my name?"

"A friend told me. She says you know my sister and I'm trying to find her."

"What's her name?" Steadily he was dealing the cards.

"Crystal Lloyd."

Peppy stiffened. He stopped shuffling and just gawked at Elandra. Patrons started complaining about him holding up the game, but it was clear his mind was not in it anymore. Viewing his reaction, Elandra didn't know whether to be pleased or frightened.

Peppy tapped a young guy who was standing next to him. They wore the same blue and white uniform.

"Will you cover for me for a few minutes?" Peppy asked.

The guy nodded, checked out Elandra, then grinned at Peppy. "Sure."

Afterwards Peppy motioned for Elandra to come with him. "I know a secluded lounge. We can talk there."

Not knowing what to think, Elandra blindly followed Peppy. They went up an escalator. As she rode, she didn't know two pairs of eyes were watching her. One pair looked out of concern and the person followed her. The other pair looked out of curiosity. By another route, that person followed, too.

When they arrived in the lounge, Peppy closed the door and locked it behind him. Once again, Elandra didn't know what to think. Facing each other, they both became comfortable on the sofa.

"Why is a beautiful woman like you asking for so much trouble?" were his first words.

She smiled out of nervousness. Peppy didn't return the sentiment.

"How am I asking for trouble?"

"Crystal is not a good subject to ask about in every place. So watch it."

"Why?"

"Because she became involved in a game she didn't know how to play. And don't you ask no more about it."

Alarmed, Elandra leaned close to him. "What game? And why shouldn't I ask about her? She's my sister and she's missing."

"And you could be missing, too, if you keep it up."

Her eyes narrowing, Elandra eased back slowly. "What are you telling me?"

"That your sister is in something. I don't know all the details, but I know enough."

"Please tell me."

His eyes crawled along her body, then reached her eyes. "I saw her and a girl named Trina leaving a boat one day with this older guy. They got into a car and I never saw either of them again. Rumors on the island said he's an important man in America. A rich, powerful one. And the reason I tell you to stop pursuing this is because I've seen the man afterwards, but no sight or sound of your sister or Trina. If he is as powerful as they say, and you ask too many questions to the wrong person, you'll be next."

Absorbing all this, Elandra dropped her head. She gazed back up. "Will you tell all this to the police?"

Without a thought, Peppy shook his head. "No way. And if you tell anyone that I told you this, I'll deny it."

"Don't you want to help my sister? I thought you were her friend."

"Can't be no friend to anyone if I wind up like she is."

"But you don't know where she is. My sister is alive. I can feel it!" Elandra didn't know if she was trying to convince herself or him.

"Wish I could help."

"But you can! At least tell me where I can find the guy."

"I don't know where he is. I just see him when he's out and about on the island."

"Well, can you give me a description of him?"

Blond hair waved from side to side. "Can't do that."

"Or at least can you call me when you see him, and tell me to come so I can talk to him?"

A blond head shook again. "Can't get involved anymore. Like I said, it leads to trouble."

"Nothing will happen to you if you help, because nothing happened to Crystal either."

"For your sake, I hope you're right." With that, a calloused hand eased atop hers.

But before Elandra had a chance to react, there was a knock on the door. Peppy sauntered over and unlocked it. The young boy who'd taken his place at the blackjack table was facing him. "They need you back at the table," he told him.

"Coming." Peppy nodded, then turned around. He took a long look at Elandra before leaving. She remained where she was, shaking her head, weighing all she had heard.

Not far from her though, on a level lower, someone else began shaking his head too. Fingers were dialing. The young fellow who'd replaced Peppy soon spoke into the receiver.

"Hello, this is me. I'm in the casino and I heard this woman asking questions about Crystal Lloyd." Pause. "Yes, she was asking Peppy, one of my co-workers. They came up into the lounge and talked."

The conversation went on. At the same time, Bradley was searching the lounges, trying to find the one Elandra went to. Entering the casino with some business partners, he'd spotted her riding the escalator up with a former employee of his. Peppy was no angel. The twosome worried him.

Peering into a room in the corner of the hall, Bradley was relieved. There Elandra sat alone. Her face was buried in her palms.

"Elandra, are you all right?"

The familiar voice soothed and excited. Elandra raised her head and gazed over to the doorway. Dressed in a navy blue Italian suit, Bradley Davenport was coming toward her. In light of the way she was thinking about him lately, Elandra didn't feel comfortable.

Everything about him made her want to stare as he approached: the confident walk, the way his rich skin shimmered in the subdued light, his body in that suit, his eyes, the wide, seductive mouth.

"Yes, I'm okay," she lied. Telling him about her encounter with Peppy would have been opening herself too much to him. They didn't need to know any more about each other than they already knew, which wasn't much.

The instant Bradley sat across from Elandra on the couch, his presence overwhelmed her. Elandra had felt defenseless and alone, hearing the details about Crystal's disappearance and Peppy refusing to help. Bradley being in front of her roused the urge to give in to it all, and lay her head against something safe. His chest looked exactly like such a place. How could she want so much from this stranger, this man she hardly knew, she asked herself. Because he didn't really seem like a stranger, something inside her answered. That something made her afraid.

Bradley leaned forward, his eyes firmly on hers. "What were you doing going up the escalator with Peppy? Was he in here with you? Alone?"

Not knowing where this questioning was going, Elandra was frowning. She was also trying to avoid looking directly at him. "You were watching me going up the escalator with him like a spy? You know him?"

"Yes, I know him. He was an employee of mine."

She wanted to ask what kind of employee. Yet she wanted him to think she couldn't care less what he did for a living. "I don't believe it's any of your business."

"It's not my business. I was just concerned." Bradley was noticing her skin. It was so dewy; he could imagine how it felt. "He's not a nice guy, believe me. In and out of jail. As slithery as a snake."

"Well, thanks for your concern." She gazed in his

eyes. They were still firm in hers. She looked away. His shoulder was safer. "I can take care of myself."

"Not if you're talking to that character. I hope you weren't considering dating him."

She was shocked. Was he jealous? The thought amused her. It would also confirm what she saw in his eyes sometimes. "I wasn't considering dating him. For your information, he knew my sister and I was asking him about her."

Bradley was shaking his head. "No, no, no. Peppy is the wrong person to ask. You can't trust anything he says. You need an investigator. I told you I know one who's very efficient."

But where do I get investigator money? "I'll find her on my own."

"I hope you do, and before you get hurt, too."

"What's that supposed to mean?"

"You're running around like a chicken without a head, playing amateur detective."

"Don't start with me."

"Believe me, if I started with you, you wouldn't want me to stop." His eyes lowered to her body and slipped back up to her face.

Elandra crossed her legs and leaned further back. "Tell me, Mr. Davenport, do you always have to turn a regular conversation into something sexual, or is it just with me?"

Bradley chuckled. "I was just throwing something at you that would make you less uptight." He snaked a glance at her legs. "Something that I thought you would like."

"You're saying I like you making sexual innuendos to me?"

He smirked. "You've loosened up. Is that proof enough?"

"Please." She uncrossed her legs. "You have some ego."

Eyes dipped down to her legs again, but quickly raised back up. "Usually when a woman is as uptight as you are, she's deprived and she wants some excitement. My little innuendos do that for you, since no real person is doing it."

Elandra popped up, her eyes aimed down like daggers. Was it *that* obvious she had been jilted? That she was manless? But she wanted to be that way! "You don't know nothing about what I have! And talking about deprived—" Eyes narrowed like a hawk. "I'll tell you the meaning of deprived. You pull down your shorts and there it is!"

Elandra jerked her head and whirled to the door, hips rocking hard from side to side. Watching her lovely derriere disappear, Bradley sat there, mouth open, brows raised, then suddenly fell backwards laughing.

"Oh, she got me. She got me that time . . . good."

At 11:15 p.m. Elandra arrived on the doorstep of the condo. Believing nothing was out of the ordinary, she poked through an assortment of items in her shoulder bag until she found the keys. Yet when she was about to place them in the lock, she observed something odd. The door was slightly ajar. Never thinking anyone other than Crystal had unlocked the door, she pushed it open and raced into the living room.

Except her greatest wish wasn't to be. Halting her joy was the shock and fright of who she saw. Instead of Crystal, standing in the middle of the floor was a stringy-legged, terribly dressed, middle-aged man.

"Who are you?" Elandra asked. "What are you doing in here?" As she talked, she glanced around the room for some source of protection, a bat, a candleholder, anything. "You have no right to be in my house. I'll call the police if you don't leave."

"Your house?" he said, and tugged up some stretchy pants by the empty belt loops. "This is my house. I rent it to Crystal Lloyd. Where is she?"

"You know Crystal?" Elandra's fear began to diminish. After all, who could really be afraid of someone who looked like this? Cheap, plaid knit pants, in red, white and purple, a too-short tie, an orange shirt with lint balls everywhere. A circus should have been called, rather than the police.

"Yes, she's my tenant. And she may be my *ex*-tenant if she doesn't pay the last three months' rent. I've let it go long enough. Why is she late? She never was before. Hasn't even returned my phone calls. I've left several messages, too. And I came all the way from Freeport. What's the matter? Boyfriend isn't paying anymore?"

"What?" Elandra stepped closer. "What boyfriend? Someone's paying for Crystal to live here? Is he an older guy? Someone told me she was seen with an older guy."

"He's about my age. The man who stays here with her sometimes. He looks rich enough. He probably pays it. A sugar daddy thing, you know." Yet as if he was figuring something out, he eyed Elandra suspiciously. "Wait a minute. Who are *you*? Why don't you know any of this stuff? You're no friend of hers."

"I'm her sister. I came here from New York after I couldn't reach her. I was worried that something happened to her."

"Something probably happened, all right. She probably skipped town after sugar daddy got tired. Skipped town without paying me my money."

"She didn't. I know she wouldn't do that."

"She did it! You have to get out—today! Whoever you are."

"Today? You can't do that to me."

"Oh, yes I can. I have no lease with you. I don't know you from Adam's house cat."

"Can't you have a little compassion and give me some time to find a place?"

"Nosiree. I'm a businessman."

"Okay, I guarantee I will get your money."

"When?"

Elandra hesitated. Her funds were on the decline with no income in sight. Worse, she couldn't afford a hotel. That was a sure money-eater. The only solution was to get a job while she was in Nassau. Quick.

"You'll get your money at the end of the month."

"How are you so sure if you don't know where she is?"

"Because if she doesn't give it to you, I will. I'll even put it in writing." *Dummy! What did you say that for?* "That you let me stay here on the promise of paying you the rent at the end of the month."

A grin spread across his gaunt face, revealing scattered teeth. "I'll write something up right now and you can sign it. You have a pen?"

After the landlord left, Elandra's nerves were so frayed she paced back and forth. It was too much. Everything was falling apart, starting with Dan sleeping with her boss, which led to losing her job. Now her money was dwindling fast; she had none to pay the rent. Crystal was missing after some sugar daddy was taking care of her, taking her somewhere she hadn't returned from. Most horrible of all, her baby was gone. What else could go wrong? *God, why is this happening to me?*

Six

"I needed this," Elandra told Daisy. "Just a day out to unwind."

"You deserve it."

They were settling at a window table in The Lakeview, a restaurant which overlooked vibrant blue waters and miles of pink sand. Elandra loved the picturesque view. The entire atmosphere was uplifting. Outside the floor-to-ceiling glass windows, the towering hotels that spired above various monuments contrasted against the luminous sky like a breathtaking portrait. Equally luxurious was the ambience of the restaurant. Soft pastel furnishings, brocaded tablecloths, thick carpeting and dramatic chandeliers heightened Elandra's mood, too. The best part of the evening, however, was Daisy's wonderful company. Elandra needed a friend. Daisy was one.

"Thank you so much for your help since I've been here." Elandra clasped her hands together, placing them on the tablecloth. "I don't know what I would do if you weren't so much help to me."

"You would do fine," Daisy said, noticing the waiter giving Elandra a seductive gaze. "You're determined. You're strong, and your sheer will and love for your sister will help you find her. I know it will." Daisy caught the fellow giving Elandra a far bolder stare.

Elandra ignored the attractive man's attention, while Daisy relished the whole scenario. When he finally placed all the food and drinks on the table, Daisy nodded her "thank you" to him. Contrarily, Elandra, who was usually extremely gracious, didn't even glimpse him. When he strode off, with Daisy's large eyes boring into his back, Elandra was eagerly picking up her fork and knife and digging into lobster.

Beaming, Daisy's eyes switched to her. "Come on, woman. Don't tell me you didn't notice that good-looking waiter giving you the eye?"

Elandra chewed a bit, then gazed up at Daisy. "I noticed."

"So?"

"So what?"

"So you're an attractive, healthy woman. And I've never heard you mention a husband or boyfriend."

"Because there is neither."

"Good. You're a good-looking woman, real good-looking, and all these men who gawk at you all the time and try to meet you are yours for the picking."

"I'm finished with men, Daisy." The subject made her pick at her food.

"You're just saying that because you're upset about Crystal. She's the only thing your mind and heart can hold right now. But wait until you find her, you'll change your mind. You'll be wanting to play catch-up in the woman department. If you know what I mean." She winked.

Elandra laughed dryly. "Daisy, I don't want to think about a man even after I find Crystal." She gazed down for a second, then back up at her friend intently. "My boyfriend . . . I caught him with my boss. They were making love in his office. I really loved him. Thought he loved me."

Daisy was scowling, shaking her head wildly. "Oh, no, that's awful!"

"Yes. I was pregnant."

Daisy frowned more, like something was physically hurting her. "I feel for you."

"I feel for me, too."

"Where is your child? In New York?" She took a sip of a piña colada.

"Nope. . . ." Elandra's eyes filled with water. "In heaven . . . I miscarried."

Daisy's hand flew up to her mouth. "Lord, no!"

"Yes, there is no more baby." A tear slid to her chin.

Daisy reached in the napkin holder and held one out to her. Elandra accepted it, dabbing at her cheeks.

Clear-eyed, she smiled at Daisy. "We all have crosses to bear. I'm bearing mine now."

"Losing a child is just too much to bear. I'm so sorry about the baby."

"You have no idea how sorry I am. I ache for my child."

"I heard that's how it is."

"It's a pain you can't even describe."

"I can't imagine it." Daisy took several more swallows of her drink, then set it hard on the table. "But I will tell you that you're lucky for being free of a man like that."

"Don't I know it."

"If you're giving respect and love to a man, you deserve it back. And I tell you this because of my own relationship with my husband."

Elandra picked up her fork and prodded the lobster. "Sometimes though, I think part of it was my fault."

Daisy was chewing. "Why do you say that?"

"Because." She nibbled a chunk as well. "Because I let him do things to me and treat me in a manner that I knew wasn't right. I should have known what I wanted out of a relationship. But I just wanted someone to love me no matter what he did to me."

"That's a problem lots of women have," Daisy

agreed. "They want love so bad, want a man so bad, they'll accept any kind of treatment from him. But you can't let men treat you any kind of way. If it's not in his nature to treat you with respect, get him out of your life. You lose your dignity the minute you let him disrespect you and get away with it. Your man had turned into a dog. A real dog. And if you act like a doormat, he's going to walk on you. Don't ever surrender your respect and you'll always be acknowledged for who you are. We all want to be those kind of women."

"I wasn't."

"A lot of women aren't. It would be so much better if you came into a relationship feeling complete and ready, and physically, mentally, spiritually and emotionally together. But this is not a perfect world and all women are not going to enter a relationship that way."

"That's for sure."

"But even in that case, there are men who won't hurt you no matter how weak you are, or how insecure you are, and how low your self-esteem is. Those are the men who know themselves. They understand that women are as imperfect as they are, and though we've come a long way, we're trying to make our way in the world the best way we can. As long as you share their kindness, their care, their understanding, their warmth, those men just want to love you and help you be the best that you can be."

Elandra pondered that. "Are there really men like that?"

"Of course. I married one."

Elandra drifted off into the horizon. "I don't know, Daisy. I've been hurt before. I don't think there are any more of those men left, and right now I'm too tired and shattered to even try to find out." Their eyes met again.

"Sounds like you're giving up."

"I have, on men. I really mean it when I say I'm finished. It hurts too much."

"But next time may be the right one."

"There won't be a next time."

Daisy tilted her head forward. Finger waves glittered in the room's light. "You mean to tell me that a young, healthy woman like you is going to live your whole life on this earth without experiencing the sweetest taste of all in life, the taste of romantic love?"

"Yes, that's exactly what I'm going to do. That taste has not been so sweet to me."

In awe, Daisy sat motionless. "You look and sound like you really mean that."

"I do! I won't let any man get near my heart again. Never! No one is going to use me again and put me through all that hell, making me feel like . . . like . . . Oh, I can't even describe it, it's such a horrible feeling. They're all the same"

"How are you going to live?"

"What do you mean?"

"I mean, what's going to give you happiness? A career, or money, or just things?"

"Many women live content lives without romantic love in it." *I will too,* she thought. *I will too.*

Daisy peered down, and hoped her ignored food hadn't become cold. After picking up a chunk on her fork, she twirled it in butter sauce and frowned at this woman whom she was becoming increasingly attached to. Elandra's way of thinking was a grave mistake. Yet after her recent experience, how could Daisy convince her otherwise? The answer was simple. She couldn't. She could only pray that time would show her differently.

They had shifted their conversation to strategies for finding Crystal when something at the entrance of the restaurant distracted Daisy. It compelled her to stop in mid-sentence and gape in that direction. Wanting to know what was so interesting, Elandra looked that way also. However, when she saw that it was Bradley Davenport that had struck her friend's excitement, she quickly turned back around. He was entering the restaurant with two other men. All were immaculately dressed and carrying briefcases.

"That's a pain in my butt," Elandra remarked.

Daisy looked at her shocked. "Who? Bradley Davenport?"

"You know him?"

"Of course, woman. Everybody knows that man. Why is he a pain in your butt?"

"Because everywhere I turn up, he's right there, bothering me."

Tittering at this, Daisy's gap-tooth smile was dazzling. "You're lucky. He's gorgeous. And a real good man. He's famous, too."

"He's famous? No, he isn't."

"Yes, he is."

"How?"

"A businessman. That man is one of the richest men on the island. A self-made millionaire. A poor boy who made it! He built all kinds of businesses from scratch, from the ground up—hotels, construction. You name it, he's in it. He even owns the hotel I work for. You just have to admire him."

"Him?"

"Yep."

Elandra glanced back at Bradley. The waitress was escorting him and the other men to a section that was out of their sight. She returned to Daisy. "I knew he was involved in something out of the ordinary."

"Woman, where have you been?"

"On this island."

"No, you haven't! You haven't really been on it if you don't know about that man."

"I accused him of being a drug dealer."

"A drug dealer?" Daisy's shoulders shook as she broke into laughter. "No, no, my dear. Far from it. If he's into drugs, it's the legal kind—pharmaceuticals."

Elandra was stunned. She had guessed that his pockets weren't hurting, but never that he was one of the richest men on the island—and smart enough to build near empires.

She focused on Daisy. "He has really been getting on my nerves. And everywhere I turn up, there he is. Now even tonight. I come to a restaurant and out of all the restaurants in Nassau, he walks in the door."

Daisy couldn't hide how funny this was to her.

"What?" Elandra asked. "What's making you look so silly?"

"He's a good-looking man. Ooh, what a body, and that face, those eyes, that strong jaw and lips meant for pleasing." Daisy raised a mischievous brow. "Don't tell me you haven't noticed?"

Elandra refused to admit the truth. "He's all right."

Daisy grabbed her stomach, laughing. When she stopped, she was searching Elandra's eyes. "Your mouth is saying one thing. Your eyes are saying something else. I think our millionaire has been getting to you."

"No, he hasn't."

"Oh yes he has." She was still grinning. "Bet you been thinking about him in bed, fantasizing. Thinking about those concrete-hard legs against yours. Your soft breasts against his hard chest and him looking in your eyes."

Elandra's eyes widened. *How did she know that?* "No, I haven't."

"You're not fooling me."

"You're wrong. But there is one thing that I do need from Bradley, though."

That brow raised again. Daisy couldn't stop grinning.

"No, not that," Elandra declared.

"You sure?"

"Yes."

"What else do you need from him?"

"A job."

Elandra was surprised how easily and quickly the appointment was made. As the founder and CEO of five companies, she expected Bradley's schedule to be prepared weeks ahead of time. When the appointment was made a day later, Elandra was overjoyed. Desperately she needed a job, and God knows she would do her best at it. She greatly believed in putting your heart and soul into your work.

Stepping through the posh hallways of Davenport Enterprises, Elandra felt swallowed in warmth and luxury. Lush carpeting, extravagant art, refined scents, music and the finest furnishings, all spoke of the style which was so characteristic of Bradley.

The secretary was a middle-aged woman wearing a baggy gray suit and sporting dreadlocks. "May I help you, dear?" Surprisingly, her accent was English.

"I'm Elandra Lloyd. I have an appointment with Bradley Davenport."

She smiled and scanned her calendar. Locating the name, she looked back at Elandra. "Come with me, dear."

They walked down a long corridor at the end of the hall. The door opened. Bradley was reading the paper. Seeing the two, he put it away.

"Thanks, Phyllis."

Elandra's eyes trailed the closing of the door behind

the secretary. It was easier to look at that than face being alone again with Bradley. Sitting behind the desk, he looked so powerful and she felt so strange.

At the same time, Bradley was wishing she didn't look like she did. In the soft pink fitted suit, her body was voluptuous perfection. Making her more luscious was how the color brought out her skin, and the way her hair was so carefree, and the exotic upward slant of her eyes. An intense urge overcame him to ease around the desk and be closer, as close as he could be. Nonetheless, good sense knew better. Bradley rationalized her effect on him. It had been so long since he was with a woman. Not since Kim.

Her eyes finally met his. "How are you?"

"I'm fine. And you?"

"Good."

Neither smiled. He was observing her as if she were odd. "Aren't you going to sit down?"

"I was waiting for you to ask me."

"Sorry for my bad manners."

Elandra sat and examined everything to avoid him. The artwork, the awards, certificates, and degrees, the pictures with other well-dressed people. All the while, he was staring.

"So you want a job?" he asked, reeling her attention to him. "And you told my secretary you have seven years of secretarial experience?"

"Yes, I do."

"Does that mean you don't believe I'm a drug dealer now?"

"I'm sorry about that. All the pressure with my sister and other things in my life made me say and do things I normally wouldn't."

"Is that right?" He sounded and looked skeptical.

"Yes, that's right."

"You know, I was really surprised when my secretary

told me who was trying to get an interview. I don't usually do interviews. Personnel typically handles that. But I juggled some things around so I could see you. I knew this would be really interesting."

"Interesting? How so?"

He leaned forward, searching her eyes. "I wanted to know how you would act now that you wanted something from me."

"What do you mean?"

"I mean, would you be nicer?"

"I'm nice to you. Nice as I could be under the circumstances."

"I think you're nicer now. Your whole demeanor since you came in here is different."

"What are you getting at?"

"How did you find out that I was in a position to hire you for a job?"

"A friend of mine told me."

"What else did that friend tell you?"

"Nothing, but that you were a successful businessman."

"So that translated to rich?"

She was bewildered. "I don't understand how this is an interview."

Tensing his forehead, he reclined in his chair. "But I do understand how you're operating."

"What?" In his demeanor there was thriving hostility. She couldn't understand where it was coming from.

Suddenly he was angry. "Now that you know I'm wealthy, you want to be nice and friendly. You want a job, probably want everything I can give you. Right?"

Elandra couldn't believe what she was hearing. What was wrong with him? She stood and headed toward the door. "I should have known better than to come here and ask you for a job. I didn't want your life. Just a job to keep a roof over my head. I should have known you wanted to demean me. You want me to beg. But no damn way!"

She had just touched the door handle when a large hand came down upon hers. Instantly warmth riveted through her. Elandra pivoted around slowly. Bradley was looking down at her, his face just inches from hers. Regret showed vividly in his face.

"I'm sorry, Elandra," he apologized. "I had no right to accuse you of being a gold digger. It's just that . . ." But he couldn't tell her what happened. With such a strong attraction to her, he couldn't share any of himself, his life. He already felt himself treading in deep waters he had vowed never to venture into again. "It's just that something happened in my life and it's hard to trust people."

He sounded sincere. Then she remembered. She remembered how he'd scared her at the yacht the first day they met. He was ranting about women and how they took and took, driving a man crazy. "Are you talking about a woman, Bradley?" He was so near and something about him so overpowering she could hardly get her words out. "Has someone hurt you?"

He didn't answer right away. He merely felt his body heating, his eyes unable to move from hers. Why was he feeling like this? After all he had been through, he'd sworn no one would get close to him again. Even so, there was something about her—vulnerability, honesty—and somehow he knew she would understand. Though he wouldn't take the chance. It took too long for his heart to mend, to have it shattered again by the next pretty face that came along.

He retreated several steps until he was resting against the desk. "I'm not going to answer that question because you and I should keep everything on a professional level, Elandra, if you're going to work for me."

Her face lit up. "You mean I have a job?"

"As my assistant."

"But you haven't even seen my résumé. You didn't give me a chance to show it to you."

"I don't have to see it. My instincts tell me all I need to know."

She was glowing. "You won't be sorry, Bradley. When I have to do something I put my all into it."

"That's good. I'm very passionate about things I do, too."

"Where will I be working? Here at the office with your secretary?"

"No, most of the time I work from home. I have an office there for you. And about salary . . ." He reached across the desk for a pad. A figure was scribbled on it. He put the amount before her.

Reading it, Elandra was so excited she could hardly breathe. "Thank you for that. You're very generous. I was about to get thrown—I mean, I needed a job real bad."

When Elandra left, Bradley stood precisely where he was, remembering her as though she were right in front of him. He knew he shouldn't have hired her to work so closely with him. Then again, how could he not? There was something about her that made him weak, that made him forget what he had been through. And when it felt like it was choking him, when it felt like that he was losing control and maybe putting his emotions on the line again, it made him do imbecilic things, like accusing her for no reason at all of being a gold digger, like he had earlier. When would the pain stop completely? But how could it, when Kim was trying to be a part of his life again?

Thinking of her, Bradley stepped behind his desk and removed the latest letter from Kim. He had been carrying it around in his jacket pocket, reluctant to open it, reluctant to take that painful trip into the past.

Why was she reopening such anguish? What had happened in her life to cause such a turnaround? Regardless of her reasons, Bradley recognized he had to confront his own demons. *Read it and be done with her.*

Dear Bradley,

I'm writing you again, because I can't stop thinking about you. I can't stop remembering the love we had, the passion we shared. Over and over I recreate how you used to make love to me. Oh how my mind lingers on how you kissed my toes, and ran your full bottom lip along my calfs and then reached my thighs, planting tiny kisses along them.

Remember how I screamed from the sweet agony and then you fulfilled me more, treating me to the delights of your hands and lips, and the nectar from your soul. Wasn't it heaven? Don't you remember? How can you forget? I can't.

No man has ever made me feel the way you did. And I know no woman can ever give you the passionate love I gave you.

We can have that again. We can have all that delicious love we made again and even better. I love you so much. I can give so much more. I hope when I see you, you'll have softened toward me. I hope time will have healed the wounds. I know it's made me smarter and so clearly I can see what a grave mistake I made. I hope you'll want to feel everything we felt before.

I will be seeing you soon, and you will love me again. I know you will.

Love,
Kim

Seven

Looking perfect and feeling comfortable was important for the first day of work, Elandra thought. A plain white silk top, beige skirt and beige pumps did the trick. Afterwards, she studied every inch of her face in the mirror. Sleek skin stretched over an oval face with doll-like cheeks. Full lips were highlighted with "Ruby Fire" gloss. Long-lashed eyes were sensuous and exotic. All was surrounded by hair which was soft, wild and healthy. A turn to view the front of her, a swivel to view the back, a pivot to the profile and Elandra was ready to leave.

A handbag was slung over her shoulder. Elandra opened the door and was surprised by an elderly gentleman facing her. Standing there in the early morning sunlight, he wore a white suit and matching wide-brimmed hat. His fist raised, he was just about to knock on the door.

"Are you Elandra Lloyd?" he asked with pleasant island enunciation.

"Yes, I am. And who might you be, sir?"

"Your chauffeur."

From that, Elandra lost her balance a bit. "You're my what?"

"Your chauffeur, Ms. Lloyd. Bradley sent me."

"You're kidding." She couldn't help smiling. "He sent a chauffeur for me?"

The man rubbed his whiskers. "That's right. Says I'm to pick you up in the limo every day unless otherwise instructed. My name is Richard."

The ride to Bradley's home would have been breathtaking enough, even without the comforts of the limo's stuffed cushions, its red wine and raspberry fragrance. Powdery beaches, crystal waters, colorful flowers and palm trees lured her attention out the window, all of it making Elandra feel like she was beholding heaven on earth.

When the driver rolled onto the manicured land of Bradley's estate, Elandra was truly in awe. She had grown up in the servants' quarters of a rich family's estate, but the house and grounds were nowhere near as lavish and enormous as Bradley's abode.

Richard escorted Elandra inside the house to his boss' office. Strolling through the immense home, she was glancing at everything. Striking pastel art deco furnishings were mingled with many earthy antiques. Unquestionably the furnishings were expensive, but equally cozy. While waiting alone for Bradley to come downstairs, Elandra even began to imagine how it would feel to live like this. Nice, she thought, to have such comfort greet you every day, and never have to worry about bills, or the cost of things, but merely treating yourself to whatever whim you had at the moment.

The pondering transported her back to days when she was a child. Her dreams were such fantasy then. An actress, an astronaut, a pilot, a doctor, anything Elandra could see herself being. Now seeing all Bradley had accomplished, she wondered what would have unfolded if she had persisted dreaming big. Moreover, what if she had acted on it? What would her life be like now? Then there wouldn't be the slightest problem in hiring an investigator to find Crystal. That being as it may, she knew dreams were dreams, and reality was real. Reality was the world and all its problems. Reality was realizing that dreams rarely came true. At least that's what her mother had always said.

"Ready for your first day?"

The exhilaration brimming in Bradley's voice swung Elandra around to his direction. Coming toward her, he was wearing a T-shirt and jeans, dressed totally unlike she had ever seen him. Reflexively Elandra's gaze traveled across the width of his chest and lowered to the snugness of his pants, then raised quickly, realizing how she must have looked doing this.

"Yes, I'm ready," she answered. "Ready and rearing to go."

"Good." He was looking at her and smiling, dimples denting his cheeks, as if he wanted to say something else, but didn't know how to.

"Your house is beautiful," she complimented him. "You're so lucky."

"Lucky?" He was tickled. "I don't think luck had anything to do with it."

"It didn't? I would consider myself lucky if I had all this." Her arms spread out to emphasize the point.

"No, it wasn't luck." He rubbed across his chin. "Not at all. I worked like a dog, worked crazy hours, worked when other people were enjoying vacations, holidays, worked when all I had to drive me was my belief."

"So how exactly did you do it? What steps did you take?"

"Steps? How *exactly* did I do it?" Pondering the question, he looked off. "I did it by following my heart." He gazed back at Elandra. She looked hungry for his every word.

"Your heart?"

Automatically she relaxed on a nearby sofa. Loving her curiosity, Bradley sat across from her.

"Yes, my heart. Doing what I loved and believing in

myself enough to stick with it, even when the going
was tough."

"But how did you start everything? I'm just amazed.
I knew a well-off family, but they had nothing like what
you have."

She scanned the room. While she did, Bradley
watched her. He loved her honesty. Many people
wanted to impress him and put on airs, especially
women.

"First off, I came from a poor, single-parent home
in Florida."

That drew her back to him. "So you're originally
from Florida?"

"Born and bred."

"And what happened next?" Anxiousness made her
lean her elbow on the couch and her palm against her
cheek. "Something great had to happen."

"Next I did extremely well in school."

"You were an A student and a jock, weren't you?"

Dimples pinched his cheeks as he grinned. "That I
was."

"But how did you get from there to where you are
now?"

"For one, those good grades helped. I was offered
scholarships. I always had an interest in business, and
knew I wanted to study it. So when I had the chance I
did very well. Then when I graduated I worked one
year for a hotel chain as a manager. After that, I had
a strong desire to run my own. I was obsessed with the
idea. The only thing I needed was capital."

"Where did you get it from?" Her eyes were glistening with her smile, soaking in every inch of him.

"Not from myself. I can tell you that. I had about
$300 in the bank and I knew no hotel empire could
be started from that." They both smiled. "So I knew I
had to get the rest from investors. You see, in school I

learned the importance of a good business plan when you have an idea. I did one, presented it to investors and they offered me my first deal. I had to give them many shares of the company, but after I worked hard, and harder and made a profit, I paid them back and bought them out. After that deal, I reinvested my profits in another business. I just made sure that my business idea was so sound, it wouldn't lose. The rest has been history. I've been blessed. But you know what?"

"What?"

"Working hard at something you like is fun."

She giggled. "I've worked hard at all my jobs, but it was never fun."

"Because you weren't doing what you liked. No, *really* it is. You get all charged up. You know, do what you love and the universe will respond abundantly. You'll be rewarded not only financially, but it will fill you up inside with so much joy and contentment, you'll be eager to get up the next day and do it all again."

His conviction staggered Elandra into speechlessness. So much so, she could only stare and think about what he said. She knew Bradley knew what he was talking about. Proof of that was him living his dreams. What she had really wanted to ask him, though, was where did he get courage like he had, the courage just to act on faith when all around you in the world was saying what you wanted could never be. Stopping her was the notion that the question sounded too silly. Elandra believed she asked too many foolish questions already.

She was wrong. It was her deep interest and candor which made Bradley see her in a clearer light. It felt good to communicate so easily like this with her, no battling, no insults, solely two people getting to know each other, taking off the layers, and slowly showing each other who they were. Each one felt more at ease

with the other. There was a serenity in the air between
them. In that brief moment Bradley convinced her to
believe he wasn't that bad after all. Nevertheless, there
was a growing silence amid the looks they were giving
each other, which before made her increasingly uncomfortable. Elandra felt they had become too personal. Her guard was down too far.

"Enough about that interesting stuff," she said interrupting the quiet and changing the subject, "tell me
about my job and what I'll be doing so I can start doing
it."

Work was a thrilling experience. Never a dull moment in the world of Davenport Enterprises. Bradley
owned three prestigious hotel chains, a construction
company, a high-rise apartment complex and a realty
company. Meetings were constantly being set up that
would likely generate million-dollar deals. Hotel service
was continuously being enhanced so that thousands of
customers would receive all the value they paid for. The
construction firm was effectively building low-cost
housing and offices for hundreds of people. Much the
same as the rest, the realty company was successful too,
selling homes, some at the cost of one million per
home. Elandra was amazed that the little messages she
took, the letters she typed, and the minutes she tran-
scribed all contributed to sustaining this thriving empire. It was electrifying for her to be part of such power.
Added to that, when Bradley asked her to accompany
him to a construction site, asking her opinion on some
things and making notes, it made her feel important,
appreciated, like what she thought truly mattered. It
gave her such a high.

The feeling lingered. That evening as she leaned on
the terrace banister, Elandra didn't feel like going

home. It was a little past nine p.m. They had been working since eight in the morning. The high of it all was still bursting inside her. As well, Bradley seemed to be still floating, too. Elandra heard him in the house, still making business calls, being the ultimate workaholic. *That's how he got where he is,* she thought, and gazed up into the sky. Stars were everywhere.

Finally she heard silence inside. Before long, Elandra heard footsteps coming up behind her. She turned around and smiled at him, then gazed back at the sky. He came next to her. Positioning himself against the banister, his eyes aimed upward, too.

"You weren't kidding when you said you're a hard worker," he complimented her. "I never would have expected you to stay so late, and work so hard, too. Thank you. You were a dynamo today."

Hearing that, Elandra looked overjoyed. It glowed all over her as she perused the stars. "No, thank *you.* It was a really wonderful day. I wasn't worrying as much about Crystal or thinking about—I mean, it took my mind off of many things. Working on all your enterprises is so invigorating."

"I'm glad you feel that way. I feel the same way."

"In just one day I feel like I missed so much before."

He glanced at her, then looked back up. "Why do you say that?"

"Because my other jobs bored me to death."

"Why didn't you ever try to do something that really got your blood moving?"

"Because I thought I was doing the best I could do."

"Didn't you ever dream about doing something you loved?"

"Oh, yes, especially in the middle of the day, when the work I was doing was so mundane. When I was alone, I would get up and look out the window, and wonder what else was out there for me. Then I would remember what my mother used to say to us, rest her soul. Crystal and I always heard it when we were growing up."

"What did you hear?"

"To know our place."

"Your place?" Frowning, Bradley's eyes fell down hard on her. "What is that supposed to mean?"

The stars were still captivating her. "She discouraged us from going for big dreams. She was a maid and believed that was the best she could do. I think her upbringing had a lot to do with it. Plus, this particular church she went to had much to do with that thinking. They believed your riches and happiness would come from heaven. Therefore she shared that philosophy with us. She didn't want us to be disappointed and devastated when we didn't make it."

Bradley was ripping inside hearing this. "You know that's wrong, don't you, Elandra?"

She hunched her shoulders. "Who knows?"

He clutched her arms, lightly jerking her to face the intensity on his face. "Your mother loved you, of course. You were her daughter. But she was dead wrong about knowing your place. Your place is as high as you want it to be."

"But that's not how I was raised, Bradley." Her tone was weary.

He shook his head. "It doesn't matter. Somehow along the way the spirit was beat out of your mother. Life does that to people sometimes. Giant obstacles are in their way and they just get tired of fighting for their happiness and they settle. But don't you settle. You can have everything you want, all the joy, all the excitement, all the riches . . ." His eyes searched deep in hers. "All the love."

Warm brown depths lured her inside them. With him looking at her like that, holding her arms so forcefully and gently at the same time, she could almost believe anything he said. They were so close, she could smell the masculine scent of his cologne. Inhaling it reeled her a step closer, where her eyes met his lips. They were moist and trembling, and when she gazed back up into his eyes they were lingering in hers, and then lower to her mouth. Elandra knew she was entering dangerous territory as much as Bradley did. With a great effort, each one eased back.

Bradley swallowed the excitement which had built in his throat. "So do you, ah . . . ah understand what I was saying to you?"

"Yes," Elandra answered, tossing some hair back off her eye. "You're saying that I don't have to settle for doing just anything with my life. That I can have my dreams."

"You can, Elandra. Don't let anyone ever tell you that you can't again. You have everything it takes inside of you, to be anything you want, do anything you want."

She nodded, then noticed the driveway below. Richard was leaning on the door of the limousine. "I better leave now. I want to get an early start tomorrow. Plus, I'm anxious to check my machine for messages. Maybe the police have some word on Crystal's whereabouts."

She walked off into the house, with Bradley escorting her downstairs and outside. When the limousine drove off, Bradley leaned in the doorway, digging his hands deep in his pockets.

"Crystal," he whispered and searched the starlit sky. "We have to find you and get you back to that sister of yours."

The next morning when Elandra entered the house to begin working, she was greeted by Bradley along with a rotund gentleman. She had noticed the blue Lexus Coupe outside and assumed a business associate had stopped by.

Both men stood when she approached them. Bradley came nearest, putting his arm around her shoulder. "Elandra Lloyd, this is Myron Tate. He's the private investigator I told you about."

Uneasily, Elandra smiled and shook the man's hand. Yes, she needed a private investigator to find Crystal, but first she had to work long enough to get a paycheck. Following that, she had to pay back Crystal's rent or get tossed out.

"Nice to meet you, Ms. Lloyd," he said in a voice that was clearly American.

"You, too."

The two became comfortable on the sofa, while Bradley stood nearby.

"I hear your sister is missing. Bradley here has told me as much as he can, which isn't much. I need much more information from you."

Instead of answering, Elandra dropped her face in her palms. Bradley and Myron eyed each other at the odd behavior.

Bradley knelt down beside her. "Elandra? Elandra, what's wrong?"

Slowly she raised her head to look at him. "I might as well be honest with you guys. I can't afford an investigator right now."

Bradley smiled. "Is that all?"

"That's enough. My finances are not in the best shape. I . . ." She almost told him about getting thrown out of the apartment, but she was too embarrassed.

Myron smiled as well, showing a boyish smile. "You don't have to worry about that, Ms. Lloyd."

Elandra was puzzled. "What do you mean?"

Myron gazed over at Bradley. "Your boss has taken care of it."

"My boss?" She gazed at Bradley. His eyes were firm in hers.

"Consider it a gift, Elandra," he said, "and I don't expect anything in return. I'll put that in writing if you wish."

Myron blushed. Elandra smiled.

"But I will pay you back. I know it's expensive."

"No price is too high for your peace of mind. You're ah . . . you're a fine employee."

"I can't tell you how much this means to me."

When the meeting was over, Myron Tate headed to his car, contemplating the first lead he would work on to start the case. After sliding his stout form upon the driver's seat, he started the engine, then looked up in the mirror to back out of the driveway. That's when he saw eyes that snapped his head around. The young man from the casino had been hiding in the back seat.

His lips were thin, and balled up in anger. Venom spewed from his tiny eyes.

"Who are you?" Myron asked, more outrage than panic showing on his face. "What do you want?"

"I was sent to give you a message. Don't look for Crystal Lloyd."

"What?"

"You heard what I said, big man. You are not to look for Crystal Lloyd. You are to *pretend* you are looking for her. Do you understand what I'm saying?"

"Get out of my car you little creep! I'll shred your hide to pieces. Now get!"

But the gun made him hush. Myron's gaze was glued to it, then to the boy as he talked.

"I mean what I'm saying, man. You have a daughter in Grierson, that private high school, don't you?"

Myron's mouth flopped open.

"And your wife works at the hospital on Paradise Island?"

"How—"

"Don't you mess with us! Bombs, guns, knives, fires—you name it, we can do it like the best of them. You do as we say, or else. You can run, but you can't hide. One way or the other we will get you."

"Can I give you a ride?" Bradley asked Elandra. She was stepping outside onto the doorstep one afternoon, expecting Richard to drive her home. Surprisingly, she saw the limousine jacked up on one side, the driver's head and chest underneath it.

"Something wrong with the limo? I guess Richard won't have it working for a while?"

"Probably not." They walked together along the walkway, down to the garage, where his numerous vehicles were parked.

"I guess you can drop me," she told him. "But I'm not going home."

"Oh no?" He went around to the passenger side of the Jaguar and opened the door.

She slid onto the leather seat. "No. I have to make a stop today."

He entered his side, then started the engine. "Where're you going?"

For someone who had stressed a professional relationship when she was first hired, he was being a bit intrusive. And she hoped he didn't feel because he had done some huge favors for her that he deserved to know her every move. She would pay him back for the investigator. As far as the work went, she was earning her income.

"I just have somewhere to be," she answered flatly.

He was driving off the property. Facing ahead, he tugged at his collar. "You're not going to see Peppy anymore to question him about your sister, are you?"

"No."

"Good. Because he doesn't really want to help. That guy just wants to get in your pants."

The comment was so out of place, she leaned back, gawking at him. "How do you know that?"

"Because I know him. A guy like that will say anything to get with a woman like you."

"And what kind of woman is that?"

"You know." He glimpsed her. "You know . . ." His attention switched back to the road.

"No, I don't know. Tell me."

"You know. You're not . . ."

"I'm not what?"

"You're not too hard on the eyes."

"I see." She smiled, taking in the gracefulness of his profile. She also noticed an eye repeatedly sneaking to her thigh. Placing her purse over what the short skirt didn't cover stopped his fun.

"So where do I take you?" Bradley asked. "We're getting near the main highway."

"To Alcove Terrace."

Eyes on the road, he nodded with an approving look. "That's a pretty nice area. Who lives there?"

Elandra saw him as so funny. He was still determined to find out where she was going. If she didn't know better, it would seem that he was worried about her visiting a man. If that was so, she wanted to tease him. After all, hadn't he teased her before about not being with anyone.

"A friend lives there," she responded.

"Someone you're questioning about Crystal?"

"No."

"That's a relief. Because this guy Myron is very good."

"I believe you."

He steered onto the main highway. "You plan to visit your friend long?"

"As long as it takes."

"As long as what takes?"

"Whatever we plan to do."

"Have big plans then?"

"Lots."

"You know, if you're seeing someone on this island, you could tell me who he is and I could let you know if he's all right."

"You could?"

"Sure. Because the guys on this island can get a little kinky."

"That's okay."

Finally they reached the luxurious but small condominiums at Alcove Terrace. Elandra peered at number 125. Her interest then switched back to Bradley.

"Thanks so much for the ride. I really appreciate it."

"No problem. See you tomorrow."

Bradley watched Elandra knock on the door, but wasn't in a position to see who opened it. She entered and his curiosity reached its peak. He drove away, pulling the car in a dirt road out of sight. He parked. Seconds later, he was on the porch of 125 Alcove Terrace.

Checking the other porches in the row, he saw no one—no one to gawk at him, wondering what he was doing. Hence, he proceeded to slink to an open window and peek over the ledge to see inside. Expecting to see some guy drooling all over Elandra, he was more than surprised when he saw a drastically different sight. There was only Elandra and an elderly, crippled lady. Elandra was helping her from a wheelchair to the couch. And when Bradley shoved his ear closer, he could even hear them talking.

"It's so nice to see you, Elandra."

"It's nice to see you too, Mrs. O'Grady." Elandra was carefully guiding the wavering woman down onto the sofa. "You know I can't go too many days without seeing you."

Mrs. O'Grady's cheeks raised bashfully. "It's hard to believe it was only a month ago that the Lord brought you to my door. It's like I knew you my whole life."

"I know what you mean." Looking misty-eyed, Elandra settled next to her. "Some people you just feel like you knew forever in a short amount of time, and others you've known your whole life, it seems like you never knew them at all."

"Amen." A bony hand patted Elandra's. "But I know you have better things to do than be here with me. I don't want to be selfish. So if you have somewhere else to be, don't worry about me. One of my dearest friends moved back to Nassau. Plus I can have me some wonderful times reminiscing about my Jacob, bless his soul, and how it was when my kids were here. So don't you think you have to stay with me long."

"I told you I would come and spend some time with you tonight." Elandra put her arm around the older woman's shoulder and gently squeezed it. "Since the home attendant cooked for you already, the least I can do is wash some of your clothes and tidy up the house a bit."

"You don't have to, dear."

"I want to. I love coming here, and I'm going to keep coming. Otherwise I'd be sitting home, just worrying about Crystal." She looked down, her eyes scattering. "That day when I came around ringing the bells in this area, trying to see if anyone saw my sister, you didn't have to ask me in your home and start talking to me about God and having faith. But you did." She looked up into the gray watery eyes. "It was like you were an angel, giving me that extra something to keep me pushing on to find her. It was even like my mother was sending a message through you. She always talked about God. I can't thank you enough for giving me that hope, and I want to help you as much as I can."

"God is going to send her back to you."

"From your mouth to his ears." Clearing her throat, abruptly Elandra stood. "And what's your niece's address again? I told her I would babysit on Thursday evening."

"Bless your soul, Elandra. That child is having such a hard time with all those kids since her husband died."

"Well, she can go to work that night and make some money to feed them."

"Can I give you something for doing all this?"

"Your company is payment enough, Mrs. O'Grady. I feel good doing things for people, making their lives easier, more pleasurable. When I left New York, I said I was going to stop being that way, but it's hard."

"Be what you are, child. Just be what you are."

Feeling suddenly like an intruder, Bradley crept down the steps and headed back to his car. He wondered why Elandra had evaded telling him where she was going. Did she want him to feel jealous? Did she want to seem mysterious? Whatever her reasons, he had seen another side to her. A side that truly touched his heart.

Eight

Elandra had showered, lotioned, and powdered and was relaxing across her bed, opening a book about finding missing people, when out of nowhere she was blinded by a barrage of outlandish color and clothing. Shocking as it was, the landlord was standing in the doorway of the bedroom.

Doubting her sight, she blinked twice. When he didn't disappear, Elandra leaped up like she had springs. "What in the world are you doing in my bedroom?" She hadn't heard the front door opening, nor footsteps. "You're supposed to knock, mister! Not just barge in!"

"I can do anything I please," he informed her, his attention trickling to the purple satin negligee Elandra was wearing. "It's my house."

It was also Saturday night. Elandra had merely longed to feel beautiful, even if she was in the house and didn't have anyone to look beautiful for. Not liking the way the landlord was looking at her, she swiped up a kimono that was slung over a chair. After overlapping each side, she tied the belt tight around her waist, leaving nothing exposed.

"What if I was nude or something?" she ranted on. "You have no right to just walk in!"

But walk is exactly what he did, taking slow steps forward. Adding to the spectacle, there was a strange twitch in his eye. He was winking the right, then the left. It made Elandra dizzy. And if that wasn't bad enough, he was walking differently, approaching her with a bop right out of a nightmare.

Elandra glanced at his high water pants, his polka dot tie, and that same orange shirt he'd worn before, with the lint balls. Combined with his new strut, he was unbearable to look at much longer! *What in God's name is he doing?*

"Stop right there!" she demanded. "Do you want the rent money? You can have it."

Elandra raced to the chest of drawers, wrenched open the drawer and grabbed an envelope stuffed with cash. Whirling back around, she extended it to the landlord.

"Here. Take it and go. You'll get the rest as soon as I have it."

He yanked his stretchy stretch pants higher with one hand and accepted the envelope with the other. A haggard face pointed down. Carefully he was counting the money.

After counting, then recounting, he gazed up at Elandra with a bizarre expression.

"You know you're short?"

"I know. I told you I'll give you the rest as soon as I get it."

"You're not short a little bit either."

"I've only been working a few weeks."

"It's all right. There is a way you can clear your debt."

"There is?"

In response, the eyes twitched again.

Before Elandra knew anything, she was backing away. The landlord was coming close.

"I'm not that kind of woman," she stressed. "Now you get out of here!"

"I like it when a woman plays hard to get." He was rubbing his hands together.

Soon after a flowerpot almost caught his ear. Afterwards a shoe flew across the room, but missed him. Running into the kitchen, last but not least, was the frying pan Elandra grasped. *Claanngg* it went on his forehead, making him instantly grip his head. While he did this, Elandra was on the other side of the kitchen, flattened against the refrigerator, studying him for signs of real physical harm. Did she need to call an ambulance for a concussion? However, she was certain no damage was done when those teeth glimmered again. Within a flash, the landlord cornered her. Wildly he was kissing her hand and arms. Elandra was slapping him. He didn't mind. Actually, it tickled him.

Bradley heard the slaps and the shrill smooches when he was stepping onto the porch. There was an open front window. He was stopping by to bring Elandra the wallet she had left at his house the day before. Hearing the noises, then seeing the door slightly open, made him cautious as he proceeded inside.

"Arthur!" Bradley shouted.

Arthur jumped back, shaking. "Bradley?"

Elandra was seething. "You know this worm?"

"He's been trying to get my price down on a property in my realty company for the last few months. But now I think I will decline lowering the price to his terms and give someone else a chance. I can't sell a property to a man who's not a gentleman."

Elandra sighed. "Thank goodness. He's been making me so sick I might not ever recover."

Arthur looked devastated. "I was just carried away by her attractiveness."

"Liar!" Elandra blasted. "You were just trying to take advantage because I owed you money."

Bradley stepped closer. "Owe him for what?"

"For staying here, and my sister's back rent. I gave him what I had, but I'm short. And I'm going to give him the rest as soon as I get it, but he just couldn't accept that. Here he is trying to be the Latin lover."

Bradley held in a laugh. Arthur was no more a lover than the frying pan lying on the floor.

"Why is that on the floor?"

"I hit him with it, and I would have banged him with it again if he would have tried anything else."

Bradley grinned, but swiftly tried to look seriously at Arthur. "Arthur, you can have that property for your price under one condition."

"Anything, Bradley."

"Forget what the young lady owes you and don't ever bother her about it again."

"Done."

"I want it in writing," Elandra threw in.

Bradley looked impressed.

Agreeing to their terms, Arthur dashed out the door with Elandra's wrath blazing into his back. When he was out of sight, she gazed at Bradley intently. "You made a business decision just to help me. I can't tell you how much I appreciate it."

"I was glad to do it. Arthur had no right to maul you. If I didn't get here when I did, there's no telling what would have happened."

"Oh I know what would have happened. I would have seriously hurt that guy."

"Those clothes alone, they're enough to beat him up for."

Elandra broke into a grin, then full-blown laughter. Bradley was already smiling and laughed along. When they sobered, he reached into a bag and handed her the wallet.

"You left it at my place yesterday."

Accepting it, their fingers brushed. The contact triggered such a surge of warmth inside them, it caused instant stillness. Elandra was the first to attempt to ignore and suppress the sensation.

"I forgot my wallet? I would have been lost without it. Thank you."

"No problem. I guess I'll be heading over to the hotel."

"Oh really? What's up?"

"Business."

"On a Saturday night?"

"Yep, on a Saturday night," he said playfully.

"I thought you would be out on the town, dancing at a club."

"I don't have—I mean, I'm not in the mood for that lately."

"Me either. I'm either visiting a few of the friends I've made here or going to look for Crystal or one of her friends."

"Fortunately you don't have to do that anymore. Myron will find her. I'm sure."

She looked down to reflect a second. Gazing back up, she searched his face. "I want to thank you so much for that also. You're so different than I thought you were at first."

Their eyes held each other.

"I feel the same way about you. You really surprise me." And he pictured her with the elderly lady.

The silence was discomforting as much as the heated looks. Bradley cleared his throat and shuffled toward the living room. Elandra followed.

"Guess I better head over to the hotel and take a look into the decorating."

"Oh, you mean that hotel situation we worked on yesterday. The one that was renovated."

"Exactly."

Elandra had felt so excited being involved in that project, she ached to go along.

"May I come?" she surprised herself by asking.

Bradley looked amazed. "You want to spend your Saturday night working?"

"I'm curious to see what's going to happen with the suite. I used to like interior decorating. But I kind of got away from it."

"Interesting. Very interesting."

"Does that mean I can tag along?"

"Get dressed, young lady. You're on work duty again."

Elandra ran into the bedroom while Bradley stood in the middle of the floor, feeling and looking like he'd won the lottery.

Some time later, standing in the midst of the hotel suite, Bradley scanned the newly refurbished room, and concluded, "I'm going to have to hire a decorator quick."

Instantly Elandra remembered how she loved to help decorate the family's home where her mother had worked. She was exceptional at it, too. She knew just what fabrics went with what, and what colors made someone feel a particular way. Elandra understood a room had to have a mood and an atmosphere. Everyone praised her flair for bringing life into a room. Once she'd even contemplated attending college for interior decorating. Except her mother and life's tribulations had pushed her away from it.

Yet with Bradley standing next to her, a man who felt he could do anything, Elandra felt she could, too. "I can decorate this room," she offered. "I have a great knack for things like this."

"You do?" he remarked.

"Yes, I do."

He stroked his chin and thought for a moment. "Okay, I'll give you a shot. When we're ready to decorate, I'll see what you can do."

Elandra was ecstatic.

She should have been, too. Bradley provided Elandra

with an ample budget, with which she enlisted the finest services to embellish the room. There was an artist who translated her vision to paper. Next she hired a fabric and color consultant, who furnished her with lush velvets and Chinese prints, all to invoke the perfect mood. Following that was the purchase of the furnishings and ultimately the accessories. When all was completed, Bradley walked into a room he never wanted to leave.

"This is beautiful, Elandra. It's striking. It's warm. It's extremely cozy." He turned from side to side and all around, examining the ravishing room. "You definitely have the gift."

"I'm happy you like it." The gratitude gave her the ultimate high.

"When this situation arises again, I want you to be the decorator."

"I would be happy to."

"Not only that, but I would love to pay for you to go to school for this."

Elated, Elandra clutched her chest. "Are you for real?"

"Oh, yes. That would be a worthwhile investment with all your talent."

"I can't accept that. Bradley, you've done enough for me already."

"Never enough for a valued employee."

"I'll tell you what, after I find Crystal I'll give going to school some thought. But I'm going to pay for my own education. In the meantime, I can't think about school right now."

"In that case, you'll be giving it some thought soon. Because Myron will find your sister."

Lying in bed at night, Bradley couldn't sleep. It was a problem he was having often lately. Everywhere he turned, each time he closed his eyes, there she was. Elandra was everywhere he went, even when she was nowhere around. In every atom of his being, accompanying each breath, she was foremost in his mind. The more he was around her, the more he needed to be around her. It felt good to be with her, to see her, to be working with her, to simply know her.

Being near her every day, getting to know her better and better, caused a euphoria to gush inside him that was sometimes overwhelming. It made him do things for her and want to do more. And he knew he shouldn't have. Instead of pushing her away, which he knew would be best, everything he did lured her nearer. But Bradley couldn't stop himself. There was just something about her.

New air had suddenly been breathed into his body. In Elandra's absence, he would question whether he dreamed her—dreamed her like the dreams that captivated him about her every night—dreamed her to make up for the heartbreak over Kim. But it was when he was reminded of Kim that he could keep some control over his growing emotions. Wasn't it always like this in the beginning? Kim had made him feel wonderful once as well. She'd possessed qualities that endeared her to him at first and eventually made them fall in love. Now he could see the same thing happening with Elandra. He couldn't get over how sweet she was sometimes, how caring, and warm, and thoughtful, and there was so much more. Yet he didn't want to go on. He didn't want to acknowledge these qualities. As irresistible as Elandra was becoming to him, he would fight tooth and nail not to get involved. He would fight tooth and nail not to give her a piece of his heart. However, sometimes he wondered if she had it already.

* * *

The powdery sands of the beach glittered, illuminated by the June sunshine like diamonds chopped into grains. Soft blue waters gently waved to Elandra, clapping against each other with lithe surges upward. Like a tourist capturing sights that moved by too fast, she soaked in the serenity of this world so removed from the rest of the beach, while keeping at bay the tenseness clambering through her.

She was getting too close to Bradley. She was astounded by the faith he had in her. She was nourished from his encouragement and positive attitude. But she was thinking about him too much. She was talking with him too much. She was accepting his generosity and desiring to thank him in ways they both would love. Though she vowed, *NEVER*. All that strength she had gained within herself—she refused to lose it. All the promises she made about a man never breaking her heart—she could never forget them. She could never forget them because she could never forget the pain. With Bradley, it would eventually turn out the same. When had it ever turned out otherwise for her?

Closing her eyes and opening them, Elandra knew she had to get a grip. *Had to!* If she didn't, she would be like those waves rolling out farther and farther to the midst of the ocean. She would soon be so lost in the sea of his beauty, she would no longer be able to touch the shore or even see it.

Nine

"Just let me put it in," Bradley insisted.

"What if I get hurt?" Elandra argued.

"I won't let you get hurt. I promise. It'll be nice and easy. Just relax and let it happen. You'll like it a lot."

"I don't know. It looks pretty big and dangerous. A girl could get killed riding one of those things."

Somehow, though, Elandra summoned the courage. She peered up at the Hackney pony and prepared to mount it.

"I don't need you to put my foot in the stirrup."

"I don't see you doing it." He was holding the stirrup out.

"I shouldn't be doing this anyway. I shouldn't be having any kind of fun. I should be trying to find my sister."

"You are. You're letting Myron find her. And he will. Now get on the horse."

"What if I said I changed my mind?"

"You can't change your mind. Ever since you've been working here you've been going to the stables and drooling over the horses, and saying how much you wanted to learn how to ride one. Now's your chance."

"But it's the middle of the afternoon."

"And both of us need a break. We've been working too hard."

"I'm learning that you're stubborn, Bradley Davenport."

"Sue me."

Knowing he wouldn't stop pestering her until she did it, Elandra took a deep breath and stood close to the horse's shoulder. She swerved slightly to the tail. With her left hand, she did what Bradley had instructed earlier, grasping the reins and the horse's mane. With her right hand, she gripped the cantle. Finally she placed her left foot in the stirrup.

Bradley watched, eager to catch her if she was awkward in the slightest. At the same time, there was soon an irresistible view. As Elandra bolted up to stand in the left stirrup, then swung her right leg over the horse's back, he was bewitched by round, high buttocks, accentuated flawlessly by white dungarees.

"Lord, you're so good sometimes," he whispered to himself.

"What did you say, Bradley?"

"I didn't say a thing."

Inadvertently he started swallowing and quickly tried to divert his concentration elsewhere, like on her safety.

The ride went smoothly. How could it help being smooth since Elandra refused to ride, but merely walked the horse over the grounds with Bradley right beside them. Ham that he was occasionally known to be, though, Bradley didn't let her get off easy for long. Swifter than a blink, he had flung himself over the horse's back and Elandra was tightly holding on.

Her breasts and the side of her face bore into his back. Her arms squeezed around his waist. Elandra wished it didn't feel so good being this close to him, feeling his hardness, and smelling his clean natural scent, lightly spiced with some very masculine cologne. It made her bring her lips close to his ear, where the fragrance seemed concentrated, and it was so arousing she wanted her lips to vibrate sexy words across his ears.

But Elandra decided it was more sensible, it was more in line with who she was now, to be angry at him for riding the horse suddenly away like a madman. Though the more they rode, the more fun she had. They rode all over the grounds and deep into the woods, galloping over small hills, through a ditch and even through a shallow pond. Next to the pond, they stopped.

Bradley helped Elandra off Sunshine and tied the horse to a tree. Afterward they relaxed by another tree, which was right above the pond.

"Whooh! That was so much fun!" she squealed. "Let's do it again."

"Hold on now. Just hold your horses. Aren't you the one who wouldn't even let her foot in the stirrup?"

Elandra snickered. "Sue me, as you say."

Dimples pricked his cheeks. "I thought you would like that."

She laid back on the grass, facing the sky. "You know, sometimes when I'm here at your house working, it's like the rest of the world doesn't exist."

He leaned over on his side, looking down at her. "How's that?"

"It just does. The work you do is so interesting. Here you are making million-dollar deals. Most people I knew back in New York, could never conceive of something like that. People like you were unapproachable and fairy tale-like."

"But now you see I'm a flesh and blood man."

Bending over her, his eyes trailed the length of her body. Everything he saw warmed him. Made him feel more than alive. When he reached her eyes again, Elandra was locked to his gaze. But suddenly realizing what was happening, she forced herself to focus on the sky.

"Your world is so full of ease and living fantasy," she went on. "No one I know in New York could take a break from work to go horseback riding."

"Have those people worked as hard as us and deserved that break?"

Elandra couldn't answer. The response was debatable. The two of them had been working extremely hard. Not only that, but it was really fulfilling. She felt so purposeful. And more and more she was seriously considering interior decorating school.

"A long time ago, I never would have dreamed I would have a day like this."

"A long time ago when?"

"When I was the maid's daughter living in the servants' quarters. Though their home was nowhere near as lavish as yours, they had horses, too. But my sister and I weren't allowed to ride them."

"I'm sorry about that. They should have let you and your sister enjoy them, considering your mother worked for them."

"But they didn't. Yes, they gave us certain privileges, but then again, they didn't give us others. We were constantly reminded of who we were, by them and by my mother."

Bradley looked upset. Elandra noticed.

"Bradley, don't feel sorry for me. I hardly ever think about that now. Those times seem like a million years ago."

"What kept you going then?"

"Going?" she asked.

"Yes, what did you have to hope for? If your mom was tearing down your dreams, what hope did you have?"

Elandra looked off deep into the sky for a moment, deeper than he knew the sky reached. "Love," she answered.

"You were in love?"

A sad expression coloring her face, she shook her head. "With the family's son."

"And how did it turn out? Is he waiting in New York for you still?"

"No, we were over a long time ago. He was my first love."

"I take it he loved you very deeply."

"I'll never really know the answer to that."

"Why not?"

"His parents sent him away when we told them we were in love, and asked them to sign for us to get married. I never saw him again. But my mom always told me if he really loved me, he would have found some way to contact me. And his mom told her that we were wrong for each other. Translation—she didn't want her son marrying the maid's daughter."

"Did he tell you he loved you?"

"So many times. I believed him. When that was over, I should have given up on the love game right then."

"Why?"

"Because I should have."

"No, you're holding something back."

"I am not. Enough about those gloomy days."

"But do those gloomy days have to do with these days, with why you were so cold before?"

He was asking too many questions, getting too close to tempting her to unburden herself so he too could eventually abuse her after she trusted him. Elandra tried to raise up, but she was forced down by his chest over her and his face inches above her own.

Bradley beheld the sun shimmering in her eyes. Staring into them made his blood pound as emphatically as his heart. God knows he had never seen eyes like those and he knew he never would again. He ached to look into them like this forever. More arresting, it was how those eyes stared into his that made the moment truly unforgettable.

At first Elandra had squirmed slightly to slide out of the awkward position with him, but as she did the softness of her breast brushed against his chest. A spark flickered. From her lips to the pit of her stomach it flamed, a tingling of urgency in her blood as their bodies connected and eyes locked in need.

Bradley drew her closer, and Elandra couldn't fight. Luxury was being wound in his thick arms, as coppery pools of lust held her gaze in its welcome fire.

With a mouth so round, puffed and plumped, her lips appeared as if juice would burst from the slightest prick of a bite. Moving his face closer, he dared to find out.

However for Elandra a flash of Dan intercepted. Elandra sprang up. Briskly, she distanced herself from Bradley.

"Bradley, we're heading into dangerous territory. Territory I would rather avoid."

Reluctantly he shook his head. "Me, too. It's better to keep things uncomplicated."

"Exactly. We're here on this beautiful island, in this beautiful setting, and we've been working so hard, working so closely together every day. I'm under pressure to find Crystal and you're under pressure because thousands of folks depend on you for jobs and you have million-dollar deals, and we just felt needy. We're human."

"Right. Right." He shook his head. "Absolutely right. We'll forget it ever happened. And it won't, not ever again."

"No, it won't," she agreed.

"We don't want to do that."

"*Noooo.* Let's go back to the house."

"Yes, we have lots of work to do."

"But I'll walk," Elandra pointed out.

"Why?"

"Just feel like walking."

He nodded. "Okay. I'll see you at the house."

In moments, he galloped off on the horse and Elandra dropped to the ground, her heart beating as fast as she had ever felt it. It made her return to the fascination of the sky. "God, what is wrong with me?" she asked.

The fingers ran along Elandra's jawline and up across the swell of her lips. Faintly the two middle ones parted them, drifted away, replacing themselves with his mouth. His lips and hers barely brushed. Softly pressing and lingering, they were intent to savor the feeling. It was more than lips making her insides come alive. It was breath near breath. Cheek near cheek. Chest near chest. Heart and soul she bonded with him. They touched each other in places no one ever touched them before. It was the magic people wait their entire lives for. It felt so good and right, throughout every fiber of her being, Elandra knew it was meant to be. Not soon enough, their hunger to express more overpowered them. Elandra welcomed all of his love.

When her lengthy lashes fluttered apart, she realized the dream had come again, the dream which had strangely teased her over and over since she had arrived on the island. Unlike before, this particular night was different. Before, she couldn't distinguish the man's face because some of his features weren't seen. This night was different. She could see them. She could see Bradley so clearly.

God help her, he was more a part of her than she wanted him to be. How had she let this happen? But sometimes she wondered. Maybe, just maybe, he wouldn't be like all the rest. Undoubtedly he was different than any man she had met. Even without his wealth, he possessed qualities she always dreamed of a man having—but never had she met a man who possessed them all. And certainly he was attracted to her. Every time he looked at her, desire screamed from him. Except she wanted more than desire. She wanted more than she'd ever had before. So Elandra pondered a question over and over. Should she give him a chance or just let it go? Or did she have a choice? Wasn't he already so deeply inside her she was breathing him every second of her life?

Elandra sat at the desk, proofreading a letter Bradley was writing to an American travel agency, detailing new brochures he was having printed. In the middle of doing so, an approaching figure attracted her attention, raising her eyes ahead. Walking up the lengthy hall perpendicular to her office was a tall, slender, striking young woman with very short hair and chiseled features. She wore a light blue sleeveless pantsuit, a matching bag and off-white high-heeled sandals.

When finally she stood precisely before the desk, Elandra was entranced. The dewy, flawless skin and sculptured features made her look beautiful enough to be a model.

Elandra greeted her with a pleasantry. "How are you this afternoon? I guess you're here to see Bradley?"

The woman didn't return the cordiality. Neither did she respond to the greeting. Instead she asked, "Where is Phyllis?"

"Phyllis?" But quickly Elandra recalled the name of the mature lady who had held the position prior to her. "Oh, Phyllis is retired and relaxing on Paradise Island."

The stranger nodded coolly. "And who are you?"

"I'm Elandra. And you are?"

"Kim Rothwell."

"It's nice to meet you." Elandra extended her hand. Her hand was untouched. Elandra was surprised at the rudeness. The woman's hands remained firm at her sides except for an occasional tug at a handbag strap. Her doe eyes were cold as she peered at Elandra. Regardless, Elandra didn't let this sway her optimistic spirit. Every day of working with Bradley was doing more and more to uplift her.

"Is Bradley in his office?"

"Actually he stepped out to get us some lunch."

"How long should it be before he returns?"

"About a half hour." Then Elandra tilted her head downward, examining her daily calendar. She knew Bradley was the ultimate professional and wouldn't dare leave someone waiting if they had a meeting with him. Not seeing the name Kim Rothwell, she gazed back up. "You know, I don't see your name in the appointment book."

"Because it isn't. This isn't business." She patted the back of her hair. "This is personal."

"Oh," Elandra remarked and didn't know what to think. Even so, she was determined to be congenial to any of Bradley's associates. "Ms. Rothwell, you can take a seat right there and wait for Bradley if you like." With her head, she pointed to a leather sofa in front of her desk.

Kim glanced back at it, then at Elandra very oddly, before stepping over to the couch. Once seated, she crossed her legs and folded her arms. From where Elandra sat the stranger appeared so bored, she thought small talk would pass the time.

"Beautiful day, isn't it?" Elandra commented.

"The sun always shines in Nassau," Kim replied. "Even during the rainy season."

"Well I love the weather here whether rain or shine. I guess this island grows on people. Makes you never want to leave." Elandra's eyes swirled in the air dreamily.

Kim detected something. Merely the island's beauty didn't make you look like that.

"So how do you like working for Bradley?" she asked. Kim was studying Elandra's face intensely.

"I love it. Working for Bradley is the greatest experience."

"Is it now?" Kim's long neck stretched forward.

"Oh yes. I can't believe how wonderful he is—I mean how wonderful working for him is."

"I see." Kim unfolded her arms, then folded them again. She leaned to one side. "What makes it so wonderful?"

Elandra thought the question was strange, but then again, maybe it wasn't. "The work is interesting, and he's nice."

"What did he do that was so nice?" Kim's lips curled to one side.

This is an interrogation. And it's becoming more and more bizarre. She's lucky she's Bradley's friend. "Giving me a job for one. Encouraging me to follow my dream for another."

"And what's your little dream?"

Elandra took offense to the word *little,* but was determined to be polite. "Well, I really enjoy interior decorating, and he let me decorate two hotel rooms."

"Is that right?"

"Yes, that's right."

"I thought you were an administrative assistant."

"I am, but he has faith in me. You see, I always wanted to be a decorator and he's giving me that chance."

Elandra was still talking, but Kim had already heard enough. The words became a blur against the concern in her mind. Kim knew it didn't take a rocket scientist to figure out that something was going on with Bradley and this assistant. The way her face lit up when she talked about him spoke volumes. And sure, she was pretty in an obvious way. Nevertheless, Kim felt she was no match for her. Bradley would be hers again. If he felt anything for this lowly assistant, it would change. She would see to it. She thrived on a challenge.

Kim hadn't realized what a treasure he was before, back when she betrayed him. So God help her, she sure realized it now—he was the best thing that ever happened to her. Never again would she let him get away.

Ten

The buoyant scent of violets staggered Bradley. Coming up the marble pathway leading to his doorstep, it slowed his pace a bit and halted him twice. Recalling the fragrance from a particular period in his life, the reaction didn't stem from him feeling good. On the contrary, the scent annoyed him. He made a mental note to tell the gardener not to plant that flower anywhere near his home. Surely that's where the fragrance had to come from. Neither Elandra nor the maid wore such a floral cologne. Furthermore, Bradley had no appointments for the day. Therefore no client could have been wearing a violet-based perfume upon entering the house.

Oddly enough, the violets became stronger as Bradley made wide steps down the long hallway toward Elandra's and his office. Though as he saw her beautiful face radiant at what he held in his hand, other thoughts were pushed aside. Finally standing before her desk, he handed her a dozen roses.

In the haze of her excitement, instantly Elandra forgot the woman who had gone to powder her face. She was too entranced. Her mouth had gaped open, her hand clutched her chest. "What's this?"

"Roses, you silly rabbit," he teased.

"For what?" Elandra laughed out. Scrutinizing their beauty, she was fascinated.

Much the same, Bradley was captivated as well. Something inside him filled up watching her. It filled him up with sensations so pleasurable he never wanted them to go away. "This is for being such an excellent employee and working so hard."

"You didn't have to do this, Bradley."

"I don't do anything I don't want to do."

Her eyes raised to his. The warm brown depths she was becoming addicted to couldn't get enough of her. Whatever he saw seemed breathtaking. Elandra felt soft and feminine and entirely beautiful.

"Thank you," she said, the strength and humor in her voice quelling to a whisper. "You're so sweet."

"I can be even sweeter."

His eyes ran across her face, winding up at her lips. Hungering to feel and taste them, he stepped around to her side of the desk. Their eyes never left each other as he moved. Neither did they move when he stopped.

"Bradley I . . ."

"Bradley what? Say what you want to say to me, Elandra." His brow furrowed with his building emotion. "Let it out. There are things I want to say to you, too. Very, very important things."

"There are?"

"Oh, yes."

It was at this same time the stranger exited the powder room. The dense carpet muffled Kim's pumps as she strolled to the reception office. Once reaching the room, she stopped dead-still in the doorway. Shock and excitement overcame her at the sight of Bradley. Her heart drummed in her chest. In dark gray pants, a white shirt and tie, emphasizing his robust physique, he was awesome and more sexy than she remembered. No sooner than she recovered from the shock of seeing him, though, did she realize what he was doing. Bradley was standing there, apparently enamored by his assistant. Resting on the desk beside them was a bunch of roses. It all made a vein in Kim's temple bulge. Yet she strived for the facade of calmness.

Kim patted the back of her hair, licked her lips, then called, "Bradley?"

Hearing the unforgettable sound, the alluring, fluent voice, Bradley was paralyzed for a moment. He couldn't speak, nor maneuver around to the sound, which astonished him. The impact of *her* in this room with him was unbearable. Bradley just stood there, facing Elandra, but now not seeing her. He only perceived the anger that was suddenly choking him.

The scent of violets was a mystery no more. Violets were Kim's favorite flower and had eventually become her most cherished fragrance. When they were a couple, she even hired a chemist to create a special perfume solely for her. Ever since they broke up, Bradley could barely stand violets, smelling them or seeing them. But right now it wasn't the fragrance that he loathed—it was the woman wearing it.

Slowly he curved around to face her, and she was more beautiful than he wanted her to be. Dewy skin, delicate features, the superbly toned body. Nonetheless, in this case, Bradley thoroughly understood beauty was skin deep. Never forgetting what she did to him, he addressed her with all in perspective. "You have some nerve coming here."

"Hello, darling," she said, overlooking his bitterness. Her interest was in how Bradley relished what he saw. A woman who never lacked male attention, Kim knew when a man desired her, even if his mouth swore he didn't. His eyes told her all his lips didn't.

Across from her, Elandra stood nearly immobilized, baffled by Bradley's rudeness. Where was it coming from? In bewilderment, she frowned at him. "Bradley,

I was so taken with your roses that I forgot to tell you this young lady was waiting for you."

"She's not waiting for me, because I don't want to see her."

"Bradley, don't say that," Kim protested. "Give me a chance." She stepped closer to him. "It's been years since we've seen each other. And this is how you treat me?"

Open-mouthed, Elandra moved back, gaping at both of them. As she stirred away, Kim glided closer to Bradley, so close that somehow she managed to wind up where Elandra stood. Elandra inched back further and further until she was near the door.

"We have nothing to talk about!" Bradley blasted. He turned his back to her.

"But we do. You know we do."

"We don't!" His shoulders raised even higher and dipped low as his breaths became harsher. "Woman, go back to where you came from before your feelings get really hurt."

Witness to Bradley's behavior toward this woman, Elandra somehow felt like an intruder on something extremely private. She shoved some hair off her eye to get a good look at a Bradley she hardly knew. "I think I'll leave early. I'll work from home on the notebook computer you gave me."

Kim squinted at Elandra. "That's a good idea that you leave."

Bradley snapped around. "You don't tell her when to leave!" He was so loud and enraged Elandra could hardly believe it was him. "This is my house, damn it!"

"But we have things to talk about," Kim insisted.

"We have nothing to talk about and you're the reason that's so. Now get out and live with it!"

The woman continued pleading her case about talking to him. Quite the contrary, Bradley was adamant

about her presence not being wanted. In the midst of
the struggle, feeling more and more insignificant, Elandra quietly slipped away, down the hall and out onto
the lawn. She saw Richard waiting by the limousine.
With a smile, he graciously opened the door. She was
more than eager to step inside.

Back in the house, Bradley watched out the window.
However, he chose not to stop her. It was better that
she not hear any more. Bradley was still too embarrassed to talk about it. How would her image of him
change once she learned what had happened to him?

"Bradley, you're not listening to me," Kim intercepted his thoughts.

"Because there is nothing to listen to."

"I need you and I still love you."

"You love yourself, Kim."

"I love you, Bradley."

"Then again, you do love someone else," he thought
aloud, his gaze narrowing on her. "You love the man
you left me for. The billionaire."

"We're over. Divorced."

He chuckled. "Over and divorced?" Digging his
hands deep in his pockets, he paced around the room.
"You're over with him. Now you come back to me."

"Don't make it sound like that."

"Like what? Like you're running from man to man.
Like you're running from rich man to richer man? He
was a billionaire, wasn't he? And me? I was just a millionaire. But more than that, I was just the man who
loved you more than life itself. I would have died for
you, I loved you so much. And for what? *For what?* To
have you leave me? Leave me the way you did—as cruel
as you did."

Kim searched everywhere around the room, like an
appropriate excuse lay somewhere within it. "I am truly
sorry. I just wasn't mature then. But I've learned so

much since then, Bradley. I had a good man and I traded him for a man I didn't love. Bernardo was old enough to be my grandfather and life was so boring. The days were long and the nights even longer. It's so hard pretending to be happy when your heart screams that it isn't. When we did anything, there was no real joy in it. When we talked, there was no connection. I never even understood his dull humor. And when we made love, it was nothing like it was when you and I were together. Oh, Bradley, don't you remember?"

Yes, it was hard to forget at first, he thought. However, slowly, but surely someone else was the woman he held in his fantasies.

For him, it was satisfying to know Kim suffered, too. Even so, he felt the pain was too unequal. Moreover, he knew he could never forgive.

"The way you did it was so cruel," he told her. "My family, friends, everyone saw my heartbreak. You humiliated me. I wouldn't have wished that on my enemy."

"Bradley, what can I do to make up for it?"

"That's just it. Some things you can't make up for. You can't bring a dead body back to life. You can't become a child again after you're an adult." He paused, burning his eyes into hers. "And you can't wipe out of my mind what you did to me. It's there, Kim. I can't erase it. And the way you did it, the way you did it, is the worst."

Kim hung her head, regret wrenching her insides. "I see." She looked up. "I guess I better go then. If you change your mind, and want to talk and get together, I'm staying at Mama's."

Bradley was so angry, he started not to ask about her mother's health. Yet he knew that was wrong. He did care about Kim's mother. Throughout the ordeal, Mavis Rothwell had expressed her deepest regret about how her daughter destroyed him. "How is your mother?"

"She's not doing too well, actually. But she would like to see you, Bradley. She thinks you would have made such a fabulous son-in-law."

"I wouldn't mind seeing her either. She was very kind to me after . . ."

Knowing what he was about to say, Kim bit her lip, then tried to look more pert.

"She read in the paper that you're having a big Fourth of July splash. She was telling me about it. She said that you were having those boys over and all their families, and just about everyone of importance in Nassau."

"There is no such thing as of importance. Everyone is important."

"Sure. You're right as usual."

"I think you better go."

"I will." She made a few steps toward the hallway. A thought spun her around. "Mama would sure like to come to the barbecue."

"She can come. Tell her nurse to bring her."

"She doesn't have a nurse."

"Oh no? Why not? I thought she was very sick."

"Insurance pays for just so much. We can't afford a nurse."

"What?" Disbelieving her, he twisted his lips sourly. "Trying to hustle again?"

"No, Bradley. Honestly we can't afford a private nurse."

"With your love for the finer things in life, I know you didn't divorce Bernardo without getting a hefty settlement."

"You're wrong."

"What?"

"Bernardo . . . Bernardo's finances and assets were seized . . . by federal authorities."

"Seized? What for?" He was frowning.

She gazed down ruefully, then back up. "It turned out that Bernardo built much of his fortune illegally. White-collar crimes. He's being prosecuted."

Bradley smiled dryly. Yes, it was for a hustler being jailed and losing his fortune, a man he held no love for—a man who stole the woman he loved, but moreso the irony. She left Bradley for a man with a greater fortune. Now there was nothing. But then a clearer picture formed of why she wanted to be with him so badly. The smile wiped completely away.

"So he's a criminal and you get the hell away from him as fast as you can, which is sensible. But then you run to me—to where some money is."

"It's not like that. I didn't even have to tell you the truth about Bernardo's finances, but I did. Doesn't that prove something?"

"Proves you're a little smarter at your game."

"You're wrong about me."

"Oh, but yes, I'm right." Knowing what she had done to him, Bradley just stared at her for a moment. He wanted to say *Serves you right*. Yet it didn't serve her mother right not to have a nurse when she needed one. Mavis Rothwell was innocent.

"I know how it looks, Bradley," she went on, "but it really isn't that way."

"What other way is it?"

She sighed. "Hard times brings out things in people. I was unhappy with Bernardo. Then I was flat broke. Now my mother is sick. How can I not become more humbled?"

She had a point, but he didn't care. Whatever excuses or problems she had didn't matter to him anymore. Breaking his heart as brutally as she had, severed all ties.

"May I bring her, Bradley?"

He was hesitant, his gaze searching everywhere but at her.

"Mama would just feel so much better being at this beautiful mansion once again."

I don't want to see you again. I want to forget you like I had almost managed to do before today. You bring too much pain to me.

"And those boys. You know how much she loves children."

I've been feeling so good lately. Who wants his greatest heartbreak gallivanting before his face, her presence teasing him about what a fool he had been?

"I don't think it's a good idea," he stated plainly.

"Please, Bradley, for my mother. I'll keep a low profile. And if you want, I could even leave her here and pick her up." Though Kim had no such intention. She was planning to attend that barbecue and serve her palate with much more than the food.

"My mother, Bradley. My mother. She may die soon."

The words awakened his compassion. It was true that her mother was extremely sick. Through the social grapevine he had heard about her hard times with her health. The added stress of being financially strapped must have been an extra burden. Bradley thought of his own mother. He worshipped her. No way he could stand her living so miserably.

"Ms. Rothwell can come," he finally agreed. "But don't read anything into this about you and I. Because nothing is there."

"I won't. Thank you, Bradley."

Elandra was supposed to be home working, but she was too restless thinking about that woman with Bradley. Who was she? Was she the one who hurt him so bad that he was cold to her at first? She was certainly attractive, Elandra thought. And as gorgeous as she was, Elandra could see that she was conceited. She didn't seem at all like Bradley's type. Of most concern to her now, though, was what were they doing. Something hadn't felt right in the room between them. It made Elandra uneasy.

She gazed in the mirror, stroking her cheek with one of the roses he gave her. She inhaled it and admired its radiance. Afterward her glance caught sight of the other roses laying on the bed. Didn't roses mean love? What was it he wanted to tell her? Would this woman's appearance in his life stop it? For as much as she hated to admit it, this was more than a crush she was feeling. This was something she had fought to the death not to happen. Now she stood at that mountain, ready to take a chance, a leap at love's door. But now with this stranger turning up, would Bradley?

Thinking about it, debating if she should follow her growing emotions or just not bother, Elandra felt confusion. She had to get out of the house. She had to concentrate her energy on something really constructive. First thing that came to mind was finding Crystal. In Myron's daily report to Bradley he hadn't turned up anything, but had a few good leads. Perhaps she could speed up the process. Remembering the guy from the casino, Peppy, who had given her some information, Elandra rushed to her closet and removed a lovely jumpsuit. As she held it against her body in the mirror, she thought about calling Daisy to accompany her. Except she remembered this was Daisy's one night of the week to work.

"I see you're back here," Peppy remarked to Elandra hours later. "I hope to see me." He dealt the cards as he talked.

"Yes, I'm here to see you."

A sly smile curled his lips. "I aim to please."

"Then will you please me by telling me anything else about my sister's disappearance."

An ear leaned closer, but it wasn't Peppy's or Elandra's.

"I told you everything."

"Did you tell the investigator, too?"

"What investigator?" A winning hand made him lean over to rake a bunch of chips to the other side of the table.

"Myron."

When he raised back up, he glanced over at Elandra. "Never heard of no Myron."

"Myron Tate. You had to hear of him. I gave him your name."

"Didn't I tell you I wasn't talking to no police?"

"He's not the police. He's a private investigator."

"I don't care who he is. I'm not talking. Matter of fact, I don't even know if I should be talking to you now. You have a big mouth." He peered over at her harshly, before shifting his focus back to the table.

She was angry and couldn't hide it. "You're a chicken."

"A live one," he added. "And if he does come in my face, I'm not telling him nothing."

Elandra rolled her eyes at him and stomped off through the crowd. Eyes followed. Eyes filled with hate. Eyes that saw a threat. They weren't Peppy's.

Eleven

It had been three days since Kim Rothwell came to see Bradley, leaving in her dust a difference in him. That's the way Elandra saw it. Since the visit they hadn't discussed much outside of work. No long conversations about their lives. No long talks about their dreams. None of that nourishment she was starved for about having a positive outlook on life and believing in yourself.

They hadn't discussed the subject of Kim, either. Elandra sensed she was a touchy topic and didn't bring her up. Prying and digging in someone's personal business wasn't her style. Instead she waited for Bradley to impart what the story was. After all, she believed they had become closer. Or was that solely assumed? As the silence lingering in the air between them indicated, their growing affinity toward each other was possibly all in her head. It was as if something had happened to make him close himself off from her.

This was in the back of her mind as she and Daisy enjoyed the good food and great outdoors at Bradley's Fourth of July barbecue. The estate was packed with folks from seemingly all walks of life. The two women sectioned themselves off several feet so they could chat without interruption. Underneath an evergreen tree full of mangos, Daisy nibbled on a rib while Elandra sipped a cup of soda. Crystal dominated their conversation.

"So Peppy wouldn't give up any more information?" Daisy asked.

Elandra was lightly holding her straw, drinking some soda. "He didn't give me any more," she said between sips. "Coward."

"Maybe he has none to give. He did tell you more than anyone else." She broke off a piece of rib and put it in her mouth.

"I think he's holding back."

Daisy was chewing. "Be glad that he told you as much as he did."

Elandra sighed. "I am glad." She took two more sips of her drink, then set the can down hard. "He's just scared to get involved for some reason. The way he's acting, you would think Crystal made a pact with the devil."

Daisy shot her an underhanded glance.

Elandra was wary of it. "What?"

"You never know. And that Trina she hung out with wasn't no saint."

"Well, I'd rather believe that Crystal is. I know my sister."

Daisy was chewing and stopped abruptly. "You *knew* her. We all change. Everyday experiences shape our lives. She's been living down here on this island miles away from you in New York. She didn't have to tell you everything in her life and obviously she hasn't. You didn't know about the relationship with an older man."

"That's true. Well, at least the investigator is looking for her."

"Now that is good. Real good."

"But I'm surprised he didn't question Peppy. I told him what he said."

"If Bradley Davenport hired him, he's an expert.

He'll get around to it." But suddenly Elandra was soon the victim of that notorious, mischievous eye.

"What? Why are you looking like that?"

"How did Bradley get around to hiring an investigator for you anyway?"

"Just being nice."

"And that's all?"

"Yes, that's all. What are you getting at?" But Elandra was amused by her suggestion.

"You're working for him, and then he hires an investigator for your sister. Must be expensive."

"Well, I told you he offered to pay. And normally I would have declined, but I have to find Crystal. I'll pay him back one day."

"That man isn't worried about you paying him back. He wants you."

"How do you know?"

"From what you've been telling me. All the goings on at this place." She looked up at the house, scanning the crowd for Bradley. Seeing mostly unfamiliar faces, she gazed back at Elandra. "All the things you two have been doing and how well you work together. Something is happening."

"I must admit, he has been really nice. And spending time with him is really wonderful."

"See. I told you that day at lunch that he rubbed you the right way." She shook her rib in conviction.

Elandra laughed and suddenly spotted Bradley. He was coming from the back of the house with some of his Little Brothers. They were laughing and joking, then joined the crowd in front of the house.

"A woman came to see him the other day," Elandra announced.

"Yeah." Daisy looked over at Bradley amid the crowd.

"Yes. He didn't want to see her. It was obvious something had happened between them, but she was desperate to talk to him. I think she was his ex."

"If you go after him, she'll stay that way."

Elandra chuckled, but quickly the glee faded. She stared at Bradley, standing far across the lawn. "That was three days ago. Ever since then, he's been different. He's hardly talked to me about anything except work. I miss that closeness we were starting to have. And I didn't tell you what he gave me, did I?"

"What?"

"A bunch of roses."

"Oh, that's so romantic. I love it when my husband gives me roses. It makes me feel like I'm a rose." She nudged Elandra. "Girl, you know what that means."

"That he's fond of my work?"

"No." Shaking her head, Daisy looked over at Bradley in amazement. She gazed back at Elandra. "Hell, that means he's serious. Seriously trying to show you that he wants to be more than friends."

Elandra sighed. "It was serious. At least it was getting there. When he gave them to me, he was about to tell me something. He said it was very important. But then that woman interrupted us. And the next time when I saw him—nothing. He was all business. It was like he hadn't said anything or given me anything so beautiful. I was about to tell him how I felt."

"And that was a big step for you. I remember how hard-nosed you were about men a few weeks ago. He's something else to change your mind like that."

"He is something else." Elandra gazed over at him dreamily. He had maneuvered near the grill and was shaking some man's hand. The man looked vaguely familiar to Elandra. Despite it, she returned her attention to Daisy. "Maybe I've been hoping for too much."

"No, you haven't." But Daisy began to squint as she speculated. "But you say you two were about to confess how you feel about each other, then this woman stops by and changes everything?"

"That's exactly what I'm saying." Elandra rested her head back against the tree and removed an ice cube from her cup. Sliding it across her neck, she shook her head. "Isn't that awful?"

"If you give up it's awful."

Elandra raised her head at Daisy. "If I give up? Give up what? I don't have anything to give up."

"From what you told me and what I've seen here today, the way you two interact, he's crazy about you."

"Oh, he's just a little more perky today because those kids are here. He loves them." They paused a moment to look at Bradley. He was wrestling with one of the bigger boys and tickling another.

Daisy was fascinated by the sight and smiled. "He would probably make a great father."

Watching him, Elandra agreed, "Yes, he sure would."

Daisy looked back at her. "So make him the father of your children."

"What?" Elandra looked at her like she was nuts. "Now you're really jumping the gun."

"I don't think so. A man doesn't give roses to someone he just likes casually. And it wasn't even a special occasion."

"He said they were a reward for my work. I do work a lot for him, and if I might say so, I do a damn good job."

"Phooey! Those weren't rewards. Those were expressions. He was definitely giving you a message. A big one." She bit down on her rib.

Elandra kind of believed that, ached to believe it, but it bothered her the way he was acting since meeting with Kim Rothwell.

"Do you know anything about this woman?" she

asked Daisy. "Her name is Kim Rothwell. Ever heard of her?"

Daisy licked some sauce off her fingers. "Not really. But I do vaguely recall Bradley being engaged to someone a few years ago."

Elandra blinked. "He was?"

"Yeah. There was an announcement in the paper."

"So what happened? Who was she?"

"I can't remember who she was." She was nibbling. "But I do recall the wedding was supposed to take place in Florida."

"That's where he's from." Elandra was toying with her straw, bending it. "I'm beginning to think this Rothwell chicky is his ex-fiancée. Was there a picture with the announcement?"

Daisy nodded. "Come to think of it, there was. She was pretty, an ex-model or something like that."

"Did she have really chiseled features and very short hair, like a tiny Afro?"

Daisy squinted her eyes again as she tried to remember. "Yeah, now that I think back, I think she did."

"That's her!"

"Who cares? He obviously doesn't want her, from how you told me he was acting."

But just then a sight emerged on the estate, amid the crowd, which grasped Elandra's attention. Watching her stand up to get a better look at something, Daisy could only ask, "What is it? Who are you looking at?"

"It's her!"

Daisy stood to get a better view. She saw a striking, tall woman pushing an elderly lady in a wheelchair. The woman looked familiar. She guessed it probably was the person in the announcement.

"What is she doing here?" Elandra asked, as both

women stared. Kim was making her way through the crowd, headed straight to Bradley.

"I don't know," Daisy mumbled.

"I do," Elandra said, trailing the woman and Bradley. "She's here to see him. He invited her. They're rekindling their affair." She sighed. "I knew it was too good to be true."

Meanwhile, a good distance away from the two, across the lawn, Mavis Rothwell was greeted with a peck on the cheek by Bradley. "The day is even more sunny with your presence, Mrs. Rothwell."

Her withered cheeks raised in delight. "Oh, dear, you're still so charming and so handsome."

"Yes, he is," Kim concurred, giving Bradley a seductive look. She patted her hair and brushed the thigh of the red short-shorts she'd chosen to wear today. She felt the outfit granted her sufficient ammunition to wear down Bradley's defenses. He did glance at her, but quickly looked back down at her mother.

"So are you still creating those crafts, Mrs. Rothwell?"

Mavis Rothwell was eager to answer, parted her lips to do so, and would have gladly responded if Kim hadn't beaten her to the punch. "Mama creates lovely crafts when she's feeling all right. When she isn't, she rests and watches television."

Bradley leered at Kim, itching to tell her he wasn't talking to her. However, he softened his expression, looking back down at her mother. "You should have gone into the craft business. You're a very talented lady. And if you have any new designs, I'd love to display them in my hotels' gift shops."

Mavis Rothwell glowed. "That's a wonderful idea."

"It is wonderful," Kim echoed, her appreciation

wandering over Bradley. "The sales will help Mama pay for a nurse."

Instantly embarrassment showed on the elderly woman's face. Touched by it, Bradley kneeled down to her level. "Your heart has been giving you trouble, I hear."

Mavis nodded while fixing a shawl across her shoulders. "Things wear out. Old tickers are no exception. Tick, tick, tick, right on out." She was striving not to be so somber, but Bradley saw the worry.

"You're going to beat this, Mrs. Rothwell. You were always spunky and a fighter to the end."

She looked encouraged. "Thank you, dear. I needed to hear that."

"And I'd like to help you."

Kim beamed.

"Help?" the elderly woman echoed. The embarrassment returned. "Oh dear, I can't possib—"

"Let me help. I want to. You need a nurse and I can provide one as long as you need it."

Mavis looked saddened. "Never thought there would come a time when I would need something so greatly for my health and couldn't afford it. But dear, I can—"

He grabbed her hand. "I know all about those bad investments your husband made before he died. I travel in the business circles, remember? You shouldn't be ashamed. Everyone holds you in the highest regard. Let me help?"

Kim lifted her mother's chin up toward her. "Please, Mama. I won't worry as much about you."

"I don't want you to worry, baby." She turned to Bradley and managed a smile. "All right."

Kim was overjoyed. "Great! Oh, thank you so much, Bradley. How can I ever repay you?" She stared suggestively.

His expression was stern. "Just take care of your

mother, that's all. Nothing more. Nothing less." He
stood and gazed down at the older woman. "Well, if
you will excuse me, Mrs. Rothwell, it's time for me to
gather my boys for a game."

As Bradley walked off, Kim was titillated by the wide-
legged, high-backed stride. What's more, she felt teased
instead of rejected by Bradley's last remarks. Kim loved
a challenge, especially one she was certain she would
win. With that in mind, her lips curved provocatively to
one side. *Look out, Bradley Davenport,* she thought. Her
scrutiny then shifted to a distant tree. She peered at
Bradley's assistant and another woman who were sitting
underneath it. "You look out, too," she whispered, her
eyes unmoving from Elandra's direction.

The games were the most entertaining part of the
day. Most watched and of those who participated, Elandra found herself involved in much of the recreation—
volleyball, races, baseball and several awkward attempts
at football. Repeatedly Bradley and she found their
paths crossing and their bodies brushing in the heat
of the excitement. There were looks that proved to
Elandra all was not lost. And when Bradley pulled her
aside, to introduce her to a gentleman who had been
staring all afternoon, he put his arm around her waist.
Nothing could express how good it felt.

"Elandra," he said, as they stood before the gray-
haired gentleman with hazel eyes. He was the man
whose hand Bradley shook earlier. "I'd like you to meet
Senator Wayne Hagans. Senator, I'd like you to meet
my extremely beautiful assistant, Elandra."

Neither man's eyes could blink for looking at the
gorgeous face. Elandra was thrilled that Bradley had
called her beautiful. He never had before.

"Nice to meet you, sir," Elandra said and extended

her hand for a shake. Instead her knuckles were caressed with a kiss.

Bradley scratched his temple.

"It's my pleasure, Elandra," the senator raved. "And your boss is right. You are extremely beautiful."

"Thank you, sir. And you know, I thought you looked familiar. Are you visiting Nassau?"

"I come down from time to time. I have some property."

"I see. I can't blame you. It's a beautiful place. I'm thinking of staying myself."

Bradley's face lit up. "You are?"

"Maybe. After I find Crystal."

"That's wonderful news." He was staring again. So was she.

But the senator suddenly clearing his throat drew their eyes to him. "Who is Crystal if I may ask?"

"She's my sister. I came from New York to find her after we lost contact."

"So you're searching for her?"

"Absolutely. I won't stop until I find her."

The senator bit down on his bottom lip. "I wish you luck in your search."

"Oh, she doesn't need that much luck," Bradley threw in. "She has the best private investigator in the world looking for her sister. And he will find her."

"Hope so," the senator remarked.

"Know so." Bradley nodded.

"But there is one thing I forgot to tell you, Bradley," Elandra added.

"What's that?"

He and the senator came nearer to listen.

"I went to see Peppy and he—"

"Didn't I tell you not to bother with that guy? He's bad news."

"But Myron is taking so long."

"Myron is a professional," Bradley defended.

"I know he is. And I'm extremely grateful that you hired him. But tell me this, why didn't he ask Peppy any questions? I gave him all the information Peppy gave me and he said he would talk to him."

"He didn't talk to him? Peppy was probably lying."

"I don't think so. He's pretty honest. At least he has been with me."

Bradley pretended this didn't bother him. Yet he made a mental note to get Myron on the phone first thing in the morning. He was curious as to why he hadn't questioned Peppy either. But then again, Peppy could have been lying.

The senator went off to mingle with associates, while oddly keeping an eye on Elandra. He wasn't the only one. As Elandra endeared Bradley to her more by playing rough and tumble games with his boys, Kim observed her. She couldn't wait to get her alone.

The moment presented itself when Elandra went inside the house to the powder room. No sooner than she headed toward the front door, Kim followed. Before long, they found themselves facing the mirror above the sink.

"Guess you got pretty sweaty out there, rolling around with those boys?" Kim commented.

Elandra smiled, then dabbed cotton over the shiny parts of her face. "I sure did. But it was fun, you know. I can really see why Bradley loves those boys. I'm falling in love with them, too."

"And they're not the only ones you're in love with."

The unexpected remark made Elandra stop dabbing and gawk at the smirking face on the other side of the mirror.

"I don't quite understand what you meant by that comment."

"Oh, I think you do. You're in love with Bradley, aren't you?"

"Look, my relationship with Bradley is none of your concern." Elandra was shaken by the words, but she didn't dare let Kim know it. She steadily moved the cotton across her face.

Kim turned from the mirror and leaned against the wash basin. She folded her arms as she sized Elandra up. "If you think you have a chance with Bradley, you're disillusioned. I heard how your voice sounded when you spoke of him the other day. I saw your eyes light up. But you're sadly mistaken if you think he reciprocates the feeling. What were those roses really for, services rendered?"

Elandra stiffened. She stopped wiping and whirled away from the mirror to eye this green-eyed monster next to her. "Bradley and I have not slept together, if that's what you're fishing for. But even if we did, it's none of your business."

"But you're wrong there. Bradley and I were once engaged and we will be again. Do you honestly think *you* could make him forget me?" Her gaze raked over Elandra. "I was his fiancée and what are you? You're some message taker and typist he took pity on."

"I'm a damn good assistant, that's what I am." Elandra stepped closer to Kim. "Not only that, but I'm also a beginning interior decorator. But most importantly, I'm a good person and a good woman, who knows how to treat a man and make him feel good. Furthermore, I must be one helluva threat to you! Why else would you have followed me into this bathroom?"

With that, Elandra strolled out the door. It slammed hard behind her. Lips drawn and fists balled up, Kim took several deep breaths. Reeling in the aftermath of those last words, she couldn't move right away.

Twelve

Many hours later, when the baby blue mist above coalesced with the orange-red that swathed the sky with twilight, Bradley indulged himself in the splendor from the suite's terrace. Quietly beautiful, the view was the opposite of the emotions dancing inside him. Excitement had him shaking. The barbecue, the entire day, had brought more than he imagined. He couldn't calm his heart down. One image ran through his mind—Elandra.

He hadn't expected such simple activities with her to be so much fun. Side by side partners in the relay race. Tumbling for a ball with the boys. Even the way she ate turned him on. Not a piggish eater, not a shy one, either; Elandra liked to eat and didn't mind if anyone knew it. Often throughout the day Bradley had observed her savoring a chicken leg or a rib. He was glad she enjoyed the food. He was glad she enjoyed herself, period. Everyone loved her, particularly Senator Hagans. Bradley had seen the lust in his eyes.

"Your ears must have been burning a few minutes ago," Richard declared, his heavily accented voice lacing through the air like an entrancing song, making Bradley swerve around.

"And why is that?" Bradley asked, coming into the house where his chauffeur was. His tone was frisky.

Richard was sitting on the couch relaxing, his cap

beside him. "Elandra was talking about you very much during our drive to her house."

"Was she?" A grin spread across Bradley's face. He eased onto the loveseat across from him.

"Oh, yes."

"What was she saying?" Anxiously he leaned forward.

"Oh, that you're such a great host. That you really know how to throw a party. That she had so much fun with you. And the list goes on. She was very happy today."

"She was, wasn't she?" His dimples showed clearly, his eyes glazed with images of earlier in the day. "And wasn't she dirty?"

"After all that rolling and tumbling with the boys. Oh, yeah."

"I loved how dirty she was."

Richard sniggered.

"No, really," Bradley said, laughter breaking in his words, too. "Most women would have been too worried about getting their clothes and hair messy. But not her. She dove right in there with my boys. She loves them. I can tell. They love her as well."

Richard tilted his head forward. "What about someone else? Does he love her, too?"

Suddenly Bradley's expression darkened. "Love is a very strong word, Richard."

"Because it's a strong emotion."

"Love is something I've tried to avoid since . . ." He looked off toward the terrace.

"Since Kim."

Bradley's gaze met his. "I don't have to tell you what I went through when she did what she did."

"It's time to move on, Bradley."

"I know."

"Can't move on if you're holding the pain of the past."

"I've been letting it go."

"You haven't tried hard enough. If you had, it would have been gone. Then you would be with that lady you think about all the time."

"How did you know I think about her?"

"I'm nice and seasoned with the flavors of the world. You don't live to be seventy-six years young and not learn nothing. I can see how you look at Elandra. I hear you talking about her when she's not around. I hear that sound in your voice. I see the restlessness you have when she isn't here. You have deep feelings. So does she. Everything you do, she does, too."

"It's hard, Richard. I can't get her off my mind." He leaned back into the couch. "I want to . . ."

"You want to be more than her friend and employer. Of course you do. She's a very beautiful, sexy woman and just as beautiful inside."

"God knows she is. You ever closed your eyes and saw a person so clearly?"

"My wife, rest her soul."

"Well, I can close my eyes and see Elandra so clearly. She's on my mind no matter what I'm doing. When I wake, when I sleep, when I work, when I'm at a meeting doing business. All the time she's laying somewhere in my mind."

"Make your fantasies come true, Bradley. Life is short."

"I want to. I really do."

"But you're letting that pain hold you back."

"You don't understand, Richard. You and your wife were together since you were sixteen."

"Bless her soul, we were."

"You should be grateful you never experienced having your heart shattered. Especially like mine was. The way it happened."

"I can't say that I did experience such suffering."
He rubbed his whiskers. "But I wouldn't let what Kim
did to me rule my life. Do you realize how much power
you've given her? You're an intelligent man, Bradley.
Can't you see that?"

"I guess I didn't look at it that way."

"Start then! You've been moping around, not letting
any woman get close to you. Now here comes this perfect woman, everything you ever dreamed of, and
you're scared of getting involved and letting her know
how you feel."

"But Richard, it's hard for you to put yourself in my
place. When someone does what Kim did to me, it just
breaks you. No, it kills you. You don't want to ever, ever
feel that hurt again and you do everything to avoid it.
It's torture like nothing else I've ever known. You give
all that you have, all that you are, your total heart and
soul, and someone tells you it's not good enough. That
no matter what you are, it's not good enough for them.
It hurts like hell. Do you know how many times I
laughed on the outside, but inside I was really crying?
Can you imagine that? It hurting when you laugh?
Some women think men don't hurt, that we just do the
hurting, but they're wrong. All of us aren't dogs. Many
of us want the same things women want—to be loved
like we're the most precious gift God could give someone in their life, and we ache to love the same way
back."

Peering down, Richard was fumbling with his cap.
He never knew how deep the younger man's pain went.
It touched him. Even so, he didn't want to see his
friend missing out on one of the greatest joys of life.

Dark, glossy eyes gazed into Bradley's. "You're right
that I don't know what you've been through, son. But
I know one thing. If you miss out on the taste of love
in your life, you're missing one of the sweetest joys God

has given us. Don't you want to know how it feels to love a woman passionately, with all your heart and soul and have her love you back that way? Can you really say you don't care if you miss that in your life? God knows, I wouldn't trade the love I shared with my wife for all the riches in the world. It's a magic you have to feel for yourself. You can't truly describe it."

"Believe me, I want what you had. I was almost ready to take that leap, too, until Kim showed up."

"Why was she here today anyway?"

"Because she arrived on the island the other day. She stopped by, trying to get back together, and asked could her mother come to the barbecue."

"So Ms. Kim didn't realize what she had until her well ran dry."

"I don't know what's her game, but I'm not interested. But Mrs. Rothwell has been sick and she never did anything to me. So I let her come."

"I've heard about her health and that's very kind of you. But I must give you my opinion, if you don't mind."

"Lay it on me."

"That woman is trouble. If you're thinking of reconciling, don't."

"I'm not."

"Don't get tempted."

"I'm not."

"You sure?"

"Yes, I'm sure. There is one woman for me. You know that."

"That's good, because I didn't miss those red shorts Kim wore today." He fanned as if there wasn't enough air. "I prayed to God to forgive me for my fantasies."

Both men laughed.

Bradley sobered, his eyes hazy with a sight in his mind. "Yes, she can be very seductive. I remember how she would just look at me and I would melt. She is a very, very beautiful woman, but I can see beyond that now. Elandra has taken hold of me and I can't shake her off no matter what I do."

"She's really under your skin, huh?"

"Like you wouldn't believe."

"Oh, I believe. The question is, when are you going to ask her out? Don't let her get away. Another guy will snap her up so fast."

"Oh, I know that. You should have seen how Wayne Hagans was looking at her today. We were discussing Crystal and he wouldn't budge an inch. And that's another thing, I must find her sister for her. I have to talk to my investigator, too. Apparently he hasn't been as thorough as I hoped."

Elandra gazed appreciatively in the mirror. Doing so, she picked up a can of oil sheen to spray the long, shiny spirals that framed her face, then turned to get a view of how her dress fit. The white, clinging mini classically accentuated all her curves.

Afterwards she grabbed a beaded purse off the bed, then took a deep breath as she left the bedroom. When she saw Bradley suddenly rising from the sofa, obviously delighted at how she looked, Elandra still couldn't believe he'd asked her out on a real date.

"Wow," he said, his smile, sparkling like his eyes. He looked like a little boy who just opened his most desired present at Christmas.

"I guess that means you like my outfit."

"I like *you* in the outfit. A dress is just a dress until the right woman is wearing it."

"Flattery will get you everywhere."

"Everywhere?"

"Uh-huh." She inspected his dark Italian suit. It was

molded so perfectly to his ultra-masculine form, she ached to touch him. But she restrained herself. "And you look pretty wonderful yourself."

"I'm glad that you think so." His smile faded as his eyes delved deep in hers.

Elandra explored, too. "Anyone would think so."

During the car ride to dinner, Elandra was so nervous she made an effort not to bring up the important matter he'd mentioned the other day. She discussed work, the boys, the barbecue, her new feeling that she could shoot for big dreams—and anything that strayed from the tension she felt building between them.

At The Pier, a lavish oceanfront restaurant, Elandra ordered lobster, salad and rice, while Bradley relished their Southern dishes. Again they had exhilarating conversation about everything except what was building between them.

Following dinner, they took in a concert on a cruise ship. Elandra enjoyed the Caribbean sounds, but she enjoyed Bradley most. More than once, he put his arms around her and she prayed for strength not to melt. She couldn't remember anything feeling so good.

When they arrived on her doorstep, she was still talking about how great the music was, when she noticed Bradley wasn't talking. He was staring at her like she was something rare and beautiful he had never seen before.

She was staring as well. "Why are you looking at me like that?"

"Because you're a beautiful woman, Elandra Lloyd."

"Any woman would look beautiful if you were looking at her like you're looking at me now."

"No, not any woman. You're not any woman."

"I'm not?"

"No, you're not." His hand eased atop hers. "You're a rare jewel."

"You know, you really make me feel like I am." She was tingling from his touch, feeling warm, warmer.

"Believe me you are. Not only are you extremely beautiful . . ." He toyed with her fingers. "But you have a good heart. The determination you have in finding your sister shows me how deep your love goes. When you love someone, you give your all, don't you?"

She looked off, thinking of not only Crystal, but of Dan. She gazed back at him.

"Yes, I guess I do."

"I want to be loved like that."

"You do?"

His face came nearer. Their eyes locked and lingered.

"Remember when I gave you the roses the other day?"

"How could I forget?"

"Remember how I told you that there was something important I had to tell you?"

"Yes." Her heart raced.

But as the next word was about to fall from his lips, a crash inside the house startled them.

"What was that?" Elandra whispered, and immediately searched her purse for keys.

"No need," Bradley said, tapping her arm, ceasing her movement. He had slightly pushed the door. It was already open.

"Stay out here," he advised and proceeded in the darkened house.

But she felt protective, afraid for him. "No," she whispered and followed closely behind.

Bradley was angered by her not listening, was even going to make her stay outside. However, when they flipped on the light switch, saw the horribly ransacked apartment and the man with a cap hiding his face, running and flinging his legs over the windowsill, Bradley took chase. Elandra was screaming. Among the hysteria, she reached for the phone and was about to dial. Except what she saw on the wall, astonished her more than she already was. Fingers froze. Scrawled on it was a message in red spray paint: DON'T LOOK FOR CRYSTAL.

Bradley relieved her somewhat by running back into the room. "I couldn't catch him," he managed between huge breaths. "He got away."

She raced to him and hugged him. Burying her head in the hardness of his chest, she admitted, "At least you're all right."

He loved the feel of her this close to him, on him. Bradley trembled to take her in his arms and love all her fright and pain away. Nevertheless, they had to call the police.

It took everything to ease out of her grip. "Don't worry, Elandra. I'll take care of everything."

"You will?" She then looked hard at the wall behind him, the one with the spray paint. Seeing her agonized expression, he was compelled to see what she saw.

Bradley spun around. "What the hell?" he murmured, reading the message.

"What is going on?" Elandra asked, frantically. "Why is someone doing this? What has happened to my sister? What was she into?" She was overwrought.

Bradley didn't answer the questions, but quickly dialed the police. After he hung up, he pulled Elandra to him, her back against his chest. Stroking her hair, he promised, "We'll find your sister. I give you my word. And don't worry about this place. I'll take care of everything."

"Bradley, you don't have to do all this."

"Ssh," he said, stroking her temple with gentle caresses. "I want to do this. I care about you, Elandra. More than you know."

Her head raised up at him. "I . . . care about you, too."

"And I'm not going to let you stay here alone, with people doing things like this." He scanned the room, then met the tears forming in her eyes. "You're coming home with me. I have a beautiful room my mother decorated, all frills and feminine ornaments. You'll be very comfortable there. And I'll be right down the hall. All you have to do is holler if you need me."

She nodded. "Okay. Thank you." A tear ran down her cheek.

"You don't have to thank me." Long fingertips met her cheek. Tenderly he wiped the tears away.

Thirteen

Myron Tate's heavy frame perched in the exact same place as the last time he'd visited Bradley's house. In spite of it, this time his expression was much different. Gone was the confidence he'd exuded when Bradley gave him the assignment of finding Crystal. Replacing it was the anxiety-filled man, who practically shook as Bradley paced back and forth.

"I've called you here today, Myron, because I'm not satisfied with the work you've done in finding Crystal."

"I'm doing my best," Myron responded. He removed a hanky from his pocket and harshly wiped at the beads of perspiration clustering on his forehead. "This assignment has not been easy."

Bradley stopped pacing. Glaring lines set between his brows. "Since when did you shrink from a challenge?"

"I'm not shrinking from anything. I'm just telling you, it's been hard finding her." He folded the hanky another way and wiped across his neck.

Bradley cocked his head warily to the side. "And what about Trina? Did you have any luck on information about her? She can lead you to Crystal, I'm sure."

"No luck there either."

"And Peppy?"

"Who—I mean, what about him?"

"You tell me about him," Bradley demanded, knowing he was about to lie.

Myron looked more uncomfortable. "I—I haven't had any luck with him either."

"Been hounding him a lot, huh?"

"Yes, but no luck."

"On his back all the time, huh?"

"Yes, but like I said, no luck."

"You're a damn liar!"

Myron wiped his forehead briskly. "What's wrong?" His pores gushed with sweat.

"You haven't even been to see Peppy."

Alarm raised Myron's temperature even higher. "Yes, I have."

"Want to accompany me to the club and ask him that to his face?"

Resigned to being caught in a lie, Myron shrugged his shoulders and looked everywhere but at Bradley. "I'm sorry," he apologized. "I'm a little sloppy, I guess, in my old age."

"You're not old. And you're not sloppy. But something is not right here. Spill it!"

"What do you mean?" Perspiration rolled beside his temples.

"I mean, I'm no dummy. After Elandra's apartment was ransacked last night, I know we're not dealing with something minor here. Somebody got to you, didn't they? Somebody with influence. Somebody dangerous."

Myron was now drenched with perspiration. He stood, dabbing the handkerchief all over his face. "If you want to fire me, Bradley, fire me. But I can't do any more than I've done." He stretched the sticky shirt away from his skin.

"Who got to you, Myron? I know they had to, or otherwise you wouldn't have been so slack. Did someone pay you a large sum of cash to hinder the investigation with Crystal?"

Myron longed to tell Bradley the truth. They had not only been associates via business, but were good friends as well. Despite it, he shuddered at the slightest threat to his family. Not only had the guy showed up in his car with a gun, but his wife and children had been followed by mysterious men. To top that, a black rose and a dead bird were mailed to his home.

"Bradley, no one is after me. I guess I just don't do my job as thoroughly as I used to."

"You're fired."

Myron hung his head. "I figured that."

Moments later, as Myron was heading out to the walkway, Elandra glanced at him on her way to the study. "That's Myron, right?" she said approaching Bradley.

"Yes."

She looked hopeful. "Any word on Crystal?"

Frowning, he rubbed his chin. "No. Actually Myron is too slack on the job. I'm hiring another investigator."

"You are?" The thoughtfulness made Elandra step closer. Bradley's gaze linked with hers. Even in a distressed state, the warmth inside his eyes touched her profoundly. "Bradley, why are you doing so much for me?"

"Because I'm paying you back," he answered matter-of-factly.

"Paying me back for what?"

His countenance softened. "For being so beautiful to look at."

She looked embarrassed. "Oh my . . ."

"For being so good-hearted. For just being you. You make me feel so good." He was whispering, his eyes slipping slowly across her face.

It all made her want to admit what had been held

back on her part. "You make me feel good, Bradley. Never has anyone gone to so much trouble for my happiness. You make me feel so special. Since I've been around you, I feel like I can do anything."

"You can. The power is all inside you. You just have to believe."

"I do. You made me believe. You make me feel like I'm priceless, and only worthy of the best."

But just then Richard emerged in the room, clearing his throat at the intensity reeking in the air. "It's time for me to take you to the airport, Bradley. Your suitcase is in the car."

Remembering he had an out-of-town meeting, Elandra buried the disappointment that fact hit her with. "Oh, that's right. You have a meeting today. I won't see you until tomorrow evening."

"Yes. I wish I didn't have to go. I'd rather be here with you."

At that she paused, elated and staggered. "No, you go. I know how important that meeting is. I set it up."

"But you do remember the alarm procedures I went over with you? I can show you again."

"No, you go. I have the alarm down pat."

"I wish you could come."

"But I have that appointment with all those consultants today. You shouldn't have hired me to decorate that renovated room at the apartment complex." She smiled. "I can't believe I'm decorating like a professional."

"You are a professional."

"I'll see you tomorrow."

"Sure."

"And I'll try to reach the new investigator while I'm in the limo."

"Thank you."

Bradley picked up his briefcase and headed out with

Richard. Elandra watched him leave, even as they got inside the car and drove off. She wandered around the mansion, enjoying its plush comforts for a while, before dreamily thinking about Bradley until her heartache soon replaced him. She dialed Daisy. After telling her what had happened with Myron and accepting Daisy's solace about it, Elandra asked, "What are you doing tonight? I want to go to another place where Crystal or someone who knows her might be."

Determined amateur detectives again, Daisy and Elandra wandered into The Wall Flower Pool Hall that evening. As soon as they entered, their first reaction was to scan the place for any sighting of Crystal and Trina. When that proved unsuccessful, Daisy probed every corner of the mid-sized pool hall for friends of the two women. While she was doing this, Elandra tried to do the opposite. She didn't want to look around and kept her eyes down. From corner to corner, men were ogling them like they were steak in the middle of a famine.

Daisy turned to Elandra. "No sign of Crystal or Trina, of course. Don't see anyone who knows them either."

"Good thing they don't know these people." Elandra was daring to look around as she spoke. An urge overcame her to run and cover up her body. "They look like they could eat you alive."

"You're not kidding."

"Let's go."

"Best idea I heard all night."

But as they headed out the door, someone Daisy brushed by made them stop in their tracks. A very muscular guy with browless eyes was fascinated. Elandra held her breath, for he smelled like raw fish was rubbed all over his body.

"I know you," Daisy said.

"I know you, too," he agreed, his uneven lips curling up. Gold teeth were everywhere.

"You're Trina's brother, aren't you? You used to drop by the hotel desk?"

"You're Trina's brother?" Elandra asked.

"Yeah," he answered in a voice laden with huskiness. Sheer joy bloomed across his features as he appreciated Elandra's face, then afterwards all the nooks and crannies of her body. "You're a friend of my sister's?"

"Sort of," Elandra answered.

Once again, his eyes couldn't stop roaming. "My sister has good taste in friends. My name is Angel."

"I'm Elandra." She had to hold her breath again.

"And I'm Daisy."

Angel acknowledged both women with a nod of his head, but kissed solely Elandra's hand. *Yuck,* she thought.

"Can I buy you a drink or something?" he asked.

Elandra started to say no, but Daisy was giving her a signal. This guy could lead them to Crystal if they handled him right.

All three sat at a booth. The fellows flanking the walls and those playing pool were still gawking. Angel relished the attention.

"A beautiful woman brings out the beast in these men." He winked at Elandra.

"Oh really?" she remarked.

"Big time." He scanned around. "Don't you see how all these men are looking at you? They can't keep their eyes away."

"I guess women don't come in here often," Daisy threw in.

"Not any this beautiful." He was staring at Elandra. Nervously she smiled. "So how's Trina?"

"Fine, I guess."

"You don't know?" Daisy asked.

His eyes remained on Elandra. "I know that I'm looking at the most beautiful woman to ever grace this island."

Elandra blushed. Daisy made a head motion for her to keep it up.

"I'm glad you think I'm beautiful," Elandra commented. "You're not hard on the eyes either."

"You think so?"

"It's obvious."

Grinning, he leaned across the table. "So when are we going out so I can show you off?"

Never, Elandra swore under her breath, but simply smiled at him. "Oh I don't know. Maybe if you help me, we can go out sooner. Then I won't be so stressed and worried about something. I'll feel free and just want to enjoy myself."

"Name it."

"I want to know where Trina and Crystal are."

Instantly the grin wiped off Angel's face. His features hardening, he leaned back in the yellow vinyl cushions of the seat. "You want to know where they are?" It sounded like a curse rather than a question.

Elandra tried to overlook his tone. "I can't find my sister. I've been staying at her place and she hasn't been home and hasn't called. And last night someone ransacked the place and put a disturbing message on the wall."

Angel's hardened features now formed a hostile glare. "Don't ask any more questions about them."

Elandra was frightened and baffled. "But I need to contact your sister because she was last seen with mine."

"You don't need to do anything, but keep your nose out of where it don't belong." He uttered this without raising his voice, but with as much rage as she ever heard.

She didn't understand him and was even more puzzled when he stood from the table and couldn't get away from them fast enough. He joined the mass of men playing pool and didn't look their way once.

When Elandra arrived home, she didn't feel like waiting for Richard to escort her to the door after he put the limo away. In light of the ransacked condo, it was a suggestion he and Bradley had agreed on for her safety. Nonetheless, too many troubling thoughts about Crystal were running through her mind. Mindlessly, she hopped out of the car and headed up the dark path to the door.

A sound made her steps slower.

"Who's there?" She peeped around.

No answer.

She made another step.

A sound again. Bushes rustling. Unsteady footsteps.

She stopped. "Who's there?" Her heart was heaving her entire body.

But quickly realizing the perpetrator was intent on scaring her instead of speaking, Elandra began walking faster toward the doorstep. An unwelcome, familiar stench made that pace even quicker and shockingly, a heavy hand yanked her by the back of the hair, making fire burn into her scalp. She screamed from the sudden pain, and the fear of all the unknown torture, which could happen. But it was being spun around to confront her tormenter that made the real terror claw at her heart.

There Trina's brother Angel stood. His eyes were seething, even as he eerily smiled.

"Don't you ask any more questions about my sister or yours. You hear me? I was sent here to give you that message."

"What is wrong with you people?" Panic felt like it was pulling her vocal cords to a whisper.

"What is wrong with you, thinking you can tease me and get information?"

"I wasn't teasing you."

"You *were* flirting." The grip tightened on her hair. Fright numbed her pain. Tears welled in her eyes. "I wasn't."

"You were and you should never tease me. But you'll know that soon enough."

As if the scene was plucked straight from her worst nightmare, Angel let her go, but only so that the men emerging from the bushes could surround Elandra. They were men from the pool hall. There was at least ten of them. Angel probably made eleven.

"This is a warning from our boss," he went on, stepping nearer. Elandra backed away.

"Don't you ask anything more about Crystal or Trina. Don't you even go to the cops or you'll get worse than what you're about to get. Then again, it's not bad. Actually you'll enjoy it—a lot."

The laughter roared. As it chopped through Elandra's consciousness, awakening her more and more to the fact that one of the greatest tragedies was about to happen to her, she prayed and prayed. Richard was parking the car not too far away. She estimated he would come soon. He could help her. He had to. She prayed for that. Just in time, God did answer and he provided more than Elandra asked for.

Like a mirage of water and food in a barren desert, two welcoming figures were dashing toward them.

"What the hell is going on?" Bradley roared.

Richard was with him in every step. "What in God's name is this?"

When Bradley reached the men, they were in for a surprise. In the blink of an eye, he pulled out a gun and fired among them repeatedly. They ducked, ran, shouted, scattering about until they disappeared into the darkness.

Richard and Bradley reached Elandra. Richard put his arms around her, while Bradley gazed in her face. "Are you all right? Did they hurt you in any way?" He was putting the gun in his pocket.

"No, I'm not hurt." She rubbed a sore spot on her head. "Thank you for saving me." Tears cascaded down her cheeks.

Bradley quickly removed a hanky and dabbed lightly along her skin.

The gentle pressure made her calm. "How did you know to come? You were supposed to be away tonight on that trip."

"Something told me to come back home. I canceled the meeting."

"You canceled it? That was a very important meeting. The guy is hard to get an appointment with."

"That doesn't matter. You matter. Something told me you were in trouble or could be in trouble. So I rushed back."

"I shouldn't have gone to that pool hall with Daisy."

"Pool hall? You went to a pool hall?" Bradley tried not to look upset as he heard that.

"It was called The Wall Flower. We were just trying to find out about Crystal or Trina."

Richard shook his head. "That's no place for a lady like you."

Bradley's scowl bared total agreement. "He's right about that."

"But can you believe that guy is Trina's brother?"

"You're kidding." Bradley's voice raised an octave.

"Yes, he is. His name is Angel. And he actually warned me not to look for them. Said something about his boss told him to give me a message."

"Don't you pay any attention to a word he said."

Bradley reeled her into his arms, resting her cheek against his chest. "I hired a new investigator today. He has to find out what's going on. He has to. If he doesn't, I damn sure will. Now let's go inside and call the police."

While Richard showed concern, equally he was observing the interaction. Heart warming it was, the way Elandra and Bradley were looking at each other, the way they so easily touched, the tenderness, the caring, the emotion so strong it lay heavy in the air. Witnessing it, sheer joy brightened Richard. He didn't have to worry about his young friend anymore. Bradley was tasting the deliciousness of romantic love, even if he didn't know it yet.

Fourteen

The police, along with the new investigator, had left the estate, their pads filled with details, information, and descriptions of Angel and the other potential attackers. Richard was gone shortly thereafter. The maid joined him in his departure. Elandra and Bradley were the sole two sitting in the living room. Her head lay against his shoulder. His arm slipped firmly but gently around hers, his hand clamping around the top of her arm. Silence enclosed them.

"You're okay?" he broke the quiet.

"Uh-huh, I'm okay." Elandra closed her eyes tightly then opened them. As much as she worried about Crystal, she worried why did it feel so good and natural to be near Bradley like this. Inhaling his sumptuous cologne and placing her head on him, Elandra wondered why did she ache to touch him all over? It shouldn't be this way, she chided herself. She shouldn't be feeling this way. After all, her world was shattered into pieces. Crystal was still missing. There were even those who wanted her to remain that way. The condo had been ransacked. If that wasn't enough, *she* had been attacked.

For Bradley the moment was equally baffling. On one hand, he knew this woman, who was lying on him, feeling so soft, feeling so good, making him feel so strong, hard and masculine, was part of him whether he wanted her to be or not. In one swooping breath it seemed she had entered his life, bringing all that was her, all that addicted him. In light of the torment he'd survived with Kim, he tried to avoid the building desire. It was a futile effort. There was no escaping, shaking, or ignoring what existed between them any longer. As much as Bradley fought it, it wouldn't go away. With this, he pondered what Richard had spoke to him about. Could he live the rest of his life without the taste of romantic love? Could he really do it when a woman like this was guilelessly weaving inside his soul?

"Elandra, we need to talk." His voice slipped into the peacefulness of the air.

"You don't have to assure me about Crystal again," she told him, not budging from her position on his shoulder. "Don't worry. I know they'll find her." Her gaze aimed straight ahead.

"No, I'm not talking about Crystal. The situation with Crystal is being handled. The other situation isn't."

"The other situation?" She knew what he was talking about. It made her feel lighter. Now she could hear it openly, honestly.

"The situation with us," he said, and she felt his body tensing.

"You sure you want to get into this?" Her limbs were suddenly quaky.

"So that proves you feel it, too."

Bradley peered down at her. Her head still rested on his shoulder. For Elandra was afraid now to see his eyes, fearing how weak they would make her, when she still wasn't sure of the direction she should go with him. "Do you feel it, Elandra?" His fingers grazed her arm.

She nodded slowly. "Yes, I feel it."

He took a deep breath, then swallowed. "Something is happening between us that we can't deny."

Get 4 *FREE* Arabesque Contemporary Romances Delivered to Your Doorstep and Join the Only New Book Club That Delivers These Bestselling African American Romances Directly to You Each Month!

No Obligation!

WE HAVE 4 FREE BOOKS FOR YOU!

FREE BOOK CERTIFICATE

Yes! Please send me 4 *Arabesque* Contemporary Romances without cost or obligation, billing me just $1 to help cover postage and handling. I understand that each month, I will be able to preview 4 brand-new *Arabesque* Contemporary Romances FREE for 10 days. Then, if I decide to keep them, I will pay the money-saving preferred subscriber's price of just $16.00 for all 4...that's a savings of almost $4 off the publisher's price with no additional charge for shipping and handling. I may return any shipment within 10 days and owe nothing, and I may cancel this subscription at any time. My 4 FREE books will be mine to keep in any case.

Name _____

Address _____ Apt. _____

City _____ State _____ Zip _____

Telephone (   ) _____

Signature _____ AR1197
(If under 18, parent or guardian must sign.)

Terms and prices subject to change. Orders subject to acceptance by Zebra Home Subscription Service, Inc. . Zebra Home Subscription Service, Inc. reserves the right to reject or cancel any subscription.

The truth raised her up from his shoulder and finally she braved his eyes. "You're right. Something is happening between us."

Bradley slid his arm off her and shifted so he could face her better. "I've been trying to tell you something for a while now. But it's been really hard. I want to be honest with you."

"I feel the same way. I want to be honest with you as well. Sometimes there is something about you that tells me that I can be open with you. Then other times this little nagging something holds me back. But right now, I want to talk. And I'd like to start at the beginning. I want to tell you why I was so distant and defensive when you first met me. That's not the way I really am."

"I know. You're really the person you are now."

"How do you know that?"

"The same way you know things about me."

"I do know things about you," she admitted. "Of course, what I see, but since I've come to know you I can sense things about you, about how you're going to feel or react to something."

"That's the same way I feel about you."

"Pretty amazing stuff," she laughed out, but seeing the intensity in his expression, her amusement waned.

"Don't be nervous, Elandra."

"I'm not nervous."

"You are." His eyes never leaving hers, he lifted her hand and caressed it. The palm was wet. "Sometimes when you're nervous, you laugh. That's something I've learned about you."

"You know me, don't you?" The way he looked at her filled her with that familiar warmth, only this time it was far more acute, concentrating in her lower belly. "I'm just scared about where this might lead. I don't want to get hurt again." Having revealed that, she turned her head aside.

Warm fingertips skimming her chin guided her back to him. "Someone hurt you a while ago, I know, that rich woman's son. But you're talking about something more recent, aren't you? I can see it in your eyes. It's still so fresh."

With the anguish of what happened weighing on her so poignantly, Elandra couldn't sit as she revealed everything to him. Hence, she stood and strolled toward the terrace. Watching her closely, Bradley followed.

It was easier to look at the sky when she told him. Under the stars and the moon, Elandra wouldn't have to fret over a look screaming to her about being a fool. Under the stars and moon, she didn't have to see the pity, either. Sharing what happened between Dan and her was draining. Mostly though, it seemed as if it happened a billion years ago—and to someone else. Thinking back, she almost didn't recognize herself. Changes had occurred without Elandra even realizing it. Strength and pride and love for herself had somehow filled her when there was little before. Even so, pain was like a dead body. If you dug it up, uncovered it and faced the reality that once blood and flesh had enlivened those bones, for that instant you would feel the sorrow. Digging up the heartache with Dan and the loss of the baby was digging up dead bones. It brought the agony all back.

Fortunately though, neither was there pity or belittling after everything was told to Bradley. When Elandra gazed at him, she saw something safe. Throughout his entire being emanated a strength and integrity she could hold on to. Zealously he grabbed her by the arms, pulling her toward his chest. Laying her head against its hardness, Elandra cried softly as he stroked her hair.

"That Dan wasn't a real man," he stated, his voice drowning in emotion. "He didn't deserve a woman like you. No real man, who knows who he is and has respect for himself and women, would treat someone like he treated you. And the baby . . ." He shook his head.

"That was the only decent thing about Dan. He gave me a baby. But now it's gone."

Her sobs became louder. Hearing them, knowing their source, tore at Bradley's heart. Every measure of her sorrow he felt.

Gently he lifted her face to meet his. "Your baby is in heaven, Elandra." A long finger blotted a tear. "And I won't even tell you that you can have more. Because I know one life will never replace another." A thick thumb softly whisked the water away. "But I will tell you life is going to be beautiful again. Some things are beautiful right now."

"This feeling," she breathed, her eyes searching his features, then languishing at his lips. She ached to kiss him. She ached to be closer than close. Even so, Elandra needed him to be honest, too. A small part of her was still unsure about him. She needed answers.

"What about you, Bradley? What happened? What have you not been telling me?"

He took a deep breath before scanning the skyline. Elandra followed his line of vision, until she realized he was seeing a place she would never see. It was the place inside where his pain dwelled.

"Kim was my fianceé," he began.

"I figured that."

"We met here on the island through her father. He and I had business dealings. He liked me and introduced me to his daughter. I was immediately attracted to her, too. Her looks grabbed me and I thought something about me grabbed her, too. Only I didn't know what it was then." He chuckled dryly. "If I had only known . . ."

"You and Kim seem different," Elandra commented and studied him. He was still captivated by that place.

"We were. I saw that right away. I overlooked a lot, too, in her character. I was just so overwhelmed by her beauty and her sexiness, I guess, and she was so much fun. At any gathering she was the center of attention. I was so proud to be with her, to know that she wanted me when she could have anyone. Then that bittersweet emotion set in before I even realized it. I fell in love. God knows why. I guess love is just one of those things that you can't explain. You can't really say why you fell for someone. You can't pinpoint what it is they did for you or to you, that made you feel such emotion. *You just feel it.* It's just felt. Because so many times after we broke up, I asked myself, what did I see in her?

"Anyway, I asked her to marry me. She accepted and prepared for the wedding. In doing so, I gave her anything and everything she wanted, access to all my bank accounts, and also privileged information on high-stakes business dealings I was doing. I shared everything with Kim."

"So what happened?"

"What happened?" That place still held his gaze. "The world ended, that's what happened. I headed to Florida that morning, where our wedding was supposed to be. My family and hers waited patiently at the church. Over 500 guests we had. Then as we tried to kill time because she was late, my best man went out in the anteroom and happened to see the paper. He looked through a few pages before he came to a page that astonished him. Like someone was dying, he then called me in the room. I rushed in and looked at the paper, and couldn't believe what I saw. There on the society page, was a picture of a newly married couple. They'd eloped. Kim had married some old billionaire the night before."

Stunned, Elandra's hand flew up to her mouth. "My God . . ."

He looked like something was funny, but Elandra knew it still hurt. It was in his voice. "And days later I found out something else. Not only did she marry him, but she took a huge portion of my money with her, and also gave him my privileged business information. That deal would have brought me into the billionaire stratosphere. Instead it netted him that worth. Not that he needed it. Not that he needed it *then*."

Elandra's mouth dropped open as she shook her head. "That was so cruel. Now it makes sense."

He looked over at her. "Now what makes sense?"

She stared at him. The strain of the story made him look like a sad little boy. "Now I understand why you said what you said to me the first time I saw you. On the boat. You were yelling about women robbing you."

"I'm sorry."

"I understand, Bradley."

"I shouldn't have taken it out on you. I shouldn't have taken it out on anyone. I almost lost my mind after that. I had to recoup all my financial and business losses and stay focused on that, while dealing with the betrayal and the humiliation, but most of all the heart-break."

"I could never do something like that to you."

He just stared at her.

"What? Why are you looking at me like that?"

"Because now I know that you couldn't do something like that to me. Right now, right this minute, looking at you, I know you couldn't. Before I was scared that you would. I was resigned to forget all about women."

"But now?"

"Now I see things differently. There's just something about you, Elandra." And his voice dipped low and husky. "And it's getting to me. Right inside here." Gently, he picked up her hand. What she felt was the insane rhythm of a heart. It matched her own.

"I see things differently, too, Bradley. I was scared, too. I was so scared of feeling that pain again. That pain of giving your all to someone to have it thrown in your face. It hurts like hell to give all your love to someone, and have them just throw it away like it's nothing. But right this minute, I feel I can trust you. I used to think I'd rather die than risk feeling love again, because it is a risk."

"Not with me it's not, Elandra."

"Can you promise me?"

"I can promise many things." His eyes fell down the length of her body and crept back up to her eyes. There was a glow in her face that made him warmer than he already was. "Can you promise me, Elandra?" he asked. "Can you promise that you will always be who you are now? Because who you are now could never, ever hurt me."

"Yes. And I can promise that I'll always . . ." Her head dropped. She was so afraid to say it.

"Say it," Bradley pressed. "I'll say it first." Cupping her cheeks, he raised her face up to his. "Love me like I love you."

The first feather-like touch of his lips against hers was for Elandra like a dream she had waited a lifetime for. With it, he gripped her face more firmly, while she wrapped her hands around his waist. Tingles in her blood seemed to race downward to an ocean of need in her lower body. Excitement flooded her and sensations of pleasure overwhelmed her.

Their bodies writhed lightly with the sweet invitation

of the kiss and the mounting desire it aroused. His mouth was soft, and skillful too, in the way it savored the feel of hers before faintly coaxing her lips apart with teasing motions of his tongue. Bradley slowly shifted his weight from one leg to the next, the mounting craving in his loins sending him into a frenzy for more of her. He couldn't get enough.

Their bodies grew tighter, locked by the soaring heat of the kiss. Fervently their mouths tangled. Insatiably, tongues sashayed over each other and in the blissful chasm beyond their lips. Deep-throated kisses unleashed a hunger each had never known. Air was all that made them come apart.

"Do you know how long I've wanted to do that?" Bradley asked, his chest rising and falling dramatically with his breathing.

"Not as long as I did," Elandra panted.

"Oh, you make me feel so good." He crushed her to him, and she caressed her face into his chest. He leaned his head back, inviting her lips to the taste of his neck. Her mouth and tongue relished the sweet cords of his throat, while her senses exploded so pleasurably from the provocative scent he emitted. Never, never could she get enough. The heartbeat plowing in her chest, hairbreadths from breaking through skin, proved that. His carnal moans urged her on, lowering her lips until she reached the first few scattered hairs on his chest.

Haplessly a ringing phone dragged them from their fever.

"Let it ring," Bradley insisted, a moan lingering in his voice.

Trying to catch her breath, Elandra eyed the phone skeptically. "But it may be the police or news about Crystal."

"You're right," he agreed with a nod and stepped toward the phone.

After listening a few moments, she saw him nodding his head.

"Who is it?" Her lips mouthed the words. "What?"

Bradley was trying to listen to both. "Okay. Okay," he said to the person on the other end of the line. "I'll be there in ten minutes."

When he hung up, Elandra didn't know what to think. Bradley's expression was hard to read.

"It's not about Crystal and it wasn't the police," he said, and moved about the room, gathering his jacket, briefcase and a few other belongings. "It's business. I'm going to The Hotel Mandarain. There's a problem. I'll be back as soon as I can, and I'll put all the alarms on. And you have my beeper number." He paused to look at her. "When I come back, if it's not too late, maybe we can pick up where we left off."

The next morning when Elandra woke, she hurriedly showered, lotioned her skin with a citrus fragrance, then sprayed lightly behind her ears a citrusy perfume. Wanting to look pretty for Bradley, afterwards she dressed in a long, floral sundress and sandals with a short, skinny heel. As she walked down the stairs, she was eager to see Bradley, since she fell asleep before he returned home. Obviously he'd worked later than both of them hoped. Except when she entered the study, there were two voices. Neither was Bradley's. She panicked, seeing Richard and a scrawny stranger.

"Where is Bradley? Did those animals get him?"

Richard smiled. "Oh boy. You have it bad, don't you?"

"Got it bad?" she echoed. *What had Bradley told him?*

"No, nothing is wrong with your beloved Bradley, my dear. He's still working."

"You mean he didn't come home last night?"

"Nope. Still at the office. Called me to bring him a change of clothes."

"Oh, I see." But she was uneasy about what he implied, even if it was the truth. "Did Bradley tell you anything about us?"

Beaming, the scrawny man was going from face to face.

"Nope," Richard answered. "But *I've* been telling both of you about each other. You two have it bad for each other and wouldn't admit it."

Elandra was glowing. "Well, you're not up to date. Last night things changed."

"Did they now?" Richard laughed heartily. "Now that's what I like to hear. Two wonderful young people showing that they care deeply about each other."

"Amen," the lanky man injected, making them all chuckle. "And allow me to introduce myself." Outstretching his hand, he stood and approached Elandra. "I'm Gregory Mitchelson. I'm the new investigator Bradley hired."

Elandra glowed even more than she already was. "I'm Elandra."

He shook her hand. "Nice to meet you."

All three relaxed on the couches.

"Bradley told me to report any news and that's exactly what I have."

"You do? So quick?" She was amazed.

"That is fast," Richard added. "Weren't you hired yesterday?"

"Time is crucial, and every minute should be taken advantage of."

Elandra liked the way that sounded. "So what do you have?"

"I talked to Peppy. He might be willing to give up some more information if we keep pushing him."

"That's great!"

"But the best news is the new lead I have."

"What is it?"

"I'd rather not say, but it may lead me straight to Crystal and soon."

Elandra shot up in the air shouting, "Thank you, God!"

"Let's not get our hopes up yet," Richard reasoned.

"Sorry, Richard," she bellowed, "I'm tired of feeling down. This news and some others that I have makes me just want to shout."

It was about a half hour later when the two men went to their destinations and Elandra headed to hers. All the good tidings popping up deserved a celebration. Richard told her Bradley would return home by six. Armed with this news, Elandra made plans. She would ask the maid to leave early. She was cooking dinner for Bradley tonight. There would be scrumptious food, candlelight and plenty of romance.

Strolling down the produce aisle in the market, Elandra had picked up two bags of carrots and an eggplant and was turning around when she bumped into what seemed like a sudden wall that appeared. Gazing up at who was in front of her, she met a pair of familiar hazel eyes.

"Senator Hagans," she acknowledged him, throwing her vegetables in the cart.

"Hello again, Ms. Lloyd. And it's Wayne to you."

She beamed. "Well, Wayne, I see you remember my name. Call me Elandra."

"I remember more than your name. I remember you. You are truly unforgettable." He smiled, but it was a bizarre smile to Elandra. Somehow his eyes didn't hold the same cheer his lips did. It made her feel strange. She tried to shake it off.

"Out shopping today?" Elandra asked.

"Just picking up a few things."

"Me too."

"How is your search going for your sister?"

She was surprised he remembered that. "Great! The first investigator we hired was slack, but Bradley's found one who has a lead already."

"A new investigator. Hmm." He scraped the corner of his graying mustache.

"That's right. And I'm on clouds. Hopefully I can see my sister very soon." She happened to notice the clock. It was getting late and she wanted to have enough time to prepare dinner exquisitely. "Well, Senator—I mean, Wayne, I'll tell Bradley that I saw you."

"Do that." And there was that odd smile again.

Elandra pushed her cart spryly up the aisle. However, as she did, the strangest feeling came over her. It compelled her to turn around, and when she did, oddly enough, the senator was standing where she'd left him. Except not only was he standing there, he was watching her. It wasn't a lustful glare, either. No, it was something that was difficult to describe.

Upon arriving at the mansion, Elandra hurried to the kitchen, anxious to get dinner started—steak, brown rice, creamed carrots, string beans, chicabob and for dessert, pineapple cheesecake.

Almost five hours later when Bradley arrived home, the aromas hit him, but he saw no one in the study or the living room. In the dining room, he nearly passed out at all the beauty. Candles on the table. Trays exquisitely designed with an eggplant and chicabob appetizer. Champagne chilling in a decorative bucket. The finest silverware, all beautified by those platters of steaming food. To top it off, soft music played in the overhead speakers that were dispersed throughout the mansion. But still, the most alluring temptation was the woman wearing a red dress.

"Do you like?" Elandra asked, and spread her hands out to the elaborate table.

"Oh, I like all right." Yet he wasn't looking at the table. He was gawking at her. "When can I have?"

"Now."

He almost leaped at her, but Elandra jumped back playfully. "Not before dinner."

Bradley's lips curved up slyly. "If you insist. But I can go for dessert before dinner."

"But I want you to experience my culinary skills. I went to a lot of trouble. I don't usually cook, you know?"

"You don't?"

"No, I was a fast food junkie in New York."

"Well, that's all the more reason why I appreciate this." His eyes scattered over the table before he stared back at her. "The table looks lovely. The food smells good."

"Wait until you taste it."

"Anything for you. I'll be right back. Let me go wash up."

Bradley hurried up the stairs while Elandra finished setting the table. When he returned, he was wearing a black shirt and gray pants. The first three buttons of the shirt were open. Not wearing any cologne, he smelled sensuous and clean.

"Looks good," he said, sitting before a plate piled high with food. These were his favorites, he thought as he scoured the table.

Elandra sat across from him. He began uncorking the champagne. The prettiest ballad was playing.

"Any word from the police?" she asked. "Ooh, I like

this song." She was smoothing her dress beneath her thighs and buttocks. She didn't want it to wrinkle when she stood.

"Not yet," he told her and popped the cork. "But I'd rather forget about them now. There's just you and me, and this great meal you've prepared. I appreciate it so much."

Her head sashayed to the music. "And I appreciate you. I hope the steak is tender enough. I never cooked steak before."

"Really?" He eyed the juicy brown meat. "Oh, it looks just fine. Don't underestimate yourself."

He poured her a glass full of the foaming drink and then one for himself. Their wrists intertwined as he gazed at her to make a toast.

"To a new beginning," he said. "May it lead us up a road of happiness that will never end."

"That's beautiful." Elandra's eyes were soaking up every inch of him. "And let me do one."

"Please do, beautiful lady."

"To fairy tales. Those aren't just fictional characters in those stories little girls read as a child. Those heroes do exist. They do. I'm looking at one."

The words made him place his hand on his chest, where his heart was. Afterwards, gazing into each other's eyes, they took a sip of champagne.

"Umm," Bradley purred. "Good. Very good. But not as good as your lips."

"You sure?"

"Oh, yes."

"After dinner, you can test again, then compare."

A devilish laugh escaped from him and Bradley picked up his fork.

The steak was the first to be tasted. Rubbery, hard to break with a fork, and equally as hard to break with the knife. Dauntless as he was, still Bradley put it in his mouth. Chewing harshly, he strived to look pleasant, for Elandra was watching him closely. Even when it felt like basketballs were inflating his cheeks because the meat was just too leathery to swallow yet, Bradley maintained the smile. He maintained it and he chewed, and chewed, until his jaw muscles performed what was tantamount to a thousand sit-ups.

Sitting across from him, Elandra ate slowly. How the food tasted to her palate really didn't matter. It was more important to observe Bradley. Pleasant-faced as he was, it was clear he was having a hard time with the steak. Perhaps the rest of the meal was better.

"Try the rice," she suggested, munching half a raw string bean. "I put a lot of gravy on it. Do you like gravy?"

Finally he swallowed. After such an effort, he paused for a moment, then answered, "Sure."

"Try it."

"Okay."

The rice was prepared better than the meat. Smiling, chewing, and looking at her, Bradley nodded in approval. More and more he ate. She was happy that he liked it. The sight urged her to eat heartily, too. That is until Elandra heard him crunching. It couldn't be her rice, she thought. Nonetheless, there were more crunches and more. Even so, Bradley looked pleasant. He continued eating, until everything was finished.

"What a meal," he declared, dabbing his mouth with a napkin. A new ballad floating from the overhead speakers made his head sway faintly.

"I'm glad you enjoyed it. At first I thought you didn't like it, but you obviously did. You finished it all."

Barely, he thought.

"Need some help putting the things away?" he offered.

"No, I'll put everything away and we'll snack on the rest later."

Hesitantly he nodded. "Sure. We'll do that." He grabbed the champagne glass and didn't stop drinking until it was finished.

Elandra was amazed. "Wow, you sure were thirsty."

"All that food makes you thirsty."

She smiled and began removing the dishes from the table. Scurrying around the kitchen and connecting dining room, her back was to him. He remained at the table, relaxing back in his chair, admiring the view.

"You know, I can make dinner for your guests when you invite them over," she volunteered.

"No!" Bradley exclaimed before he realized how he sounded.

Elandra spun around. "What do you mean no?"

"I mean, you don't have to do that. You don't have to go to all that trouble."

She stepped over to him. "You didn't like my cooking, did you?"

"Sure I did."

"No, you didn't. I can see it on your face."

It was on his face. Sitting there, observing her, Bradley couldn't get over how the rice crunched like crackers, how chewing the steak was like chewing a basketball, how the string beans and carrots were raw when they were supposed to be cooked, and how the cheesecake was sour. But the crazy fool in love that he was, Bradley ate it all. Thinking about it, he could no longer bury the humor inside. He burst out, howling with laughter.

"What's so funny?" Elandra asked.

It was too much. He couldn't express it. He turned sideways and bent over in convulsions that made him yowl.

"What's so funny, Bradley?" She was getting really mad. Her eyes squinted like the sun was in them.

It was hilarious to him. He tried to utter words, but Bradley found it all the more hysterical.

"What's so damn funny?" she screamed, her stinging tone somehow sobering him.

"You," he admitted, chuckles edging his voice. "You can't cook worth a poot. But I love you so much I ate it anyway. Crunchy rice, steak tough as rubber." He threw his head back, and laughed some more. He wanted her to see the humor of it all and laugh with him. She didn't.

Not believing his nerve, Elandra was fuming. After all the trouble she had gone through, he was making fun of her.

"Well, I'll never cook for you again! That's for sure. I knew it wouldn't work! I'm out of here." She stomped off toward the living room, intent on going upstairs and gathering her belongings.

"Where are you going?" Snickers weaved through his words. He was following her.

"Out of here, like I said. I knew it wouldn't work."

Realizing how serious she was, Bradley reached Elandra and whirled her around. Rage breathed in his face.

"You're not kidding, are you?" he asked.

"No. I'm leaving."

"Because I teased you about your cooking? That's ridiculous."

"Because you don't appreciate the small things in life. Like someone taking time to do something special for you. It just tells me so much about your character. You're so rich, you don't know how the common folk live. I can't make you happy. And I won't even try!"

"That's what this is about, isn't it?"

"What are you talking about?"

"You're not furious because I didn't enjoy your cooking. You're furious because you know we were about to take our relationship to another level and you're scared. You're scared to death. I want you so bad, and you want me just as much, and this is your excuse to run."

"I'm doing no such thing." Except she was scared. Offended, and so scared. "And who said I wanted you? And what relationship?"

"Didn't all we talked about mean anything to you?"

"I was fooling myself."

"You're fooling yourself now. How can you throw everything away because I didn't like your cooking? Because of something that trivial? I ate it, didn't I?"

"Don't do me any favors!"

"I'm not! Elandra, I don't want you for your cooking." His gaze firmly in hers, he clutched her arms. "I want you for yourself. Unless you have a burning desire to do so, you will *never, ever* have to cook. Hell, we have a maid."

"You have a maid!"

"What's mine is yours." And he whispered, "My heart and soul are yours. And you know they are."

Fifteen

Elandra turned her back to him, her lips quivering but no sound escaping. All his accusations were true. Fear was guiding her. Although at the same time, Elandra did believe she possessed his heart. Deeply it was felt. It rang in everything he did for her, in every look, in every touch, in the way he spoke her name, even in the air between them. When weighing those factors, her defenses relented, allowing Bradley to move closer. Hot breath fell down the back of Elandra's neck and along the sinews in her shoulders. It roused tingles. It stirred heat in the blood. Elandra desired him more than she ever had before. What was she going to do?

"I want you," he whispered, his lips so near her ear that his breath stroked it. "I want you in the way any man wants a beautiful woman, lustfully. But it's more than that. It's more than carnal needs being met. It's love." Caressing her cheek with his thumb, he was never more serious. "I'm in love you, Elandra. I may have taken a while to let you know it verbally, but I think I've been showing you. I did everything I knew how to show you that I care, to show you that I won't hurt you. And it took so long because I was afraid you would hurt me. But now I know you won't. I love you. I love you. But you . . ."

Slowly she curved around to meet his gaze. "Bradley, I am afraid. Ninety-nine percent of me is sure you won't hurt me. But there is that one percent that remembers what it's like to have a knife in your heart. To give yourself so freely and have someone break you into a billion pieces, leaving you with an ache that you can't take any medicine for. It just stays with you twenty-four hours to make you suffer."

"I know the feeling, Elandra. I've been there, remember?"

"If you know that, then you know it's that part of me that's deathly afraid. I don't want it to be that way, but at times I just can't help it." She paused, searching his face. "On the other hand, I'm tired of being afraid. I love you, too. And I ache to show you how much, but I need time."

"I don't want to pressure you." He brushed hair off her eye. "I want you to do things when you feel ready, when you feel that it's right and you're comfortable with it. I can wait. I'll wait forever for you."

"You're amazing." Her pinky traced his jawline. "You're just an unbelievable man. Sometimes I wonder if you're real or did I imagine you, or am I hearing or experiencing something that's all in my head."

"Whatever is positive which I bring to your life, I'm glad. And I want you to know it's not in your head. Everything between us is real."

Her pinky reached his lips, tracing them softly. "It is real, isn't it?"

"Oh, yes." Both hands caressed her cheeks. "We both feel how real it is. Our bodies don't lie."

For that moment after, they were entranced by each other. So much so their eyes asked the question about dancing to the impassioned harmony and their eyes spoke the answer. Because of their bickering before, the tunes blended into the background. Yet as their bodies mingled together, their lips merely trembling, the sound was everywhere. It exploded through their senses. A stirring ballad, beginning calmly, but captivating like the beauty of a sunset, it held depth. Passion poured from the piano, the saxophone and the violin. The vocalist's emotion could be felt, transporting the listener with her expression from the sweet and pure of love until it built to a raging inferno.

Bradley's arms wrapped around her back, flattening her chest against his. Elandra sighed faintly from the glorious feeling and the wild thumping of his heart. It lured her face into the curve in his neck. Burying her face there, she was intoxicated by the unique scent that was him. Excitement throbbed in her lower body, then reached up, shaking her heart. Unable to resist touching him more, her arms circled his waist, her hands climbing the bone in his back. Like this, Elandra heard the music thundering around them, even if soon it was drowned by a music all their own. It reverberated in her heart. As they began to sway, it was one with his, rumbling fast, passionately, with a life she had never known.

He slumped toward her slightly, tightening the embrace, shutting his eyes, letting his body's curves mold with hers. Elandra closed her eyes, too, letting her hips rock carefully with the amorous rhythm of his. Feeling weightless and dreamy, she was further excited by his love pressing into her flesh, proving how ravenous he was for her. It overwhelmed Elandra. Her limbs ached for more.

"I need you," he rasped, hugging her so tightly. "Elandra, this feels so good, so right."

She squeezed him just as hard. "I don't want to ever let you go, Bradley."

"You don't have to." Eyes still closed, he nestled his nose in her hair. A strawberry fragrance streamed at him. "I'll always be here for you, to hold you like this. I want to please you, Elandra. I want to make you so happy."

"You do. I'm happy right now. With all that's not right in my life, you're still making me so happy."

"I wanted to hold you like this for so long. I kept telling myself that I didn't."

"I did the same thing. I didn't want to love you, and told myself I didn't, but my heart knew better."

His hands slid up and down her back. "I can make you feel so good, Elandra. Like the woman that you are. So loved, so appreciated, so desired. When you love someone like I love you, you can just . . ."

Bradley released his hold just enough to gaze in her face. She was so beautiful he could hardly stop himself from throwing her on the floor, and loving her like this was their last night alive. Control was the key. He balked at doing anything to scare Elandra away. They had come too far to regress. Despite the agonizing desire that screeched to be released, he would wait. A woman like Elandra was worth waiting your whole lifetime for.

"Good morning," Bradley whispered, several hours later. Facing her, he leaned on his elbow, the sunshine streaking through the curtains having nothing on his smile.

She sat up some, wiping the last remnants of sleep from her eyes, and catching his gorgeous face between her fluttering long lashes. "Do you wake up this happy all the time?"

"Waking up to you every morning, I'll be this happy all the time."

That made her blush. To elude the embarrassment, she scanned the living room. "I guess we danced ourselves right off to sleep. Thank goodness this couch is a big one. I'm a wild sleeper. I might have kicked you or flung an arm somewhere painful in less spacious accommodations."

Dimples pinched his cheeks. "You slept like a baby snuggled next to me."

"It was nice, Bradley." Her expression was as sincere as her tone. "It was nice just to dance and cuddle with you until we fell asleep. Thank you for not pressuring me about making love."

"I told you, I'll wait as long as you want. But at least I don't have to wait for this."

His mouth lowered toward hers, his lips stopping only an inch from her face. Softly his middle finger brushed her lips, before his tongue gently induced them apart. The sweet nectar of him triggered inside her an ocean of need. Combined with the strong pressure of his arms around her, Elandra felt herself drowning in ecstasy. When had a man ever kissed her like this? *Never,* the eruption in her heart resounded, *never.*

"You are so beautiful, Elandra. So beautiful," Bradley confessed, his lips taking a moment to recover, his eyes absorbing her.

"And you're everything I ever dreamed of in a man. You aren't just a gorgeous package outside, you're just as pleasing inside."

"I'm crazy about you," he moaned, and crushed her to him. Tenderly he kissed all over her face with little pecks. Lightly they pressed across her warm skin, eventually reaching her trembling lips. His craving for her made him delirious. He fingered her lips' silkiness before being thrilled by kisses over his nose, cheeks, lips, and chin.

Not able to withstand any more, in one leap Bradley smothered her lips, forcing his tongue beyond them into the sweet taste inside. Instantly his need for her was more aroused. Enraptured, he clung to her with every breath, taking all the joy that he could. Delicate as a brush of wind on a summer night, he kissed her one moment. Then the next, passion made him ravenous and harsh. Shivers of pleasure raced through Bradley, rousing him to embrace her tighter. The rapture was almost unbearable. It was no wonder he almost missed the clock. Through his love-drugged eyes he happened to glance it.

"Oh no!" he said, springing back from her, hopping up from the couch.

"What's wrong?" Elandra asked, alarmed.

"I'm late."

Her head shot up at the clock. Panicking, she gawked back at him. "You are late. That meeting I scheduled."

"Oh boy." Bradley began hurrying toward the doorway. "I better go shower and get dressed."

"Yes, you better do that."

"But not before you do one thing for me."

"What's that?" She was trailing him.

He twirled around. Bradley clutched her shoulders, kissing her hard and long. When he released her, Elandra looked drunken. Seeing the expression, Bradley loved the effect he had on her. He wanted to stay there with her. He wanted to stay there with her and see it again . . . and again. But time was his concern now.

"The one thing I want you to do is accept a dinner date for tonight. Meet me at The Chateau Restaurant at eight p.m. Richard knows where it is."

She was elated. "I'll be there."

"Great. Just great." Heavy, quick footsteps sped up the stairs.

Meanwhile, downstairs Elandra swiped a pillow up from the couch. Hugging it to her middle, she laughed aloud and began dancing around provocatively. In her mind, it was last night all over again.

* * *

When Bradley saw her entering the restaurant, all else in the establishment became a blur. Striding toward him among the mirrored walls, Chinese carpeting and huge chandeliers, Elandra wore a soft yellow dress, ankle-strap sandals of the same color, and a floral pastel bag.

"Am I early or late?" she asked. He stood, then came around to pull out her chair. "Thank you kind sir," she teased as she sat, then watched him relax across from her.

His eyes were sparkling. "You look so beautiful."

"I feel beautiful when I'm with you."

She blushed.

"You embarrass easily." He seemed spellbound.

"No, I don't," she denied playfully.

"Yes, you do. But that's going to change. I'm going to teach you how to accept a compliment."

"You are, huh?"

"That's right. Because you're going to get plenty of them."

She blushed again. "I was thinking about you today."

"I was thinking about you, too. I loved dancing with you last night and holding you this morning."

"Actually I loved it so much, I feel guilty now."

"Guilty about what?"

"About feeling so good when Crystal is still missing."

His expression turned pensive. Bradley reached across the table and placed her hand inside his. "I told you I will find her and I mean it. And you shouldn't feel guilty. Besides, the new investigator has a new lead already."

"I know, but I still feel guilty." She gazed down in her lap, then back up at him. "What if when he finds her, she's . . ." Elandra looked down again. She couldn't say it.

"Dead," he finished her sentence.

Her head shot up. "It is a possibility."

"But we're not going to let it be. One thing I learned in my journey to becoming wealthy—always think positive until you have no other choice but to think otherwise. Then you just deal with the cards you're dealt. Whatever happens, the man upstairs will give you whatever you need to make it through."

"You're right. You're always right."

"Don't worry, we'll find her. We have the investigator, the police. I've even had flyers made up and people are handing them out right now. A reward was posted. Fifty grand."

Stunned at his generosity, Elandra clutched her chest. "My God. You did that?"

"Of course."

"I can't tell you how much I appreciate it."

"Your kisses tell me that."

She smiled. "What would I ever do without you?"

"If I have my way, you won't ever have to find out." He leaned across the table and kissed her. When they came apart, neither was smiling, just smoldering.

"Like I said before, you're amazing, Bradley Davenport."

"Amazing like the lady in my life."

She chuckled. "You're spoiling me. I could get used to all this sweet talk."

"That's my plan."

"And I really do appreciate what you're doing for Crystal."

"I know you do and I'm glad to help. I'm even going to use my contacts to find her."

"Your contacts?"

"Yes, you know—the people in the so-called high places that I know."

"Speaking of people in high places, I saw the senator yesterday."

"Where?"

"In the supermarket."

Bradley's eyes widened. "The *supermarket?*"

"Why is that such a surprise?"

"Because Wayne Hagans has people that do everything for him. He's disgustingly rich and takes full advantage of it."

"What do you think about him?"

Pondering the question, Bradley rubbed his chin. "He's okay, I guess. He's done a few favors for me and I've done a few for him. Otherwise, I wouldn't say he's my best friend." He peered at her. "Why do you ask?"

"I don't know. Yesterday when I saw him, he gave me the strangest, weirdest feeling. It's hard to describe, but it made me very uncomfortable. He asked about Crystal."

At that moment, a waiter interrupted, placing menus in their hands. Also at this time, a pair of eyes scrutinized them from across the room, and had been scrutinizing them for a while. Kim had been seated at a secluded table ever since Elandra walked in. What she saw repulsed her. The affection Bradley and Elandra shared was obvious. Undoubtedly their relationship had reached another level. But so what, she thought. Never had there been a man whose heart she couldn't win. Bradley Davenport would be no different. He'd lived and breathed her once. He would again.

The waiter had just placed the meal on the table and sauntered away, when Bradley and Elandra were treated to an unexpected visitor.

"Secretary and boss out for a night of dinner?" Kim inquired, surprising them, drawing their attention up to her.

"Hello, Kim." Bradley spoke, stiffly. He then chose to ignore her by sampling a morsel of food.

"How are you, Bradley?" She was lit up like a bulb.

Without glancing at her he replied, "I'm fine and you?"

"Extra fine," Kim responded. "Can't you see that?"

"Have no idea." Not bothering to look up, he was digging into the meal.

A tacky, tacky, tacky woman, Elandra thought. It was all the more reason to enjoy Bradley snubbing Kim. Elandra glowed.

Disappointed, Kim directed her sight across the table. "And how are you, Elaine?"

Elandra glanced at her nonchalantly before tucking a white napkin in her lap. "It's E-lan-dra," she pronounced.

"Oh, I'm so sorry. It's such a different and difficult name. Very hard to remember and articulate. I would find it sort of irritating and cumbersome, not even feminine."

"Doesn't matter what you would find," Bradley said, gazing at Elandra, then glancing at Kim. "Because if you don't mind, my date and I would like to be alone."

"Your date?" Kim disguised the hurt that jerked inside her. "Your secretary is your date now?"

"Actually she's more than my date." Big, warm hands reached across for Elandra's. "She's the love of my life."

Kim's face went blank. "I see."

"Yes, you do," he said, staring in front of him, stroking Elandra's knuckles. "So you'll understand why we would like to be alone."

Kim looked down at the eyes fastened on each other. "I ah . . . I, ah, just stopped at your table to tell you thank you."

Bradley frowned at her. "Thank me for what?"

"You know."

"I know what?"

She eyed Elandra, then him. "You know? I don't

know if I should say." She nodded her head toward Elandra.

Certain that she was trying to stir up trouble, Bradley was angered. "Anything you have to thank me about, Elandra can hear."

Elandra was loving this. "Be my guest, Kim."

Kim yearned to slap the smirk off of the lowly competition, but curled up her lips instead. "I, ah . . . I just wanted to thank you for what you did for my mother. You know, the nurse. I appreciate it and I know you did it because you care."

"I care for your mother," he stressed. Afterwards he returned his attention to the beauty in front of him.

"Right," Kim remarked, seeing that neither was paying her attention anymore. They were enthralled by each other. Frustrated, she walked away.

Bradley and Elandra continued dinner, eating, laughing, chatting, teasing, staring, kissing, feeding each other. And while they did this, Kim never really went away. Hunched over her table, she watched and waited for the opportunity she was hoping for. It presented itself nearly thirty minutes later, when Elandra practically bounced to the ladies' room. Kim followed.

"Think you have him hooked?" Kim charged upon opening the bathroom door, stepping beside Elandra before the mirror.

"Not this again," Elandra sighed and shook her head. She searched through her purse, fumbling for a powder puff. "Please don't tell me you're singing that song again."

"Yes, it's this song again. I had to set you straight." She peered in the mirror at Elandra. "You'll never keep him. Only in your dreams."

Elandra was powdering a pretty nose. "I'm not about to fight over Bradley with you. First of all, women shouldn't have to fight over men like primitive cave people. Second of all, there is not even anything for you to fight about. Bradley doesn't want you."

At that, Kim's lips twitched. Eyes grew hard as marbles. "You have some nerve!" She faced Elandra's profile, poised for attack. "You may think you've snagged Bradley, but it won't be for long! He wants me." She beat her chest. "Can't you see it in the those brown, glittering eyes when he looks at me? All that desire. It's there. Why else do you think he has so much anger? Because feelings are still there. Why else do you think he is paying for my mother's nurse?"

"Because he's trying to help a nice, sick, elderly lady."

"Wrong! Because he can't get over how *nice* her daughter was." She raised a brow. "And I mean I was *nice* to him. Nicer than you could ever know how to be."

With that, Kim wrinkled her upturned nose and wiggled her narrow hips out of the room. For Elandra, the door couldn't close behind her fast enough. Standing at the mirror, she tried to finish fixing herself up. Powdering away any shine on her dewy complexion, smoothing the slightest wrinkle from her dress, playing with her hair so that it was even more sensual. It was all an effort to forget what was dumped upon her. Except as much as Elandra wanted to omit the words from memory, some of the assertions remained. Was there another reason Bradley was paying for her mother's nurse? And why was he *still* so indignant with Kim? Was there *still* something there? But when she went back outside and returned to the table, thrilled by the way Bradley looked at her, Elandra felt secure again. No man could look at a woman the way Bradley looked at her and not feel something precious. He did love her. The love closed around her as magically as his embrace did soon after.

* * *

"Why did I let you bring me here?"

"Because you want to know the future," Daisy answered Elandra. She was holding her with one hand and knocking on the door of a little white house with the other.

"This is crazy," Elandra thought aloud. "I'm here to see some voodoo lady because I'm scared of losing Bradley. No, I'm going back home." She whirled around and started toward the car.

Daisy jerked her back. "Ms. Holloran is a well-respected psychic on this island. And if you want to know if you should proceed with Bradley, or even if you are going to find Crystal, she's the one to tell you."

"This is silly. I never believed in this hocus pocus."

"It's not hocus pocus," Daisy argued. "This woman is really on target. And what's the alternative, you going crazy with those dreams you've been having lately?"

God knew, her dreams were like nightmares lately. If she wasn't seeing Crystal in some coffin, she was seeing the revolting sight of Bradley and Kim making some hot love. When the tiny, frail woman opened the door, Elandra knew she had better go inside. Her mind would give her no rest.

The house wasn't at all decorated in the fashion Elandra envisioned for a psychic. She'd expected beads, potions, too much furniture, crystal balls. She saw none of those. Instead pastels, art deco furnishings were ravishingly blended with antiques. There was lots of space between each piece. One large plant added a special touch of elegance.

"What can I do for you today, Daisy?" She sounded much younger than she looked. "Sit."

Settling upon a beige sofa, they did as invited to do.

"You can do for us a little of what you do best," Daisy responded.

The infirm-looking woman smiled, revealing paper white teeth. The smile gave her face a vibrancy. "Lay it on me."

"My sister is missing," Elandra began, "and I want to know about her . . . like is she okay and . . ." Elandra was reluctant. She felt silly.

"And she wants to know about her boyfriend," Daisy finished.

"All right," Ms. Holleran said, as if each was a normal request. "Let's see what we can do."

Ms. Holloran lifted Elandra's moist hand, flipping the palm toward the ceiling. There she stroked it gently, drawing circles. All this she did while gazing into Elandra's eyes. Suddenly she began frowning. "Your sister is in big trouble, isn't she?"

"Yes." *Of course she is. I all but told you that.*

"And she came here and she met a man."

"Yes," Elandra answered. *Women meet men all the time. Anybody knows that.*

"That man hurt her terribly. She felt used. She felt shattered, like her life was over. She may have even wanted to take her life."

"Take her life," Elandra gasped. "No, not Crystal."

"She may not have done it," the woman went on. "She thought about it, but she decided to do something else instead. She decided to punish, but that's where she was punished."

At that point Ms. Holloran squinted, an odd visage covering her face. It bewildered Elandra, making her want to know more. "Say it. You want to tell me something else."

"I do." That being as it may, Ms. Holloran knew Elandra couldn't handle the oppressive evil she felt swallowing her sister. The devil had crossed her sister's

path and somewhere out there a woman was the victim
of tragedy. But Ms. Holloran could sense how Elandra
would handle such news. In such a hysterical state as
she would be, Elandra truly couldn't help the one who
needed her. At times, it was better not to be honest.

"I see darkness of the spirit over your sister. She's
not feeling as she should be."

Elandra didn't think that was any help. Anyone
could have told her that, but she didn't want to insult
the lady. Definitely a skeptic now, she decided to humor
her with another question. "So what about my boyfriend?"

"What about him?"

"Does he love me? Or does he love another woman?
Is he going to leave me for her?"

Ms. Holloran mused for several moments. "I draw a
blank there."

"Why?"

"Because what is happening with your sister is strong.
What is happening with you and a man is fragile. A lot
depends on how much each of you are willing to give,
or to let go. Then it will be stronger and I can see it more
clearly. I can't tell you anything more."

"Wow, she sure was a lot of help," Elandra mocked
Daisy, as they left the little white house.

"She's usually more helpful," Daisy said. She was extremely disappointed.

But the frail woman was watching from the window.
Reflecting on what she sensed about Elandra's sister,
she closed her eyes and began to pray. The sensation
of evil prevailing was so strong, she wasn't able to
deeply tune into Elandra and her boyfriend.

Sixteen

When finally Saturday came, they intended to do nothing except savor each other. Their quest of pleasure began at sunrise. Elandra offered to cook again, but neither Bradley's taste buds nor his stomach could withstand a repeat of its prior terrifying experience. Lovingly he coaxed her away from that idea, and secretly sighed in relief. Hence, they ordered a fantasy breakfast from a beloved restaurant in the shopping district. On the terrace, they feasted on croissants, pineapple cheesecake, pancakes, scrambled eggs, bacon, ham, fresh fruit, soy milk and assorted exotic juices. Devouring various portions of everything, pleased as children in a candy store, they were further ravished by the spectacular view. The sky was a portrait of serenity. Stroked with blue, yellow, but mostly red, the hues draped over their skin like candlelight. The sensuous cast intensified how delicious they appeared to each other. It inspired taking full advantage of the terrace and the view. Hence, after the meal they danced. They caressed sweltering arms, backs, waists, shoulders, hands, cheeks. They kissed as if their mouths couldn't survive without the taste of each other. Before long, dawn had vanished, replaced by afternoon sun.

Later, there was a midday reggae concert aboard a yacht called *Hullabaloo*. Elandra jiggled to the sprightly rhythms, and immersed her soul in the dusky, torrid melodies when the pace slowed. Swept up in the richness of the music, she was far more mesmerized by something else, someone else—Bradley. If he wasn't enclosing her in his husky arms, making her feel like silk, he was talking to her, listening, igniting the undeniable chemistry between them. Other times, he was simply coveting her with his eyes, as if she was a rare, incredible jewel he would worship forever. Addicted, Elandra had become. Every second with Bradley was a splendorous dream she couldn't bear waking from.

Following the entertainment, Bradley felt she deserved a shopping spree. It took some convincing, too. After all, Elandra wasn't accustomed to a millionaire telling her she could have anything she wanted, a millionaire who loved her. So strolling hand and hand throughout the stores, nuzzling, playing, locking lips along the sidewalk, it was a wonder they purchased anything, they were so involved with each other. Somehow though, Elandra did indulge herself in items so stunning, it was almost unbelievable they were coming home with her. Anything her heart desired was hers.

When they arrived home, Elandra's ton of shopping bags couldn't be carried in at once. It took several trips from the limousine. When they finished, it was dusk.

"I had the most wonderful day of my life," she confessed, inching toward the stairs backwards.

Keeping up with her, Bradley strolled forward. "It was the most wonderful day of my life, too."

"Really?" She was surprised.

"Can't you tell?"

His spellbound stare told her many things, all of which reached into her heart, making it race.

"I better go up and change for dinner," she said, with a hint of laughter.

"From the way the food smells, my illustrious maid has outdone herself."

"You've outdone yourself, Bradley."

"I have?"

"Inside here," she whispered, and glanced down at her heart.

Bradley was so touched he eased close to Elandra. Feeling the heat between them blazing, she longed to move closer, to move right to his soul. Instead she willed her desire away by running up the steps. From the bottom of the stairwell Bradley watched her until she was out of sight. God knows he wanted to make love to that woman more than anything on this earth. It was all he could think about lately—when he woke up, when he lay down at night, when he worked, when he did anything and everything. As certain as he was of his own existence, Bradley knew they were meant to be together. Their lovemaking would no doubt be *the* unforgettable moments of their lifetimes. They were magical already. Above all, they were in love. *Deeply, passionately.* Yet he had to be patient. He wanted Elandra to know that he truly loved her. Whatever it took, he would do.

During dinner, Bradley shared with Elandra two important messages from the answering machine. First, there was the disappointing news from the police that they had not ferreted out Angel and his mob. On the positive side, however, there was also an encouraging message. It was the investigator informing them he was even closer to finding Crystal. Elandra was so ecstatic she felt giddy. It made her want to jump up from her chair and do all kinds of whimsical things. Foremost, she expressed curiosity about a special room next to her bedroom.

"I passed it one day when it was unlocked and the maid was cleaning it. I glanced in. There were so many books."

When they finished supper, Bradley escorted Elandra

up to the place of intrigue. Complete with a desk and a computer, the remainder of the room was filled with wall-to-wall books. Fiction and non-fiction, the subjects ranged from Shakespeare to Toni Morrison to Civil War history.

Elandra beamed, reading many of the titles. If given a choice, she would have selected the same works.

"I love to read," she revealed, scanning a row full of novels. "Books hold magic."

"Reading is one of my loves, too. As you can see." They both chuckled, surveying the hundreds of titles. "But I never knew that about you."

"Oh, yes. Books are so special to me. Thank God for them. When I was a little girl, I would read every chance I had. The stories would take me to places that I thought I would never go. I would experience things I thought I would never feel. For those moments, lost in those books, I could be anyone. I could be so happy."

"But now things are different, Elandra."

"They are, aren't they?" She stared at him. "My life is something I never believed it would be. I'm an assistant to one of the richest men in the world. I've also been decorating his luxurious hotel suites. Me, with my limited knowledge of interior decorating. It's funny how things can change." She paused as a long, thick finger pointed out some self-help books to her.

He removed one from the shelf. "This book will really motivate you. It's helped me a lot." Lost in her eyes, he handed it to Elandra.

Dazed by the sultry gaze, she accepted it. She began flipping the pages. "I'll read it when I get a chance."

"Do that."

"Is this where you received your inspiration? From this book?" She was browsing over a particular passage.

"I tried to get it anywhere I could, from positive people, from inspiring church sermons, through experiences, through my mom and so many other places."

"That's smart." She turned to another page, afterwards another. "I should have done that, too."

"But you've started over." He rubbed her hair, making her head aim up to him.

She smiled at his tenderness, before peering back down at the page. "Yes, I have started over." She gazed up at him. "And you're responsible for that."

"No, I'm not."

"Oh, yes you are. And after I find Crystal, I'm going to study interior design and who knows what else I might do? I'm going to make you so proud, and myself. I feel like my life has just begun and I can do anything."

"That's how you should feel."

"It's funny." She looked off, just staring into the air. "I used to see books like these in the bookstore, but never read them."

"Why?" He studied her closely. She was entranced by an invisible sight in the horizon.

"I guess I believed in what the person was saying, but somehow I didn't think it applied to me. It was always for other people, those luckier people. Others could make their lives into a fantasy, but somehow I believed God didn't intend that for me. I guess I never thought I was good enough. My happiness would come only when I went to heaven. I had to bear things others couldn't conceive of and weren't strong enough for. My mother wanted me to think that was my worth."

"She was wrong, Elandra."

"I know now she was, but back then, I truly couldn't grasp that *I* could do anything and be anything. It's a shame how life can beat all the spirit out of you, and take all the joy and magic out of your world, and you just let it happen. You just crumble and surrender to living all your time on this earth in misery, in lack, unfulfilled."

"It's easier to give up, especially when you're surrounded by people telling you the wrong things based on their bad experiences."

"It is easier." She turned her back to him, again scouring the shelves. "But now things are different. I'm not what I used to be."

"What are you then?" He came behind her, his hot breath floating across her flesh.

From the electricity of his nearness, Elandra closed her eyes. Opening them, she had to take a deep breath to gain some equilibrium. "I'm happy now, Bradley. When I'm with you, I feel like one of those characters in those books, the ones with love stories, where the ending is happy and the unfortunate victim gets all the things in life she was always denied."

"Like what things?" His hands softly held her arms. Again Elandra closed her eyes and opened them. She was dying from his touch.

"Like love." How much more could she take without becoming one with him? "All I ever wanted was a man to love me, to adore me like I was the most precious creature on the earth, and that's what I wanted to do to him. I wanted someone who would never betray me, who would never, ever do anything to hurt me, just love me. Someone who always saw me as beautiful, and unique, and so special he couldn't live without me."

"You have that." He curved her around in his arms, searching her face. "I do adore you. I love you more than anything. I love you more than I've loved any woman."

"Really?"

"Yes, really."

"Even more than . . . Kim?"

"Much more than Kim. Compared to what I feel now, I don't even know if that *was* love."

"I believe you, Bradley. I believe you. And I'm ready. I'm ready to show you how much I love you. I need you, like I know you need me. Make love to me."

As Bradley carried Elandra to his bedroom, she knew there was no turning back now. The time had come. The need for him screamed throughout her blood, throughout her heart, throughout her soul. There was a strong physical attraction and a deep spiritual bond they shared. In one sense, it was as if she had known him all of her life. In another sense, he was so exciting, warm, intelligent, thoughtful and loving, she never learned enough about him. And he was so much more, beautiful beyond description and mere words. She couldn't believe they only knew each other a few months. In that short time, they had grown as close as two people could be.

"I love you," Bradley whispered, while his hand crept up her thigh and moved her dress around her hips. He was standing near the side of the bed.

"I love you, too," she breathed, staring at his chest, brushing her hands across its hardness.

The words were as much a gift as the desire building inside them, between them. From his gentle handling, she trembled with anticipation and eased backward on the bed for him to grant more. More and more he stroked her. He caressed her tenderly, but with his mounting desire, the touches grew voracious and fiery.

Within seconds shoes, pants, a dress, shorts and panties lay not far from their bodies.

"You're as beautiful as I thought you were." His scorching gaze drifted from her head to the bottom of her feet repeatedly. He rested at her half-closed eyes.

"You're a dream come true." Her breath grew heavy from the beauty of his brown, glistening form. Every inch of him begged to be loved and she couldn't wait to oblige. As if he were the tastiest dessert, she couldn't kiss or feel enough of him.

"I want you," he moaned. "I wanted you for so long and now we're about to . . ." His gaze fell down the length of her body.

"Yes, Bradley. Oh yes, you can have me."

"I'm going to make you feel so good." Hot kisses rained over her lips, neck, and inside her ears. "I'm going to love you like you've never been loved before."

"I know you are. I can feel how powerful your love is. I want to feel it all the way."

Now the music of their love floated above all. Bradley moaned with gladness as she thrilled his muscles, chest, hips, thighs, and that magnificence she ached for. Like an expert in pleasure, she did this while kissing him at first softly, then deeply and lustfully.

In turn, tantalizing kisses scorched her face and lips. They carried their serenade down the length of her neck and across her chest. There he teased her breasts with a tongue that held magic.

Her body then surged with warmth when he entered her. Elandra welcomed him, feeling the silkiness of his belly and the hardness of his love. His hands were carefully cupping her face, kissing it so passionately, while his movements were slow, light and teasing.

Before long, she was panting. His chest was heaving. Their bodies swirled in spasms of euphoria. Her breasts slapped hard against his chest as their ecstasy grew to a frenzy. Hips were rocking, fast, hard, long. Tongues were thrusting, winding, tasting, licking, harshly and titillatingly. Elandra begged him to never stop. As if she were holding on for eternity, she gripped his back hard and wouldn't let go. She wanted him deeper, harder, and writhed her hips erotically to give every drop of her love.

They screamed, but not even that could do the sweet

feeling justice. Never enough of each other they could feel. Then much too soon it was all over in one shattering cry of love.

"I want Crystal to feel like this one day," Elandra said languidly into the after-quiet. Her tousled head lay on Bradley's chest while his arms enveloped her. "To feel so good and wonderful like I'm feeling right now. I just want Crystal to be happy like I am."

Dimples nipped his cheeks. "That's impossible."

"Why?" She curved her head to look up at him.

"It's impossible because we're the only two people who can make love like we just did. It was mind-bending, beyond description. Something I can't even put into words."

"Umm, you're right," she agreed, lifting her face for a kiss.

His tongue played across her lips, before entering the sultry sweetness of her mouth. Elandra moaned from the blissful feeling, only stopping to separate for air.

She took a deep breath. "You're too much."

"So are you." He paused, staring at her with a slight frown. "I've never made love like that before, or felt what you made me feel."

"I've never experienced what I felt with you, either."

"I want it every day, every night." His voice was low and husky with hunger. "Because I can't get enough. And I need some more right now."

He leaned over on her, meeting chest to chest, face to face. Elandra felt wholly feminine and pleasantly overwhelmed by his size and massive strength stretched over her. Beneath him, she parted her moist lips and brought her arms around the great width of his shoulders. Her fingertips played with a small scar on the left one. He was electrified from her touch. As well, for a moment he allowed himself to feel beguiled by her doll-like features. Less than an inch from them, he felt her breathing, he clutched her waist, and finally kissed her.

Their bodies writhing like the sinuous motions of their tongues, they had to have more. Slowly, wildly, provocatively, ravenously, they began to love again. It was only a nagging sound that distracted them. Like a noisy fly that wouldn't go away, the doorbell buzzed, the ringer growing more persistent. After a while it couldn't be ignored.

"Who's ringing that bell like that this time of night?" Bradley roared. Sharply he sat up, flipped on the lamp switch, then tilted toward the clock.

It read 3:14 a.m.

"I don't know who that could be," Elandra said, "but they sure want to see you badly."

"Damn them, why now?" And with the question, his eyes scattered over her body. It was half exposed and half covered by the mauve satin sheet. "Let's ignore it. It can wait until tomorrow."

There was an attempt to reclaim his cozy position under the sheet. Except the bell continued buzzing.

"You better go see who it is, Bradley. Their persistence makes me feel it may be an emergency."

"Then why didn't they call?" He glared at the door.

"I don't know. But something tells me it's important. Somebody is desperate to see you. Listen at how they're ringing that bell."

He nodded, threw on his bathrobe and slid his feet into some loafers. As his footsteps made heavy thumps down the stairs, Elandra was intent to relax and simply wait for his return. However, when he opened the door and she heard a familiar, irksome voice, Elandra grabbed her robe.

Flying out the bedroom door, she bumped her knee on the dresser and tripped twice on the carpet snag at the top of the stairs. Nonetheless something other than clumsiness stopped her. She pictured how it might look to Kim if she came running downstairs to guard her man. It would show she was insecure. Even so, nothing could stop her from standing at the top of the stairs, out of sight, listening.

"What do you want, Kim?" Elandra heard Bradley snap. "Do you have any idea what time it is?"

"I know, Bradley," Kim admitted, sobs piercing her voice. "But I need you. I don't have anyone else to turn to."

He scowled in suspicion. "Need me for what?"

"I have no one else." The weeping grew louder.

"Kim, what's going on?" But Elandra could hear his tone mellowing.

"My mother."

"My God, she's not . . ."

"No." She blotted her cheeks with a handkerchief, then shook her head. "She's not dead, but she's sick. In the hospital. She's critical, Bradley."

"I'm very, very sorry to hear that."

"If I lose her, what will I do? She's all I have."

He patted her arm. "You won't lose her, Kim. She's a fighter."

"She's also human. How much suffering can she take? Maybe it's her time, but I'm not ready for it to be. She's all I have. There is no one else."

"I'll stop by and see her tomorrow."

"That won't do, Bradley."

"Why not?"

"She wants to see you."

"Me?" He pointed at his chest.

"She loves you like a son. You would have been her son if I hadn't ruined things. And she's asking for you."

"Right now?" He gazed up the stairs.

"Yes," she answered, tugging his attention back to

her. "Will you go see her? Come with me . . . *now?*
Please. It could be her last hour." She dried a teardrop.

Thinking, his eyes darted mindlessly about the room
for a second. "Sure, I'll come. I have to go get dressed."

"Thank you."

Kim leaped. Before Bradley realized anything, her
arms had folded around him. With great effort he tried
to loosen the embrace, but she held him so tight, he
felt her breasts squashed against his chest.

From above, at the top of the stairwell, Elandra wit-
nessed the display of gratitude. As much as she didn't
want it to, it left her feeling ill at ease and vulnerable.
Despite it, she didn't exhibit any insecurity when
Bradley returned upstairs. Reposing on the satiny
sheets, her expression was nonchalant.

"Did you hear who's downstairs?" he asked.

"I heard." She forced a smile.

"I'm sorry, baby."

"It's okay."

"Did you also hear where she wants me to accompany her?"

"Yes. You go on."

"You're okay with that?"

"Yes, I'm okay with it. I trust you, and I know you're
just going to be kind to an old lady."

"Would you like to come with me?"

"No, you go. I can't stomach Kim twice in one
night."

"That makes two of us, but her mother . . ."

"Her mother wants to see you and you would feel
horrible if something happened and you didn't go. I
understand, Bradley."

"You do?"

"Really I do."

"You're perfect. What did I ever do to deserve you?"

He pecked her on the forehead and began dressing.

By the time the car rolled off the estate, Elandra had convinced him she was fast asleep. It wasn't so. Elandra raced up over to the window, shoving aside the curtains. Biting her lip, she followed the sedan's taillights until they vanished into the darkness.

Seventeen

Kim wasn't exaggerating, Bradley thought, treading inside the ICU room where Mavis Rothwell lay motionless on a bed. Seeing her hooked up to various machines tore at Bradley's heart. Such a caring woman had come to this.

"Mama," Kim called, wiping tears away, trying to smile. She stood near the top of the bed, stroking her mother's cottony tresses. "It's me. I'm back. I brought your favorite person."

"Mrs. Rothwell," Bradley added, hunching over the bed railing toward the frail woman. "You have to get up out of this bed. You ate all my food up at the barbecue. I'm charging you next time."

A lopsided grin accompanied a fluttering of short lashes. Soon watery, gray-brown eyes circled the room, halting at Bradley's face. "You . . . you came." Her voice was low and raspy.

"Yes, I came." He forced himself to look cheerful. "I wanted to see how you were."

"And . . . I . . . wanted to see . . . you . . . Brad . . . Bradley." Her cheeks raised slightly. "You . . . you're one . . . one of my . . . fa . . . vorite peo . . . ple."

"And you're one of mine, Mrs. Rothwell. What can I do to make you feel better?"

Her lids raised a trace more. "You can . . . you can

look . . . out . . . for Kim. I . . . I want you . . . to look
out . . . for . . . my . . . my daugh . . . ter."

At that, Bradley swallowed, striving not to show the
discomfort he felt. He knew Kim's gaze was glued to
him. He refused to look at her.

"I look out for everyone, Mrs. Rothwell."

Slowly a parched hand eased on top of his. "But . . .
but . . . I'm not . . . ask . . . ing you . . . to—to . . . look
out . . . for ev . . . ery . . . one. . . . I'm ask . . . ing . . .
that . . . you look out . . . for my . . . daugh . . . ter, the
woman . . . you . . . were go . . . ing . . . to . . . marry."

"I see." Not knowing what else to say, he looked
about the room.

Enjoying her mother's spunk, Kim patted her
cropped locks.

"She . . . has . . . no one . . . Brad . . . ley," the feeble
voice went on. "No . . . one at all . . . in this world."

"But she will," he remarked. "Your daughter draws
people to her." He glanced at Kim. She was captivated
by him. Promptly he shifted his concern back down at
her mother. "She'll have no trouble having someone
in her life."

And that someone is you, Kim swore to herself.

The elderly woman's grip tightened around his
palm. "Will it . . . be you?"

Kim laughed curtly. "Mama, you're putting Bradley
on the spot."

But Mavis Rothwell didn't find anything humorous.
Not at all amused, she was adamant. With all the energy
frailty allowed her to muster, she raised her head from
her pillow toward Bradley's. "You . . . you cared . . .
about . . . her once. . . . You can care again. Tell me . . .
you'll . . . look after her so . . . I can . . . go . . . to my
heavenly father in peace. I . . . know you're a man who
would treat my daughter like . . . a queen, with . . . un-
dying respect. Forget . . . and forgive . . . what she's

done . . . and think . . . how happy you two . . . can . . . make each other. She's . . . changed so much . . . dear. Seeing me . . . seeing me suffer like this has made . . . her humble. It's taught . . . her what's . . . important, good . . . old . . . fashioned love."

Kim feigned embarrassment, yet she was anxiously awaiting Bradley's response.

His lips moved, but he had to be careful about expressing what he felt. No way he would forget, or forgive Kim. On the other hand, he didn't want to do anything to upset her mother and precipitate a setback. A nurse, pushing the door open, with a medicine tray saved him.

"Mrs. Rothwell," she announced, striding toward the patient. "It's time for your medication. And afterwards the doctor would like to examine you."

Goodbyes were spoken. Kim thanked Bradley for coming and remained for her mother's exam. Bradley left, sauntering down the slick, white tiles of the hospital hall, his gait lacking all the spirit that came with the resplendence of the day. When he arrived on the main floor, passing the revolving glass doors, and finally stepped outside, he felt the crisp early morning air brushing across his face. It could have been a soothing prelude to the day, along with that fragrance of sea water waving from beyond the pier. Too bad he couldn't appreciate either the treasures of the ocean or the anticipation of a new day. No. All Bradley could contemplate at that moment was why this kind of pressure was being put on him *now*. Not so much Mavis Rothwell's wishes either. No, it wasn't that, which seemed most unfair. It was the simple fact that Kim was weaving her way into his world again, just when he learned that a heart ripped out of your chest doesn't mean life is over, that love is over. You could go on. You had to find it again if you were to survive and live fully. That way when it was securely in your hands, you could put it back where it belonged. It could be repaired. A mended heart could grant life anew, and you could feel what you never imagined was possible. That was, if you were nourished with the tenderest loving care.

But suddenly, as images formed in his mind, he did appreciate the air. Because of the visions, over and over he inhaled, and could almost taste the salt in the sea. For he was visualizing Elandra. Remembering her sprawled on the bed, he had a second wind. He hurried home.

Nearly three hours later Bradley was slumbering peacefully while Elandra worked downstairs in the office. She was endeavoring to get several important tasks accomplished before he awakened. Of greatest interest was contacting consultants about decorating a spacious hotel suite which was newly renovated. She wanted to impress her new love.

There was a knock at the door. She knew Bradley wouldn't knock.

"Come in," she beckoned, her focus on the computer screen.

"Gladly," an exuberant voice responded.

When the door opened, Elandra glanced in that direction and promptly pushed her monitor aside. Private investigator Gregory Mitchelson was so vivacious, Elandra was certain he had good news.

"Why, hello," she greeted him.

"Hello, Ms. Lloyd." His scrawny frame strutted to her desk, every feature aglow.

Elandra stood. "Does that look mean you've found Crystal?" Her hands folded together in a prayer position. "Oh my God. . . ."

"Close." He beamed. "Very close."

"How close?" She held her breath.

Gregory turned back toward the door. "Come in," he called to a mystery person.

Heart racing, Elandra looked and waited, inhaling, exhaling. It seemed like it took the longest time, but finally a young woman was entering the room, a young woman she had never seen before. Short, plump, with auburn hair and china doll eyes, she appeared as uncomfortable in Elandra's presence as Elandra was in hers.

Baffled at who she was, Elandra looked from Gregory's face to the woman's. "She's—she's not Crystal."

"I know she isn't," Gregory acknowledged, his lips spread in satisfaction. "But she will give you the key to this whole situation. She knows everything about your sister's whereabouts."

Elandra swerved anxiously toward the woman. "You do? Tell me then."

"She—"

Bradley unexpectedly sauntered into the office, cutting off the sentence.

"What's going on?" he asked, peering at Elandra, Gregory, and lastly the stranger. Keeping his eyes on her, he shook a finger. "I've seen you before. Around the island. One of my realty agents handled a transaction with you. Aren't you the young lady who rented my boat? It was called *FunShip* then."

"*FunShip*," Elandra echoed.

"Your name is?" Bradley was trying to remember.

"Trina," she answered in a charming island accent.

"You're Trina?" Elandra asked excitedly. She rushed around the desk, stepping right in front of her. "I've been looking for you. I've been looking everywhere for my sister."

"Where's Crystal?" Bradley asked.

"I'll tell you." Trina looked aside for a place to sit. Locating a space on a leather couch, she tucked her dress beneath her buttocks and settled onto the cool cushions.

"So where is she?" Elandra asked. She sat next to her, leaning forward. "How is she?" Zealousness brimmed in her voice.

Trina's lip wiggled as she half smiled. "She's fine. She's in Sweden."

"Sweden?" Elandra clutched her chest.

"Sweden?" Bradley echoed.

It took a minute before it sunk in. After it did, Elandra was relieved. "She's really in Sweden?"

"Yeah," Trina confirmed, then peered down at a leg that was shaking incessantly. "That's where she is. It's a long story."

"We have plenty of time," Bradley stated. He was observing the stranger closely. She was so skittish, if he blew at her, he was sure she would jump out the window.

"Go ahead, tell them," Gregory urged. "Tell them what you told me."

Trina's attention remained on her shaking leg. "Crystal and I are best friends. We used to hang out together and double date and stuff." She hesitated.

A thought came to Bradley's mind. He debated whether to ask it and finally decided to. "Weren't you a . . ."

"Hooker?" Trina answered, looking offended. "No, that's what everyone thought. I just liked to have a good time, dancing, listening to good music, going to fun places, just hanging around guys who had money to see how they lived. So did Crystal."

Elandra was nodding. "Yes, go on."

Trina glanced at her, then looked back down. "We,

ah . . . we met a lot of men and one of the ones Crystal met was a rich, older man."

"Did he pay the rent for her condo?" Elandra asked.

Trina snaked an eye at Gregory. Bradley looked at them both. She reverted back to her leg. "Yes, he paid for it."

"And what else happened?" Elandra sank back into the cushions, folding her arms.

"He, ah . . . he and Crystal were an item," she replied. "That is, until he broke it off. He was married, you see." She glanced at Gregory again. The exchange intrigued Bradley. "Crystal didn't know."

"That must have broken my sister's heart," Elandra determined somberly. Tension distorting her features, she drifted off into the horizon. "Crystal always stayed clear of married men."

"It did break her heart," Trina acquiesced. "That's why she went away. She wanted to go far away and just recuperate. I went with her. But I felt it was time for me to come back home, and it was at this time that your investigator contacted me. As soon as I hit Nassau's sand he found me."

"So when is she coming back?" Elandra asked.

Trina looked to Gregory as if his permission was needed to speak. He was simply listening. She returned to Elandra. "Crystal is going to be away awhile."

"Does she know that I'm here?"

"When your investigator contacted me, asking me about her, I called her and told her. She told me to tell you that she's fine."

Bradley was still studying Trina closely. Something wasn't right. "Does Crystal know how worried her sister is about her?"

"Since I've returned, I talked to Crystal and told her that her sister hired an investigator to find her. She said, don't worry."

"Give me her telephone number and address?" Elandra searched around for a pen and pad. Yet when she looked up at Trina to write the information down, she was shaking her head.

"I'm sorry."

"Sorry for what?" Elandra was stumped.

"Crystal doesn't want to talk to anyone right now. Doesn't want to have any contact either. She was very firm in telling me not to give information of her whereabouts."

"But I'm her sister."

"Surely she didn't mean Elandra," Bradley remarked.

"But she did. She meant everyone."

"This is really hard for me to believe," Elandra said. She was so upset she had to stand. "Crystal and I are so close. She would never not want to talk to me."

The words drew a furtive glance from Trina at the investigator once again. Bradley just observed.

"I'm afraid that's why she didn't call you all these months," Gregory elaborated. "She just wants to be alone."

Not understanding this, Elandra began pacing. Bradley's brawny arms coming around her stopped all movement. She melted into his chest.

But seeing Elandra's distress made Trina uneasy. Rubbing across her forehead, she added, "There is something else I have to tell you."

Elandra raised up from Bradley. "What's that?"

"Crystal loves you to death. Don't doubt that. But she doesn't want to talk to you or anyone because she's just so hurt and ashamed."

"Ashamed?" Elandra was frowning. "Ashamed of what?"

Trina peered downward. After a moment, she faced the distraught woman above her. "She was pregnant for the married man. But he convinced her to get rid of the baby."

Instantly Elandra's eyes clouded. "I see."

Bradley kissed each lid, then looked harshly at Gregory and Trina. "But what about Crystal's apartment being ransacked? And that message on the wall? And Trina, your own brother even warned Elandra not to look for Crystal. Said he was sending a message."

Riveted to her leg again, Trina persisted in being withdrawn. Quite the opposite, Gregory smiled.

"Bradley," he said, "the people here probably heard you asking a lot of questions and thought it was a perfect opportunity for a robbery of the condo. Thought they could throw the police off with that little message."

Bradley quickly responded, "But nothing was stolen."

Gregory hunched his shoulders. "Who knows?"

"You should. That's what I pay you for. Think I'll hold off on that check."

Gregory stopped smiling.

"And what about what happened to Elandra?" Bradley went on. "She was nearly raped." He focused on Trina. "And your brother attacked her."

At that, Elandra buried her face in his chest.

Now scowling, Trina wiped at the beads of perspiration suddenly flanking her hairline.

"Angel and I are estranged," she said.

"What about what he said to Elandra about not finding her sister?"

Gregory looked mystified. "Bradley, I don't know what the creep was talking about. But we do know where Crystal is. Isn't that what you wanted?"

"Yes," Elandra said, raising her head to look at him. "Thank you. I'm very grateful." She turned to Trina. "And thank you."

Moments later, as Gregory and Trina prepared to

leave, she grabbed Elandra's hand and stared in her eyes. "Don't worry about Crystal. She just has to recover from what she's been through. I'm there for her. Don't worry. Be happy she's alive."

Alone inside the house, Elandra was feeling comforted by Trina's last words. Standing before Bradley, she even smiled.

"You know, Trina was right. I should just be happy my sister's alive. I should be living it up. My sister is fine. She just has a broken heart, like mine was. And she's lost a child, like I did. But she's going to make it. Because I have. And she's going to fall in love. Because that's what's happened to me."

"You sure you're okay?" His hands slid over her shoulders.

She softened at his silken touch in handling her. "Yes, I'm okay. And to prove it, I want to go out."

"Out where?"

"Out somewhere fun." Her eyes rolled around, finally stopping at his. "I want to go to the beach. That's a romantic place."

"Your wish is my command."

"Just let me go change into my suit."

Elandra flew up the stairs. While she did, Bradley couldn't move right away. Rubbing his chin, thoughts raced. Something wasn't right about what had just taken place. Or was it his imagination? For Elandra's sake, he hoped all was as it was supposed to be. Because if it wasn't, he would make it right. He would do anything for her.

The sand, the surf, the sun, the overall resplendence of the island Elandra saw as gifts for a celebration. Amid his haze of passion, Bradley believed she was the reason for him to celebrate. During their day at the ocean, they played like children, burying each other in the sand, running, jumping, teasing, tickling, swimming. So spirited they were, it was well after midnight when they settled down for an intimate moment. By then the shore was deserted. The ocean's soft music was the only sound heard. On a blanket, Bradley flattened on his back, his eyes closed, his fingers tangling through Elandra's untamed tresses. Much the opposite, her body molded to the warmth of Bradley's side while she adored the sky.

She raised her palm to the sparse hairs along his chest. Gliding across them, she spoke soft and low. "You know, I used to think it was corny to look at the stars. I used to see stuff like this in movies and say 'How corny.' But not anymore. This is wonderful, lying like this with you."

"It is," he agreed, breathily. "But I know something even more wonderful." His eyes opened and Bradley raised up on his elbow. Gazing down at her, his entire being radiated his affection. "All day I couldn't get it out of my mind, how you made love to me." He lifted her hand, kissing a finger, and then another. He put each one in his mouth, grazing over them lightly with his teeth.

Elandra twitched from the sweet feeling. "I couldn't get over how you made me feel, either. No matter what I was talking about or doing, it was right there in my mind."

"No one ever made me feel like that." He was nibbling the tips of each finger with one hand. The other was stroking her thigh, rising higher with every caress.

Becoming more aroused, Elandra closed her eyes, putting her arms around his shoulders, inviting his robust form atop hers. Once in a blood-heating position, their limbs writhed provocatively, beckoning more of each other's touch, senses enlivened by the unique fragrance of each other. It all beckoned her to bury herself in the curve of his neck. It lured his fingers to slowly pull down her bikini top. Desire flooded inside her from their closeness, from his strength, from his large hands' contact with her sensitive skin.

"I want to feel you again," his voice quivered across her ear. She warmed with more delight. Then without her even feeling any noticeable tug, the top was completely off.

Instantly Bradley was lured to her breasts, hungering for them, hungering for all of her. "You're so beautiful," he moaned, switching his fascination to her lips. "So sexy."

"How else can I be when you look at me like that?" She parted her lips for his slowly approaching mouth.

"You turn me on so much. I'm going to give you all my attention, all my tenderness, all my passion, all my love."

His body pressed into hers deeper, his hands running through her hair. Bradley kissed a path along the side of her cheek until he coaxed her lips open wider with his tongue. The sweet taste of the honey beyond her lips he couldn't get enough of. Heartbeats pounded fiercely, as one. Ravenously he tangled his tongue within her mouth, his lips as demanding as the stroking that began pleasing her flesh.

Treasuring the feeling of his touch all over her, Elandra couldn't wait to experience more. Her arms drew him nearer, so near she was titillated by the hard urgency of his manhood boring into her lower stomach. A dire need for more of him coursed through her veins. Never enough of his kisses could she have. Never enough of his silken and impassioned caress all over her body. Moving her hips erotically, she cried out her extreme message.

Bradley received it and acknowledged her wishes by

reaching her bikini bottom. Carefully easing it down her leg, he further thrilled her with kisses over her belly. A craving for him blazed through her veins. She panted, urging him to raise up to his former position. She too was sliding down fabric. Not soon enough, both were bare, their bodies bathed in blue moonlight, their hearts and souls locked together in the fulfillment of love.

Moans of pleasure drowned the tide. It was a song of ecstasy, feeding the raging heat between them. They felt blessed to create this unique rhythm, harmony, a music of passion all their own. If they had known someone else was watching them, the bliss still would have been too overwhelming to stop. For a figure was frozen along the seaside. She had been coming from the hospital, terribly upset, and had hoped to gain some equilibrium among the calmness of the shore.

Kim hadn't expected this. The last thing in the world she expected to run up on was Elandra and Bradley making love. Several feet away she stood, close enough to see who the man and woman were, enjoying themselves immensely. Kim's heart was already wrenched from her mother's worsening condition. This sight made the nightmare of the last twenty-four hours come full circle.

It ripped Kim apart beholding Bradley with another woman, being as close as a man and woman could be. Did he love her? *Her love* he was giving to someone else. It was enough to kill her right then. For a second, she even debated strutting over to them, doing anything and everything to spoil their fun. Except what was happening with her mother weakened Kim momentarily. Not having the energy for anything else traumatic, she decided to walk back to her car and head home. Tomorrow, after a good night's sleep, she could think about how to get a better grasp of this situation.

Tomorrow, she would figure out the answer to getting Bradley back.

But for now, she could only regret. Never had she forgotten how Bradley used to make love to her. He was so attentive to her body, to her responses. He would kiss her like she was the food he hungered for. How she missed all that when she was with Bernardo. It was only a week after they were married that she began to pretend he was Bradley. After that, she did it each time they made love.

Soon she began picking arguments with him because he wasn't Bradley. He wasn't gorgeous. He wasn't sexy. He didn't know how to make love. He didn't have the character or wit Bradley had. He wasn't smart like Bradley. Bernardo's wealth was gained illegally, stupidly. Bradley's wealth was self made. From the ground up, he built an empire by using his head.

When she had Bradley, Kim did adore him. Yet she had learned early the importance of money, when her father gained and lost substantial amounts of cash in his business dealings. She had been rich and she had been poor. Poor just didn't feel as good. When she met a billionaire, a man far richer than Bradley, the magic he brought into her world, the ecstasy, the warmth, the kindness, all didn't matter that much. Visions of being richer than everyone else danced in her head. The high of it was so strong, she left Bradley at the altar.

Eighteen

Riding back to the mansion from a decorating site, Elandra was a chatterbox. She couldn't stop telling Richard how wonderful the interior decorating was proceeding on the main level of a new hotel Bradley built. Richard seemed quite interested, particularly so since Bradley had given him several shares in the hotel for a birthday present. Elandra could hardly wait to tell Bradley how well the decorating was progressing.

When the limousine rolled onto the estate, the two were in deep conversation. The only thing distracting from the exhilarating dialogue was the police car that passed them, exiting the property.

After the car pulled into the driveway, each hurried into the house, curious to know the nature of the police visit.

"They were here to let me know about Angel and his pack," Bradley responded to the curious faces.

"Did they find them?" Elandra asked. His serious expression lured her further inside.

"No, they were here to tell me about why they hadn't."

"I'd like to know that myself," Richard interjected.

Bradley took a deep breath and narrowed his eyes. "Said they believed Angel and that pack who tried to rape Elandra are in Florida somewhere. Their leads tell them that."

"They may never find them if they've gone that far," Richard pointed out.

"That's true," Elandra agreed, then came closer to Bradley.

Standing in front of him, sliding her palms over the roundness of his shoulders, fingering his little scar, she didn't look as upset as he'd imagined. Actually, there was a peacefulness about her. He knew it stemmed from believing Crystal had been found. He debated whether to share his gut feelings about that. It lightened his heart to see her so happy. He didn't want to take it away.

"I didn't want to disappoint you," he told her. "I wanted to get those guys for trying to hurt you."

"But I'm not hurt, Bradley. I'm fine. And I do so appreciate your caring about me so much. I've never had anyone treat me the way you do."

"Because I love you more than any other man ever could."

Richard smiled. *Ah, love is so delicious.*

But then Bradley peered at her, harshly frowning. "And it's because I love you so much that I must be honest with you, Elandra."

Richard sat, resting his hat on the end table. He didn't like Bradley's tone.

Puzzled, Elandra eased even closer. "What is it? I don't like the way you're looking."

"And I don't want to tell you this, but I have to." He took a walloping breath. "I don't believe Trina, and I think we're no closer to knowing where Crystal was than when I first met you."

"What?" Mouth hung open, she reared back.

Bradley held her arms lightly. "Baby, I hate to tell you this, but that's how I feel."

"But why? Did the investigator call you and tell you something?"

"Actually, he's one of my concerns. You see, I kept getting this strange feeling about the two of them. But for your sake, I was constantly telling myself that things were as they say. But I've been calling him, and her, and I get no answer. I had more questions for them."

"Bradley, why are you making trouble when there is none?"

"I'm not making trouble."

"You are!" She took a few steps back, easing from his hands. "I believe Trina."

"Because you want to believe her. You want Crystal to be fine and just recuperating from a broken heart."

"She is."

"I want her to be fine, too."

"Then why are you stirring up trouble?"

"I told you, Elandra, I've been calling them for days, both their numbers and I can't reach them. I even went by his business and her home. Do you know they haven't been seen for days? I asked their neighbors."

"Why?"

"Because I have this gut feeling something isn't right. They were giving each other these furtive glances."

"So? Trina was probably nervous and she felt comfortable with him."

"Elandra, you were hearing what you wanted to hear."

"I don't like the way you're sounding."

Hoping to lessen the building tension, Richard stood and walked toward the door. "I'll be in the car."

"I'm taking the Jag to a business meeting in a few minutes," Bradley told him. "I'll leave the limo here for Elandra."

Richard nodded and left the room.

"Thank you," Elandra said, not looking at all grateful. "And thank you for upsetting my peace of mind after it took me so long to get it."

"I'm trying to be realistic, Elandra. Your sister could be out there, needing your help, and you can't give it to her because someone has suckered you into believing something that isn't true."

"Stop it!"

"And what about those messages, the one on the wall in the condo and the one from Angel? The investigator didn't give me any reason that made sense."

"Stop it, I said!"

"Baby, you have to listen to me."

"I don't! And I don't like who you are right now. Aren't you the one who taught me how to be positive, and have high hopes?"

"Yes, I was."

"Well, I do. I believe my sister is in Sweden, recovering from her broken heart. And you're just being so negative. I don't like you like this, Bradley. And I don't want to hear it! It's a turn-off! *You're* turning me off."

She dashed up the stairs, leaving him in the living room alone. Pondering if he'd made a mistake sharing his opinions, Bradley was still for several minutes. When he tugged out of his contemplation, he happened to face the clock. Time had slipped away from him. If he didn't hurry, he would miss the gentleman he was meeting for a business lunch.

Up in the bedroom, from the window, Elandra watched the Jaguar until it was out of sight. Why was he doing this, she wondered. Why was he taking away the relief and peace Trina gave her, robbing it slowly, replacing it with alarm and a growing hysteria. But deep down, it was dawning on her that Bradley could be right. As much as she fought him, at heart she knew his points were valid. Trina and Gregory were behaving oddly with each other. Most noticeable, Trina was extremely nervous. Added to this, things didn't make sense. Gregory's excuses about the threats in the condo and from Angel were inane. Moreover, why couldn't Bradley reach either of them? Funny, they had disappeared, disappeared like Angel and his cronies.

Gliding from the window, Elandra dived on the bed, flattening backward on it. As she smoothed her palms against the satiny spread, she vowed not to get overwrought. After all, she had gone this long not knowing where Crystal was. That being the case, she could go longer if necessary. After all, how could she help Crystal if she was falling apart. If it turned out that her sister was still missing and the investigator and Trina were all a part of some con, she needed all her faculties to function and rescue Crystal. And if she wasn't in Sweden, she prayed that she could rescue her. She prayed that it wasn't too late. Then again, she couldn't entertain that thought. Crystal was alive. She had to be. What could she have possibly been mixed up in that would make so many people go to so much trouble? Something dangerous, Elandra answered herself. She refused to imagine something deadly.

"Thanks for coming shopping with me," Elandra said as she and Daisy strolled through the shopping district.

"No, thank you, girl. You know I love to shop. It's number three after sex and eating."

Both women chuckled and strode along the pavement. Too bad Elandra's amusement seemed a little off.

Daisy stared at her. "You've had that puppy dog look off and on today. What's wrong? You know where Crystal is, so that shouldn't be worrying you. And I know that wonderful man is treating you well."

With a sigh, Elandra faced ahead. "We had a little

disagreement earlier today. Actually, it was right before I called you to go shopping."

"A disagreement about what?"

"He thinks Crystal and the investigator were up to something."

"Up to something? Something crooked?"

"That's about the size of it."

"Goodness. Every time I turn around this scenario is sounding more and more scary. What in the world . . ." Daisy paused, seeing the upset in her friend's face.

"Go ahead," Elandra goaded. "You can say it. What in the world is Crystal mixed up in? I've asked myself the same question."

"It's just that people are going to a whole lot of trouble."

"I agree totally. And I tried to tell myself that Trina and Gregory were telling the truth. I even argued with Bradley about it. But now that I think about what was said and how they acted, and the fact that we can't reach them for more questions, I think maybe Bradley was right. They might not have been telling the truth. Someone might have been going to a whole lot of trouble to throw us off track."

Daisy was quiet for a second, then said, "That's scary."

"You're telling me. Bad thing about it, I accused Bradley of being negative and that he was turning me off. And all he was doing was just being honest and telling me the truth. He probably hates me."

"He doesn't. And girl, calling him that is no big crime. You'll patch that up tonight, *but good.*" She winked.

Elandra wanted to laugh, but couldn't. She was too guilty. "You know, he brought up such valid points. But I just didn't want to listen."

"You were in denial?"

"Guess I was."

"But it's nothing out of the ordinary. You love your

sister and you want more than anything for her to be safe. And then you had no reason to think these two would deceive you."

"But now that I think about it, and what Bradley said, I'm going to consider what he's saying. I would hate to lose him over something stupid. And I really shouldn't have said that he turned me off. He's supersensitive since Kim broke his heart."

"And how is the little heartbreaker? Has she disappeared and fallen off the earth?"

Elandra was tickled at that. "No. Her mother is sick and Bradley has visited Mrs. Rothwell several times."

"And how do you feel about that?"

"About what?"

"About him being so attentive to his ex-girlfriend's mother?"

"They were close once. It's understandable."

But what she didn't tell Daisy was how Kim always had to hug Bradley, how she had called so often for him to come to her mother's hospital bed, where she was also, and even in the middle of the night he would go. With her greatest effort, Elandra struggled not to let it worry her. She had held her tongue when she ached to say something.

"It is understandable and admirable that he cares about this woman," Daisy concluded. "Especially after how her daughter treated him. But watch that Kim. She looks like a sneaky one."

"Not sneaky," Elandra corrected. "Desperate is the word."

After Bradley's meeting was over, there were handshakes and good vibes before his associate left. Not ready to abandon the comforts of the posh restaurant, he remained at the table, engrossed in a proposal that could increase his financial worth into the billions. When it came to fruition, he pictured the things he could do: more donations to his boys, more scholarships, more low-cost housing, more training programs, more food for the starving countries, more donations in all the areas he contributed to already. Then there was the concept he was mulling around lately. Elandra was so talented she didn't even need to go to interior design school. She needed her own corporation. Bradley intended to make that happen. As soon as the situation with Crystal was settled, it would be reality. So would the other idea he had, the one which would change their lives forever.

Sipping a martini, he read further into the proposal, his expression displaying all the excitement he always received from the initial stages of a business deal. Nothing could distract him. Not even the presence who emerged so obviously before him.

Her voice alone made him look up. "That sure must be interesting?" Kim asked. Wearing a vibrant blue halter dress, she curled her lips alluringly for the object of her attention.

"It is interesting," Bradley confirmed, the spirit in his demeanor vanishing at her presence. He faced her without the slightest cordiality. "How is your mother?"

"Much better since you've been coming to see her."

"I'm glad." With that, he returned to his proposal, hoping to give her a *get lost* message. Instead, she placed a hand on the empty chair, sliding it back, and took the liberty of sitting.

Bradley's jaw tightened. "Don't you have something to do?"

"I just want to talk to you for a minute."

"I don't have time to talk. I'm a busy man. I'm trying *to recoup all my losses.*"

The words were a reminder of how awfully she'd deceived him. Regret emanated all over her. "I'm sorry about running off with that large amount of your money."

"Not as sorry as I am."

"I don't know what I was thinking."

"I don't know, either. Hell, Bernardo was a billionaire! Why did you need my money, too?" The pain rekindled, he pounded his fist on the table.

Kim winced. "I guess it was pure greed. Then also the fact that his funds were often tied up in high-stakes investments. Now neither one of us can get to any of it."

"There is a lesson there, Kim. I hope you've learned it." He looked back at his proposal.

"I did learn it. And I want to make it all up to you. I could really show you how sorry I am, and how much I care."

His head shot up. "Don't start with me."

"Bradley, just give me a chance. That little assistant you have can't possibly turn you on the way I did. No woman could make you feel the way I did. You know it."

"You're right. She makes me feel better than you did."

The words shocked her into silence, practically sucked away her breath.

"How could you say that?"

"Because it's the truth."

"No, it's not the truth. You're just trying to hurt me. You're trying to make me jealous and pay for hurting you. But I know deep down, you want me. It's all about paying me back. It's working."

"Kim, I don't want to pay you back. *I just don't want you!*"

She shook her head. "I won't believe that."

"You have to. I'm in love with Elandra. In fact . . ."

He paused, searching her watering eyes. "In fact, I'm going to ask her to marry me."

"Marry?" The notion was so heartbreaking it escaped in a whisper.

"I haven't asked her yet, but I will."

Kim felt herself shaking from her powerful heartbeat. She had to put a stop to this. The heavy artillery had to be taken out. But for now, there were other pressing matters.

"Bradley, I also stopped by this table to ask you something."

"What?"

"I need a favor."

"I don't know why you think I should do you a favor. But I'm curious about your nerve."

"It's . . ."

"I'm listening."

"Actually it's not for me. And I was planning to go over to your house tonight. But I just stopped in here for lunch and here you are. It must be fate."

"Get to the point, please."

"It's for Mama."

Now he looked intrigued. "I thought she was doing better."

"Oh she is, this is about . . . it's about . . . it's about her hospital bill."

"What's the problem?"

"The insurance doesn't cover it all, just like they didn't cover the nurse, and her finances and mine, just can't cut it."

"What is the bill?"

Reaching into her purse, she removed a folded paper. Taking it from her, Bradley examined it, then handed it back.

"I'll take care of it."

"Thank you. Thank you." She reached her hand across the table, sliding it on top of his.

Promptly he removed it. Fumbling in his jacket pocket, he was trying to locate his checkbook. Finding it, he wrote out the payment for the full amount. Handing it to her, he had no idea anyone was watching.

Elandra and Daisy had entered at what Elandra believed was the wrong time. In the vestibule of the restaurant, she saw the hand sliding atop his, the tender look in Kim's eye and the check being handed to her. Not able to stand any more, she rushed out with Daisy hot on her trail.

"Girl, what're you acting crazy for? That could have been harmless."

Elandra was moving so fast, her friend couldn't keep up. "Giving his ex-girlfriend money is harmless? Letting her hand touch his like that?"

Daisy was quickly losing her breath. "If you ask me, he removed it pretty quick. And did he *really* look happy to see her to you? To me, he looked like he was eating grass."

Elandra wasn't hearing her. She was too upset. "And where is that damn business associate? There wasn't any. He was meeting her all along."

"I'm sorry. I think you're reading much too much into this."

Elandra was steadily stepping. "And to think all I did was tell him he turned me off." Roughly she threw hair off her face. "Just that one time. That was all it took. Any excuse to go back. I knew she wasn't out of his system."

"You're confusing him with that Dan. They are different men. Bradley won't hurt you. He loves you. It's all over him. Anyone can see it when he's with you."

Elandra still didn't hear. She merely marched. "But

I won't let him know I'm on to him. I'll see what a cheater he is when he gets home."

Daisy's head aimed to the sky. "Oh, Lord. Please come down and help us this time. Please. She's getting on my nerves."

By the time Bradley arrived home, Elandra was lounging on the living room couch with a magazine. Taking in the silky nightgown she was wearing, he smiled and headed straight to her. Once side by side, he stroked her cheek.

"Have you given any thought to what we talked about concerning Crystal?"

"Lots." She didn't show any of the fury boiling inside.

"And what do you think about it?"

"You're probably right." She laid the magazine aside. "And if you are, we have to do something to really find her."

He sighed. "Good. We won't give up until we hear her voice and see her. We'll hire another investigator. We'll put out some cash, posters, flyers and my friends at the television and radio stations will give the subject some air time, too. On top of that, Richard and I can also do some snooping around."

"Great," she said, and truly was rejoicing in all his endeavors to locate her sister. It proved that he truly did love her. But try as she did, she wanted this proof to wipe from memory the scene at the restaurant. It didn't work. "How was your meeting?"

"Better than I expected." He began loosening his tie. "If this deal comes through, can you believe I could be called a billionaire?"

"That's wonderful," she said, forcing a smile. Images flashed of slapping him. "Anything else interesting?"

"Anything else?" His eyes widened. "Isn't what I told you enough?" He slung the tie over a pillow.

"Yes, I guess."

"Woman, what have you been smoking? Don't you know how exciting this all is?" He reached for her. As swift as he did it, Elandra stood.

"I'm going to bed now," she informed him. She yawned and stretched.

"Good." With a mile-wide grin, he sprung up, too. "Show me the way, sexy lady."

He slapped her butt. She flinched.

"I'm going to bed alone."

"Huh?" The curl of his lip formed into a straight line.

"I'll sleep in the room I was in before."

"But do you have to?"

"Yes."

"Oh baby, please don't do that. Baby, baby, baby, please."

"I have to do it. I'm really tired and I want to think about this Crystal situation more."

"I see." But his body didn't. Even so, he had to abide by her wishes.

"Good night, Bradley." She began walking up the stairs.

Not moving from the bottom of the stairwell, he watched her round buttocks. There was a wicked sway to them. Bradley swallowed. Climbing the stairs, the lengthy split in the back of the gown revealed soft, curvaceous legs. Breath caught in his throat. Bradley swallowed again. He could even see it all when she was out of sight, along with her cleavage. Knowing how it all looked uncovered, how she felt, how she smelled, he grew warm. He grew extremely warm. Bradley grew fiery hot. More inviting, visualizing all that succulence, topped with the most gorgeous face, he couldn't be still. He leaped into the shower quickly. Cold water was turned on full blast.

Nineteen

An eruption of laughter flew up to the window, sounding off like a ball smacking the glass. Hurling Elandra out of a restless slumber, it made her fly up to see who was being so noisy. Wiping the last remnants of sleep from her eyes, she then squinted beyond the sun to see a miniature army of boys running across the estate, scattering everywhere. With all the flurry of the past week she'd forgotten they were coming today.

After showering and dressing, Elandra came downstairs, to see Bradley and several of the Little Brothers in the living room playing some video game. Nevertheless, seeing the woman who'd frolicked with them on the Fourth of July, they fled the game and ran toward her.

"Elandra," they echoed one after the other.

"Hi, boys." She smiled, recalling all the faces.

Bradley strolled over, joining the crowd. "Hi, Elandra," he spoke playfully. "Sure was cold last night."

One of the smaller boys swerved around to him. "In this heat? It's summer, man. Are you kidding?"

A puberty-aged youth was a bit sharper. He was noticing Bradley's fascination with Elandra. "He's not talking about the weather, man. He's talking about some lip locking. Kissing and hugging. He probably didn't have any. That's why he was cold."

Some of the boys snickered. The tiniest ones didn't

understand and looked perplexed. Before long, all of them returned to the video game.

Cornering themselves off, Bradley pecked Elandra's cheek. "Good morning, beautiful."

She stiffened from their contact. "Good morning, Bradley."

The detachment had to be his imagination. "Your timing is perfect," he went on. "I was just about to go to your room and wake you up. Wish I could really wake you up." He raised his eyebrows repeatedly in a teasing gesture.

Elandra was unimpressed. "What were you going to wake me up for? It's Saturday and I'm off."

"Because I wanted you to stay with the boys while Richard and I check on a new lead about Crystal."

"A lead?" She brightened.

"Yes, a friend of mine just called me. He's one of the people I threw a little cash at, to let me know if he heard anything about Crystal's disappearance. And he told me Peppy was drunk and saying a lot of interesting things about Angel and that gang, and Crystal."

"What things?"

"I'm going to go find out. But I need you to stay with my boys. Richard is coming with me and the maid can't keep an eye on them because she's fixing them some breakfast."

"I'll watch them. They're great kids."

"You're perfect." He pecked her lips.

You're not, she thought, watching him rush out the door. She didn't know whether to kiss him or kick him.

Bradley was taking quite a while. Elandra was extremely curious to know how things were going, and could have been climbing the walls. Occupying herself with the boys temporarily filled her mind with other things—like fun.

There were games of baseball, basketball and football. If that wasn't tiring enough, she taught several of the boys how to play tennis. Recently Bradley had taught her. A few she allowed to ride horses. Others claimed to be good enough swimmers to dive in the pool. After many hours, Elandra noticed the difference in their ages. The pangs in her knees, the strain in her back and neck, screeched that she was an adult—they were children. Several times, Elandra struggled not to take a doze, for she was exhausted. They exhausted her. However, if she did, there was no telling what those boys might get into. They were mischievous.

Underneath a tree it happened, despite her noble intentions. Watching the boys bring out the punch bowl, her lids fought until they were closed. Some of the boys noticed, and tapped the rest on the arm. Giggles filled the air.

"Elandra, Elandra," she heard Bradley calling her, then shaking her arm.

Elandra tussled with her eyes to open and was confronted with a frown. Peering around and seeing some odd things, she tried to awaken herself from confusion. She had no idea what time it was.

"Bradley," she said, feeling herself waking more. "What time is it?"

"Time for you to wake up!" he snapped.

His tone felt like ice water on her face. "What is wrong with you?"

"What do you think? Look around."

Elandra did. Some things were out of order. Chairs were lying on the ground. Food was strewn in places. The boys were crawling around on the grass. So they had been wild, and she thought the crawling was an odd game, but they were kids. She gazed back at Bradley. "I still don't know what your problem is. And what happened with the info about Crystal?"

"I'll answer that," he said sternly. "But not before you answer me a question."

"What's that?"

"Why did you fall asleep? Tell me *why*? You were in charge of these kids for heaven's sake."

"I was tired."

"*Tired*? Do you know what happened here?"

"They made a mess."

"They did more than make a mess! Woman, those boys are drunk!"

"What?"

Elandra jumped up and ran toward them. Bradley hurried behind her. Stopping at the head of one of the boys, who was crawling on his belly but getting nowhere, Elandra kneeled down. Straightaway the wine's scent waved inside her nostrils.

"Kenneth?" Elandra called. "Were you drinking?"

"Hee, hee," Kenneth cackled.

"Kenneth, were you drinking?" she questioned again.

"Ah, yep."

"What?"

"Ah . . . yep." He burped. "The punch. That was . . . that was good, good punch. Hee, hee, hee."

Elandra couldn't look back at Bradley. She could feel his anger blowing against her back. Instead she inched over to another boy. He was flattened on his stomach, unmoving.

"Trevor, were you drinking?"

"Did I," he said, animatedly.

"Where did you get it from?"

"From the punch."

"Who put something in the punch?"

No answer.

"Trevor?"

No answer.

"Trevor?"

And suddenly there was snoring.

"We all put something in it," another boy injected, drawing Elandra and Bradley across the grass toward him.

Having enough of crawling, he was daring to stand. Bradley helped him up. Nonetheless, wobbly legs simply fell back down again. Leaving him there, Bradley shook his head. "They raided my bar and poured everything they could in the punch. I'm calling a doctor." He practically stomped toward the front door.

Elandra felt horrible. She called to him, "Bradley?"

Briskly, he curved his head around, showing as much anger as she had ever seen.

"What?"

"I'm sorry."

"Sure."

The boys and the doctor were long gone, before Bradley decided to join Elandra. She was sitting down in the dining room, trying to go over some of her notes on the decorating project. Concentrating was impossible.

"At least the boys are fine," she said, unable to read his blank expression. He was standing in the doorway.

"Yes, they are," he agreed, sitting across from her, removing the pad and pen from her hand. He gazed at her intently. "I'm sorry, Elandra. I apologize for practically taking your head off. But put yourself in my place. You would have been upset, too."

"I understand. You were worried about the boys."

"It's just that their parents trust me with them so much. I couldn't bear if anything ever happened to any one of them."

"You're a very responsible man, Bradley. That's one of the reasons I love you."

His fingers stroked hers. "I guess not having a father around impacted on me very much. A man should do all he can to make sure his children, and the younger generation, are well taken care of."

"I agree."

"I know you do. And a man should always do everything possible to treat his lady like she's gold."

Elandra smiled. "You do." The scene with Kim flashed, yet she was determined to ignore it. Didn't his going out of his way to find out about Crystal prove how much he adored her? It was probably harmless, like Daisy said.

"Now that that's out the way, I want to tell you what happened with the information concerning Crystal."

"I was wondering what was happening all day."

"It was pretty interesting." A pensiveness colored his face as he sank back into his chair. "According to Peppy, not only are Angel and the crew in Florida, but he practically swore that Crystal is."

"She is?" Elandra's face brightened. She leaned forward. "Where?"

"He doesn't know where. But in his stupor, he was talking plenty. Said a rich politician from the states is involved with her, and he's into something heavy. Said he comes down to the island very often. But that could be anybody. Many senators come down here."

Silence held them a moment. Elandra was sorting this out. Finally she focused back on Bradley. "You know it has to be someone involved with such magnitude like that. Why else would these people be going

to such trouble for us not to find her, if it weren't something heavy involved?"

"I'm one hundred percent with you."

"What's our next plan of action?"

"Richard and I are going to Florida. Fort Lauderdale
is supposed to be the place."

"I'm going, too."

"You're staying here and safe."

"I'm going with you, Bradley. Crystal is my sister."

He was tickled. "A stubborn, stubborn woman. But
I love you."

"You better."

With the words, eyes lingered. Mouths quivered.
Bradley leaned his head across the table toward hers,
intent on sampling her lush sweetness. A ringing
phone right after the first press of their lips, drew them
apart.

"Let it ring," he insisted.

"It might be about Crystal."

"You're right." He snatched up the phone. "Hello?"

Frowns followed. Deeper and deeper they formed as
the person on the other end chattered so endlessly.
Bradley tried to get a word in, but couldn't.

"You're at your mother's?" he finally asked, then listened. "And she's moved to 100 Martingham. Calm
down. Calm down. I'll be right over."

Thoroughly agitated, he hung up.

"Who was that?" she asked. But she already knew.

"Who else?"

"I can't imagine."

"It was Kim."

The scene in the restaurant flashed. "Her mother
again?"

"Yes. Said her condition is far worse and she feels
like ending her life right with her. Says she has some
pills and wants to take them all. She was hysterical."

"And she begged you to come over?"

"Yes."

"I see."

"Do you? Because if it bothers you, I won't go. I don't want to go. But she really sounded unlike I've ever heard her before. She was desperate."

She is, Elandra thought. *So desperate she'll try anything. But will you fall for it, Bradley? Ninety-five percent of me says no. My heart says no. But that five percent—that tiny part that can't forget that scene at the restaurant—that part that can't forget how Dan betrayed me—that part has to be sure. I'll put you to a test. One momentous test. It's the only way to know for sure.*

"Go on," she urged. "Your conscience will bother you if you don't and you wake up tomorrow and something happened to her."

"All right. I'll go over there for a second. And if she's truly going bonkers, I'll call a doctor. They can take it from there. I'm not getting involved any further. She might get ideas."

Richard was off for the evening. Therefore, Bradley took the Jaguar. As soon as his wheels rolled off the estate, Elandra hurried to the driveway and slid inside a car, too. Remembering the address as he spoke it aloud, she was also going for a visit. The incident with the boys had thrown her off the track. Now she was on it again. After all, he didn't *have to* go over there. He simply could have called the police. If Bradley was rekindling the fire with his ex, she was going to find out right now. She wouldn't play the fool any longer.

Twenty

The instant Bradley entered Kim's house he was suspicious. Though she was crying and distraught, her outfit was hardly that of a grieving daughter. On the contrary, her red silk, short, baby doll would have made his temperature rise at one time. At that moment, however, he grew cold instead of warm. Regardless, he would give her the benefit of the doubt.

"Bradley, I'm so glad you came," she sobbed. "I knew you still cared about me."

"I care about your mother. If something happened to you, she wouldn't get over it. That's why I'm here."

She dried her cheeks. "So you didn't come because you care?"

"I care about you as a human being."

Disappointment dulled her spirit. "Wow, you sure know how to make me feel better."

"Look Kim, if you want psychiatric care, I've heard of an excellent doctor in Freeport."

"Bradley, I need love. I need people in my life. I don't need a psychiatrist." She sniffled. "Can't you understand that?"

"We all need love."

"If my mother goes, who will I have? No one. That's why I want to die. I have nothing. No one to love me. There will be no one when she's gone. You said I don't have you."

"You did once."

With a tissue, she blotted her cheeks again. "Can't you give us another chance?"

Exasperated, he threw his hands in the air. "You lied, didn't you?"

"Why do you say that?"

"You sounded all hysterical on the phone, threatening to kill yourself, and now I see it was just a ploy to get me over here and plead your case again. You know how I am. You knew what your mother said about looking out for you would mean something to me."

"I wasn't lying," she countered, never noticing the door was ajar—ajar just enough for the eyes that peeped in.

"You were! That's what you do best. You're deceitful. You're greedy. You're shallow."

"I was that way. I'm not anymore."

"You'll always be that way. It's your nature, Kim. You were born that way. You'll die that way."

He spun around to leave. She grabbed him by the arm. Stern-faced, he didn't turn around.

"Bradley, don't leave me like this," she begged.

"You're about as ready to kill yourself as I am. And believe me, I'm not."

"You don't know what it's like to have no one in this world to love you."

"Your mother loves you. And you—you love yourself enough for everybody."

"We had a good thing at one time." She stepped closer, so close, she could smell his cologne. God knew, she wanted him. Not solely the money. Long ago, she'd realized she needed *him*. "Don't you remember how good it was?"

Thinking back, he paused for a moment. "We had our moments," he admitted, the tension in his voice lessening.

The eyes that were peeping couldn't blink for looking.

"I could walk into a room and you would light up."

The memory made him pause. He smiled. "I loved you so much." His voice drowned with such emotion it sounded low, like it came from somewhere deep.

"I could hold you like this." Her arms slowly came around his waist. "And you would become so tense. So excited."

No, no, God no, don't let it happen, Elandra cried silently.

"But that was then," he said, easing her hands off, turning around, "and this is now."

Disheartened by the rejection, Kim tried another temptation. She sashayed closer, precisely in his face. Lips an inch from lips, they stood.

"Bradley, you know you want to kiss me."

He stared down at her.

No, no, no.

"Baby, you know you're aching to touch these hot lips," she raged on. "Remember what they used to do to you? All over you?"

To her, Bradley was mesmerized.

"I know that look, Bradley," she went on. "Any minute now, you're going to throw me on the floor and tear my clothes off."

To her, he was more captivated.

"Aren't you?"

Her lips softly pressed against his.

The sight almost made Elandra pass clean out, if it hadn't been for what happened the second after. Abruptly, Bradley stepped over to the phone. He picked up the receiver and began dialing.

"What are you doing?" Kim asked. She was more than frustrated. She didn't wear spurning well.

"I'm calling the hospital." He was waiting for someone to answer.

"What are you calling them for at a time like this?"

"To check on your mother."

Immediately she raced to the phone. She tried to grab the receiver, but Bradley held her off. When he inquired about her mother's condition, and they informed him she was being released because of greatly improved health, he hung up shaking his head at Kim.

"So what," she said, defiance in her tone. "So what! I lied! Big deal."

"Do you know I left Elandra at a precious moment to come over here?"

Elandra's lips curved up.

"So what? That twerp can't satisfy you."

"Watch the names, Kim. I could call you plenty, like gold digger, bank robber."

"Bradley, let's not argue. Let's make love."

Not expecting anything but more pleading, Bradley was more than shocked when she slid off her baby doll, revealing all to him.

"Put your clothes on!" he demanded, picking the flimsy outfit off the floor. Shoving it at her, he didn't look at all turned on like she'd hoped. He looked repulsed.

Elandra was ecstatic.

Wiggling herself back into the nightie, Kim had never been so insulted.

"Are you gay now or something?" she griped. Never in her life had a man humiliated her so terribly.

"Just because I don't want you. Please, please, please. Give me a break."

"Something is wrong with you, Bradley!"

"You're wrong. Something is right with me. I'm in love—with Elandra."

"I don't want to hear that crap."

"But you need to. I love Elandra with every fiber of my soul. I'm in love with her in a way I never loved you. I never even thought love this deep was possible."

"Why are you saying this? Why are you so cruel? You want to hurt me for leaving you for Bernardo? You've won then. I'm hurt."

"You have to face reality. In your own sick way, you may even really believe that you love me, but sometimes when you realize something, when you realize that the pebble you thought you had, is really a pearl, it just may be too late. This is one of those times."

Elandra was jumping up and down.

"We can start over, Bradley," Kim pleaded. "If you just give me a chance, you can fall in love with me all over again."

"Kim, I don't want to be mean to you. I don't even want to get even. I just want you to let go. Let go. When you touch me, when you tried to kiss me, when you just took your clothes off, I felt nothing. Not the slightest buzz. There was excitement nowhere in my body, in my heart, my soul, my mind. No place on me was excited by you. No place ever will be again with you. Elandra is the only woman who can do that for me now. When I see her, I come alive in a way I've never known."

"You can't . . . you can't. . . ." She began sobbing.

"I love her. And I'm going to ask her to marry me."

The heartfelt confession was like a string, pulling Elandra's legs high up in the air in an exuberant jump. But when she came back down, she stumbled. Toward the door she went. It flew open and she with it, onto the floor.

She looked up at a shocked Bradley and leering Kim.

"Hi, Bradley." She waved.

"Baby, what were you doing?" He began helping her up.

Infuriated, Kim propped her hands on her hips. "She nearly broke my door in eavesdropping, that's what she was doing."

Once standing, Elandra looked pensively at Bradley. "I'm sorry I followed you, but I was just . . ."

"Just scared I would take your man," Kim taunted. She was twitching. "I knew you were insecure. You have plenty reason to be, too." She looked Elandra up and down.

"No, you don't have reason to be," Bradley corrected, caressing her chin, beholding her unusual eyes. "I love you more than anything in the world, and I admire you for going to all this trouble. It shows how much you care."

"I do care. And was that true what you said? You want to . . . to marry me?"

"This is not the place I planned to ask you, but I do. Will you marry me, Elandra?"

"You know I will."

His eyes sparkled down on her as he gathered Elandra in his arms. Not even paying attention to Kim, they headed out the door. "I want to ask you again, alone in a special place," Bradley said.

All the while they walked to the car and drove off, Kim examined herself. Whatever she was, all that she was, was no longer enough for Bradley. Her beauty, her sensuality, her sophistication, her heart were not good enough. She had lost him. Someone else won his heart. For some reason, it made her think back. It made her wonder what Bradley must have felt when she married someone else, and he was standing at the altar waiting for her. In this situation, there was no altar. There was no preacher. There were no friends and family gathered in a church. There was no reception hall. Even so, Kim knew what she was feeling now, was what he was feeling then. God knew, she would have done anything to make the pain go away. It was an ache unlike any other.

There were no more questions. There was no more doubt. There was no more worry. There was purely the magic of love and all its power. Elandra showered, powdered, lotioned, perfumed, and afterward dressed in her sexiest Victoria's Secret nightie. Propped up on a pillow, Bradley was lying on the bed. When he saw her emerge from the bathroom, he had never seen anything so beautiful, so sexy, so desirable. His heart raced. His body hardened with excitement.

Bradley reached out. Sashaying toward him, her features were as earnest as the passion pounding inside her. Elandra wanted him to take in all of her. She yearned for him to appreciate everything that he was going to get. Heaven knew, she appreciated him. Lounging atop the covers, he was a masterpiece. Rich brown skin, scintillating eyes, a graceful nose, and wide lips set lusciously in an angular jaw. Lowering her admiring look, Elandra loved the lines in his neck, and the mountain of chest and arms like melons stacked on top of one another, and legs concrete hard.

"You take my breath away," he revealed as she climbed next to him on the mattress.

"You're not too hard on the eyes, either." Her hand fell along the side of his face.

Bradley kissed a finger. "You're so beautiful." He shifted to get a perfect view of her face. "But it's even more than your looks that get to me. It's who you are inside too, your spirit, your heart, the way you love so deeply, the way you give your all to something that you do. I thank God every day for you, Elandra."

"I thank him for you, too."

"And I also let him know how much you mean to

me. I love you inside out, Elandra, and I want you to be my wife."

A tear bubbled in her eye. She blinked it away before it strode down her cheek. "I would love to be your wife."

"Hearing that makes me the happiest man alive." He pressed her lips lightly and raised back. Bradley allowed himself to be captivated for a moment, before reaching to the side in an end table drawer. A small, red velvet box was removed. He handed it to her.

"What's this?" Elandra asked, but she had an idea. She was trying to stay calm.

"Something beautiful, but not as beautiful as you."

When the box was opened, a huge, sparkling, pear-shaped diamond posed before her. Taking it out, slipping it on her finger, Bradley's clear happiness matched hers.

"I've never had anything this beautiful." Elandra was turning the diamond to various angles of the light, admiring it. "When did you buy this gorgeous ring?"

"I bought it after I told you I loved you."

"I can't get over it."

"And I can't get over you."

With his fingers, Bradley grazed her chin, luring it to his face. There his mouth inched and inched toward hers, until she felt the intoxicating feel of his lips caressing across her face. Her forehead, nose, cheeks, temples, and ears were ravished by nimble, succulent kisses. Aroused by the building sensation of them, Elandra treated him to the same. Bradley breathed deeply, letting his head fall back, inviting her lips to thrill his neck, too. After she did, he returned to his heated obsession with her face. Consuming the lush beauty of her, the unusually beautiful eyes, the smooth, moist skin, the full lips like fruit ready to be robbed of their juice, he could stand no more without tasting her.

Desperately he gathered her within his arms, his mouth covering hers hungrily. Instantly the heady sensation of ecstasy ran through her, as it did him. Elandra held on, holding on to his shoulders and back while she was wrapped sideways in his arms.

"Jesus," he moaned, as their need grew more anxious. Long and slow his lips caressed hers, relishing the feel of their smoothness. And Elandra delighted in this pleasure, the demand of his mouth becoming harder. Over and over he did this, then tasted the inside, satisfying his hunger with the sweet taste of her tongue and the exotic juice of her mouth.

Drugged by their kissing, they ached to be loved more. Gently Bradley coaxed Elandra's back against the bed while he eased to the side of her. Lingering kisses then delighted her neck and across her chest. She whimpered from the unbearable pleasure and wiggled as he whisked her nightie away. Naked underneath a hungry, burning gaze, she never felt more beautiful. Slowly his eyes traveled seductively over her body before she carried his shorts away, too. As sexy as any creature on this earth had any right to be, was how he looked to her, skin glistening, body so hard and eager.

His fingers slid across her breasts, exciting her, stroking their fullness. Elandra threw her head back from the blissful feeling, then rewarded him with kisses across his own chest. With a gaze softly caressing her, his hands did also. On the silken skin of her belly he touched her gently, kissed her gently. On the curve of her hips, he enthralled her with his hands. Along her thighs, calves and buttocks, he granted each tender loving care. Excitement surged through them both, as Elandra titillated him with kisses everywhere and anywhere. The joy was unbearable.

Finally he carefully melted his love into hers. Kissing her, he had a lusty urgency, that drew out all of her own. Flesh against flesh they thrilled each other, at times with slow strokes, then wild, voracious ones. The rapture grew to heights neither ever experienced, not even before when they loved, and when they reached that supreme height of bliss. They knew nothing would ever be the same again. Elandra made love to him with her whole heart and soul, and Bradley did the same. There was freedom that was never there before. She had finally let go of the past. No longer was she its victim or prisoner. She was a woman tasting the deliciousness of romantic love. It was a taste she knew she would taste forever. Bradley was the kind of man her heart and soul had been starving for. This was the kind of love God had intended for her to have.

Twenty-one

From the hotel suite, Elandra pressed her nose against the window, taking in the picturesque view of Fort Lauderdale. Never having visited the city before, she didn't know it was such a busy vacation spot, boasting luxurious hotels, tourist sites and the mysteriousness of the Atlantic Ocean. At the window, adoring it all, the scenery was soon phased out by the images in her mind. At first, Elandra was replaying the way Bradley made love to her before he left in the morning. He was so passionate, tender, and determined to please her with mind-bending love. He knew what excited her body better than she did, and she couldn't wait until he returned to experience the magic they created all over again. She felt so blessed.

For the rest of her life she would feel that love. She couldn't wait to be his wife. Sometimes when everything was quiet, and Elandra was evaluating her life, she still couldn't absorb the fact that she would soon be Mrs. Bradley Davenport. Never had Elandra imagined a man could love her so much, and that she could return such a depth of love. All she needed now was her special maid of honor. Bradley and Richard had to bring her back. She even stuck around the hotel instead of investigating with them because she hoped one of the people they'd passed a photograph flyer to would call or stop by. Bradley had posted a $100,000 reward for any information leading to Crystal's where-abouts. In Nassau the lesser reward hadn't proved fruit-ful. Something always thwarted anyone from coming forth. Now Elandra knew it was probably the promise of great danger. It was her most heartfelt prayer that the danger hadn't come Crystal's way. Everything they learned about Crystal's disappearance said she was in danger. However, Elandra knew miracles could happen through God. Look at what happened to her: the most wonderful man in the world had fallen in love with her. If that was possible, anything else was. And if she had learned anything from that wonderful man, it was to think positively. Always have hope.

The second image that came to Elandra was more of a fantasy. It was simply Bradley and Richard escorting a vivacious Crystal Lloyd into the suite. She prayed it would come true.

Richard and Bradley split up, beginning their search in two rental cars. They agreed to meet up at the hotel around 9:00 p.m. Hopefully one of them would have Crystal, or at least know where she was.

Bradley's search took him everywhere, to the airport, the bus terminal, the train station, stores, restaurants, then to the streets, avenues and dirt roads, where after hours places hid. When he wound up at a place called The Bottom because some folks indicated Trina's brother Angel hung out there recently, Bradley felt like he hit pay dirt.

Entering The Bottom Bradley easily saw that it was a greasy spoon pool hall. Paint-chipped walls, the worn pool tables, the scent of stale beer and man after man who looked like they tread the darker side of life.

"Is Angel around?" Bradley asked. He was asking a guy, someone in the streets described as the person running the place. With a sickly, pallid complexion, red hair and red freckles, Red was easy to pick out.

"Who's asking?" Red asked.

"Name's Bradley." Bradley put out his hand to shake.

One of Red's hands remained at his side. The other played with a toothpick in his mouth. "What you want Angel for?"

"Just wanted to see him. I'm a good friend of his."

"I'm a good friend of his, too, and I never heard of you." He slid the toothpick around.

"Yes, we're friends all right. Is he coming in today?"

"Might and might not."

Bradley noticed Red checking out his jewelry and clothes. He had tried to under-dress. He guessed he just hadn't done it successfully enough. "You're a mighty sharp dresser to know a guy like Angel. Where you know him from? That senator introduce you to him? He introduced him to some other rich guys who pay him to do deeds."

Now we're getting somewhere. "Yes, the senator did actually."

Red perked up. "You have anything for me to do? I'll do whatever it is for the right price." He inspected Bradley's watch. "I want me a watch like that."

"You can have one. Right away. That's if you'll really do anything. For the right price, of course."

"I'm ready."

"Just tell me where I can find this girl, and you can have $100,000." Bradley removed a flyer and a color 8 x 10 photo of Crystal from his pocket.

Red took one look at it and threw his toothpick away. "What are you up to, man?" He was seething. "What? I want to know now!"

Bradley maintained a cheerful front. "Why so hostile?"

"Like I said, what are you up to?"

"You do know something about this girl, don't you?"

"What is it to you?"

"Plenty. Her sister is worried about her and wants her safe."

"You better leave." Red turned his back to him.

Roughly Bradley slung him around, slamming his back against the wall. "Not until I find out where this woman is."

Tightening his lip in a hard circle, Red was beyond infuriated. "Get your damn hands off me before I have one of these fellas in here give you a few holes and slits."

The words and an abrupt silence triggered Bradley to scan around. Every man in the place was glowering at him. One went so far as to remove a knife from a back pocket.

Bradley peered at Red. "Just one more question."

"Get out of here while you can."

"What is the senator's name? Just tell me that one name and you can have the money."

Red just looked at him, as did all the other men.

Bradley looked at them, too. "If any of you know this girl, or the senator who knows her, and can give me any information as to her whereabouts, I'll give you a $100,000." Looks exchanged all around the room, as many considered the offer. Despite it, no one budged in offering information.

"All right," Bradley said, stepping toward the door backwards. "Don't ever say no one ever gave you guys a chance to get rich. One name would have done it."

As soon as Bradley left, activity resumed. However, Red didn't join the pack in lounging about, enjoying the afternoon. Quite the contrary, he picked up the phone and made a call. When he hung up, he grabbed a bag from a back room and rushed out the door.

Bradley didn't return to the rental car immediately. Instead he paced the streets and roads, still inquiring about Crystal's whereabouts. When finally exhaustion told him tomorrow was another day, he headed to the car. Driving along, listening to thoughts in his mind, he practiced what he would tell Elandra. Though he hadn't located Crystal yet, he felt he was getting close. But tonight he wouldn't talk about that too much. After all the work he did today, he deserved some loving. He wanted some. Fast wasn't fast enough to get it. Except as he sped down the highway, then realized he was exceeding the limit, Bradley mashed the brake mildly to slow down. The brake was like a broken spring. Over and over, Bradley hit it with his foot to no avail. *No, this can't be happening,* he thought, alarm racing his heart, his mind in a flurry trying to figure out what to do. *I'm not going to die,* he swore, stomping the brake again and again. Nothing happened. The car rolled faster. Then in one breath it seemed, there was a thunderous crash. Bradley's lids fluttered closed to the waving of leaves.

"What happened to me?" Bradley mouthed listlessly to Elandra. The doctor and nurse had just left the room. "These people around here won't tell me anything, except that I wasn't seriously injured in a car accident."

"Thank God you weren't. Just bumps, bruises and a little out of it for a while." Sitting, crouching over his bed, Elandra lifted his palm. "And they did tell you what happened. You were in a car accident."

"No, I mean, what really happened? How did it happen? Did someone hit me? Did I get run off the . . ." Suddenly remembering something, his eyes darted about the room. "Wait a minute. It was the brakes. My brakes went."

"Your brakes! Well, Richard is at the police station. He told them it might have been foul play so they are checking on the car. Fortunately he told me his car hasn't been tampered with."

"Thank God." He looked tense, recalling how it happened. "But my car was tampered with."

"Oh no. Did it have something to do with your questions about Crystal? It's all my fault." She lowered her head.

He raised it with his fingertips, leveling his gaze in hers. "No, it's not your fault. It's those idiots who had this done. Those same people have your sister. I know it. I'm calling the police and telling them what I know."

He picked up the phone and began dialing. As he did, Elandra decided to go get a soda and wandered down the hall. Walking, she smiled at the hospital staff and occasionally glanced in some patients' rooms as she passed. So it was more than a shock, more than astonishment, more than her heart could bear, when she glanced in a room casually, expecting nothing more than any other patient, and saw a sight that jolted her full force. Somehow it felt like the earth was moving beneath her feet.

"Crystal?" Elandra uttered, approaching the woman lying motionlessly in the bed. "Crystal, it's you," she said again, her amazement dropping to who sat beside her. "Trina? She's not in Sweden. She's here! With you!"

"I didn't want to lie," Trina defended, suddenly sobbing. She stood up, backing against a wall. "I hated telling you that lie."

"But you did." In pure astonishment, Elandra gaped at her, but was again totally absorbed by the inert body in the bed. In silence, Crystal searched her face. Yet Elandra saw no recognition. She heard none either.

"I'm so sorry, Elandra," Trina told her.

Elandra waved her off, concentrating on her sister.

"Crystal, it's me," she spoke. The emotionless face could have passed for a stranger's. The large doe eyes were weak. The full mouth, identical to Elandra's, was set in a straight line. Her hair was tousled, her limbs thin. Even so, Elandra would have known her sister anywhere.

"What's wrong with her?" she asked, turning to Trina. "Who did this to her?"

Tears welling in her eyes, Trina shook her head. "Elandra, it's so dangerous. You need to leave here and forget you ever saw Crystal."

With a handkerchief to her face, Trina turned her back. No sooner than she did, Elandra yanked her around. "Don't you dare stand here and tell me to forget my sister! With a brother like Angel, I can understand why you can't understand what it means to have a brother or sister! But that's your problem! I want to know what happened to my sister and I want to know now!"

"Please don't make me." Her eyes scattered cautiously about the room. "They are listening, maybe even watching."

"Who are?" Elandra grasped her wrist, digging her nails into it.

"I can't tell you."

"You better. You better right now! You're not leaving here until you do."

"You don't understand what will happen."

She glanced at Crystal. "I see something has happened already. And if you don't tell me what's going on, something will happen to you. Something serious, right now."

Elandra rushed to the door, and beckoned a guard from the hallway.

"Yes, ma'am?" he asked.

"I want you to witness what this young lady tells me, and I want you to watch her so she won't escape. I think she's committed a criminal act. I believe she's involved with hurting my sister here."

The security officer peered over at Crystal. Still as death, she appeared unaware of the world. He carried a somberness back to Elandra. "We'll watch her, ma'am."

Trina began to sob loudly.

"I'm going to get someone." Elandra talked over cries to the guard. "His name is Bradley Davenport. He needs to *see* this and hear this, too."

Twenty-two

Bradley and Elandra's rage aimed down at Trina as she sat crying uncontrollably before them.

"I just spoke to Crystal's doctor," Elandra informed her. "They said my sister was in a coma from a head injury. They said her speech is impaired, and so are some of her other faculties, along with amnesia. They said it may be temporary or it may be permanent. It's in God's hands. But what is most distressing to me is how she became this way. Any ideas, Trina?"

"I can't talk about it." She rubbed her streaked face. "It's dangerous."

"What's dangerous is my brakes being tampered with," Bradley snapped. "And I think you know a little about that. According to the doctors, the police told them Crystal's brakes were tampered with, too."

Elandra mellowed her anger, softening her look at Trina. "Trina, my sister is lying over there, practically helpless. I have to know what's going on. I know you couldn't have done this—not by yourself at least."

"I didn't! I swear. Crystal and I were best friends, still are."

"Then what the hell is going on?" Bradley inquired. "If you ever cared about your friend, you have to help her by telling us. You tell us now or the police later."

Finally and hesitantly, Trina nodded.

"Start at the very beginning," Bradley urged.

"The beginning is like what I already told you. Crystal and I were dating guys like I told you, in Nassau. And also like I told you, Crystal was seeing a married man. She didn't know the senator was married, though, until she became pregnant. He was furious. He accused her of getting pregnant to trap him. But she hadn't. It just happened. Plus, she loved him so, and thought he loved her.

"Anyway, he then revealed his marital status. Said he had a wife and grown children and didn't want any more."

Elandra was intrigued. "So he is a much older man? Who is he?"

Trina was silent a second, then, "Senator Wayne Hagans."

"What!" Elandra screeched, while Bradley nodded.

Trina nodded. "Yes, it's him."

"I suspected his involvement, but I don't know how!" Bradley declared. "Wayne Hagans!"

"So that's why he asked about Crystal so much," added Elandra. "I knew there was something not right about him. But go on. So what happened next? How did my sister get like this?" Sadly she gazed toward the bed. Shaking her head, she sighed at Trina. "What kind of monster hurts people like that?"

"First off, it wasn't Wayne, himself," Trina answered. "It was what his power causes." She paused as she pondered for a moment. "He's so rich and powerful, with the disguise of dignity. And he didn't love her. He just used her. He wanted her to have an abortion. He argued with her so much about it that she ended up losing the baby anyway. She miscarried."

"Oh, no." Elandra clutched her chest, and felt the burning in her nostrils that warned of tears to come. Nevertheless, she wanted to stay strong for Crystal. She needed to know everything, and have whoever hurt her punished severely.

Bradley shook his head. "What else happened? We still don't know how Crystal came to this."

"Crystal hated him. That's what happened. After losing her baby, she hated him so much, she pretended she still loved him. But all the while she was scheming. You see, our dignified senator had more secrets than a mistress. The senator is involved in high-stakes prostitution. When young women are arrested and sent to prison farms in rural areas, the senator has them prostituting. They are taken out of the prison and forced to do favors for men, or they're put in solitary confinement. Many of them are even sent abroad to foreign countries, where men pay exorbitant prices for beautiful American women. Often, too, they are sent to prison on trumped-up charges, just because they're beautiful and Wayne knows they would fetch a high price.

"But that's not all. He also has other enterprises, tax scandal, stock and bond corruption. And he has such lowlifes involved with him, the scum of the earth, who are so devoted because they know if he goes down, they will too. Plus, they want to protect their bread and butter. Wayne has mostly ex-cons working for him—people employers don't want to hire. He throws them money because no one else will. So how else will they live? By doing what they do best—being criminals. For them, it's all about survival. For Wayne, it's just about greed and evil."

"And this is supposed to be someone we look up to?" Elandra gasped.

Bradley was amazed. "And the way he maintains this is by having people working for him, who he holds some power over? But what about the prison officials, who know about the prostitution? How does he get them to cooperate?"

"By giving them a huge cut of the tremendous profits. And you see, Crystal was planning to pay the senator back in a big way for using her. She demanded that he give her a million dollars or she would hand over to authorities all the proof of his illegal activities. In the condo he sometimes shared with her, she was taping conversations he had with his cronies about the prostitution business and other activities. She was videotaping him, too. His face was right there for the world to see. Then there were the illegal transactions on paper that had his signature. But like I said, Wayne's power lay in survival and greed.

"Money is a powerful weapon. Those lowlifes that work for him will do anything to keep theirs coming. Like working you up a little bit mentally, or sometimes even physically. Before this happened to Crystal, I never heard of anyone trying to cross him being seriously hurt or killed." She glanced at her friend, then divided gazes between Elandra and Bradley. "But those cronies of his can put fear in you like no one can believe. That's why I was afraid. They threatened me. Bradley, he got to your first investigator with threats to his family, too."

Bradley snapped his finger. "I knew it was something."

"The second one, he got with money . . . and some fear."

"And what does he have you with, Trina?" Elandra asked.

"Can't you see it on my face? Can't you see it shaking in my bones? I'm just scared."

Weighing this all, Bradley and Elandra just looked at each other. Bradley cleared his throat. "But how did Crystal get to this stage? You still haven't told us."

Water clouded her sight with the memory forming in her mind. "We were on the boat, a boat called *Fun Ship*. That's where we met him and his friends often. We had parties there. Then one day we flew in his private jet. He took us here to Fort Lauderdale, where he was having an important meeting. Crystal had threatened him by then, and he had forgiven her, claiming he would marry her and leave his wife. I knew he was lying. But Crystal was so in love she chose to believe otherwise.

"Anyway, after arriving he went to his meeting. Then, later one of his cronies called and said Crystal should meet Wayne at a particular restaurant for dinner. They told her a rental car would be waiting outside of our hotel. But in reality, the call came from one of his cronies. Wayne hadn't asked her to meet him.

"The car's brakes were tampered with I learned after the accident. Crystal was thrown clear out of the car several feet, receiving very serious injuries. Wayne thought she was going to die. But it was so surprising to see how torn up he was about it. That's when I first knew he didn't have any involvement with what happened to her. He didn't know the lowlife was going to hurt Crystal when he told him how she was making his life hell with the blackmail threat. No, he didn't love her the way she wanted. However, he hated to see her hurt like this. But at the same time . . ."

Elandra's eyes widened. "What?"

"She had set it up so that if anything happened to her, all of the senator's secrets would be out of the bag. You see, Crystal signed up to be an organ donor. With it, there is a code on her file for special instructions. The special instruction file is called Senator. It would indicate where to find all the proof to have him indicted for his activities. He didn't find out about this until she almost died in here."

"My God." Elandra closed her eyes and opened them. "All this was going on . . ."

"But when he and his cronies learned that no matter what button they pushed, this code was so governmentally regulated it couldn't be erased, more than ever Wayne wanted Crystal to stay alive. On the other hand, Wayne didn't want her to recover from the amnesia and tell what she knew. The amnesia she has provides a perfect situation for him. And that's where I come in." Remorse covered her face as she looked around, then back at Elandra again. "He makes me come here to make sure Crystal doesn't get her memory back. He knows once she finds out someone tried to kill her, she'll retaliate and tell where all the proof of his activities is hidden. She had come to the point too, where she really wasn't afraid of what his power could do. I guess she felt she lost so much already, losing the baby and all. What more could she lose? He hurt her so bad, she had come to the point that nothing really mattered anymore—even her own life. So what if she took a chance on losing it. Losing the baby was the greatest thing she could have ever lost."

Elandra hung her head. "I know the feeling."

"When she is in the mood for talking," Trina went on, "and does say something that makes sense about her past, he forces me to confuse her. They have me tape our visits. Sometimes I even feel like even if I wouldn't tape them it wouldn't matter. Because I feel like they put bugs in here. That's why . . ." Rubbing her shoulders, she scanned around. "That's why I didn't think it was good to talk to you."

Bradley and Elandra were horrified. Yet they knew what had to be done immediately.

"We have to go to the police and tell them everything," Bradley insisted, ushering Trina up.

Vehemently she pulled away. "I can't go! I might get hurt, too, killed even."

Elandra clutched her by the arms. "Don't you realize you have more of a chance of getting hurt by not telling what he's done? Do you really think they're going to let you go on about your business with all you know? Do you?"

Wayne paced back and forth in a motel room as Angel watched.

"Don't worry about what you heard, boss."

"Don't worry!" Wayne stopped pacing and gaped at him. "How can you tell me that? You heard what that little witch told them. Trina told them everything." He started pacing again.

Angel smiled. "I can take care of them all. Even my dumb sister."

"No!" Wayne stopped pacing and leered into Angel's hardened face. "It's one thing to make money on the side with the prostitution, and the other deeds that stuff our pockets. But physically hurting people and murder, I told you I didn't want that! Those types of things leave a trail. A trail, don't you see that! And it leads straight to me. Everything was fine until you took it upon yourselves to start tampering with brakes and trying to murder people. This is what I get for working with ex-cons! You're losers and you think like losers!"

Angel silently cursed Wayne for the way he was talking to him. He talked to him like that often lately. Nonetheless, he didn't raise his voice, or mention how *soft* the senator was starting to seem to him and the other guys.

He hid his observations with a lopsided grin. "We just thought you wanted to preserve everything at all costs."

"Not at all costs! Did I say that!"

"Uh no, but—"

"So why the hell do you keep doing stupid things!"

Angel took a deep breath. "I—"

"The way we were going, no one would have been on to us." Wayne gestured wildly with his hands. "Who cares about whores! Every man knows we need them. But you and those fools had to go practically killing people. And if some dog sniffs up on it, they're not going to turn their head. They're going to eat it up. Eat it up because Senator Wayne Hagans is involved, and they would love to get their name in lights by bringing me down."

"So what you want us to do, boss?" His level voice revealed none of the resentment brewing, none of the visions of slicing Wayne's throat with the knife in his back pocket.

"The only thing we can do. We'll try to see if we can cut Davenport in. He's itching to get even richer. Pretty model stood him up at the altar once for a richer guy, a billionaire. Plus I know every man has his price."

"So what if he doesn't go for it? That Elandra babe isn't going to let him do that after what we did to her sister."

"Elandra has her price, too. We just have to find out what it is."

With that, Wayne smiled. Standing behind him, Angel didn't.

En route to the police station, Bradley and the two women hurried to Elandra's rental car, which was in the hospital parking lot. At that moment, the lot seemed vacant. It was a facade. Figures lurked in the shadows.

Merely a foot from the car, Bradley, Elandra and Trina were about to leap in and take off. What they didn't count on was Angel and his cronies emerging from nowhere, drawing guns at their heads. Moments later, all were crowding into a dusty old station wagon.

Richard was just entering the parking lot, hoping to get a space so he could visit Bradley. Instead he tried not to panic seeing what he did, but he vowed to remain calm and adjust his route. As long as they didn't kill them before he found out where they were headed, everything would be all right. If only they could stay alive. He would do the rest.

The shack they were taken to was located in an impoverished section of Fort Lauderdale. During the ride, Angel constantly referred to it as Graves Way.

When the station wagon stopped in front of the dilapidated property, Elandra and Bradley prayed that this wouldn't be their last place to be together. Not a place like this.

"I'm glad you came, Bradley," Wayne Hagans said, watching Angel and his cohorts shove the three inside. Each one had two men holding their arms.

"Wayne, how could you live with yourself?" Bradley spat. "Making those women prisoners prostitutes. How could you let Crystal get hurt like that?"

"The same way you do what you do, Bradley. You work hard at your job. So do I." The men chuckled.

"You tried to kill my sister!" Elandra accused.

"No, I didn't," Wayne denied with a hint of desperation. "I would never tamper with her brakes, trying to kill her. It was these goons that did that. Without my knowledge. That's what I get for working with uneducated, classless, imbeciles. They don't think. No brains at all."

Killer looks aimed at Wayne from everyone in the room.

"Well, you're not getting away with it," Bradley informed him. "No way."

Wayne's lips curled to one side. "Come on, Bradley. How's about I cut you in?"

"Get out of my face."

One of the goons stepped forth, looking angrily from Wayne to Bradley. "You let him talk to you like that? Threaten you like that? Take him out, man!"

Boisterous agreement echoed around the room from the men.

Wayne's shake of the head silenced them. His eyes burned into Bradley's.

"No. Bradley and I can do business. He knows all about the power super wealth can bring. A woman even left him at the altar because he didn't have enough of it."

Elandra noticed Bradley swallowing.

"I was there at the wedding, Bradley, remember?" Wayne teased. "This is a way to prove you're king, no matter what she or anyone says."

Bradley narrowed his eyes like a hawk. "What do I look like to you? Nothing in the world you can say, will make me stupid like you are."

"You're stupid if you pass up on the money I'm offering!"

"What? Be part of helping you exploit those women and whatever else you're doing? No thanks. You're a punk."

Elandra and the men snickered.

Wayne was incensed. He nodded to the men. Instantly guns drew on Trina, Elandra and Bradley.

Seeing the weapons, Elandra was filled with terror. She was so petrified she could barely breathe.

"All right, Bradley," Wayne said, burning his gaze upon his former friend. "I gave you a choice. You can either take it or leave it, or leave here I should say . . .

cold . . . stiff. Get my point? That goes for the women, too. I don't want to do it, but I have no choice now. You leave me no choice."

Hearing the threat, seeing Elandra's state, Bradley leaped at Wayne. The two guys holding him, yanked him back. "You better not touch a hair on Elandra's head, on anyone's head."

Elandra trembled.

"Shut up!" Wayne growled. He didn't like the way the men were looking at him. The loss of respect was evident.

Wildly, Bradley shook his head. "I better not ever get loose. You'll wish you never even heard my name!"

"Watch it, tough guy!"

"You're right I'm tough," Bradley countered. "I'll break your damn neck! Thing is you know I will too! I can see it in your eyes, you coward! You're not a man anymore."

"Why don't you take him, boss!" Angel shouted. Yet he was anxious to see Wayne get beat. Wayne had grown too soft—and too uppity. Where did he get off thinking he was better than them? What's more, Angel felt he deserved the money Wayne was receiving. He was really the leader of everything. He carried out all the action. Wayne never let his hands get dirty. Some how, some way, he would fix him. He would fix everything.

"Shut up!" Wayne commanded, never snaking his fury from Bradley.

"Let's see what you can do as a man. A *real* man. You can order these dunces around and they'll jump and say where to land. But can you really get down and dirty and show some testosterone? I think not. You're an old man. You're lower than the dirt on my shoe. You're a woosy, too. No, you're a . . ." He grinned. "Well you know what rhymes with woosy."

Outrage distorted Wayne's features. It bloomed because of the verbal attack against him, but equally for the way the men were looking at him. Scanning around the room, the insults and challenge made them regard him with something he had never seen before when he gazed in their faces. Feeling that if he didn't beat this younger man senseless, he would diminish in their eyes, Wayne slung off his jacket. Sleeves rolled up.

"Let him go!" he commanded, and Bradley was free.

"If I win, you let us go. If you win, kill us. Deal, big man?"

"Anything you say, Davenport."

"I mean it," Bradley stressed. "A deal is a deal. That is unless you don't think you can win?"

"Oh, it's a deal all right. I'm going to kick your butt."

Hands poised for attack, moving in a circle they baited each other.

Elandra was speechless. Trina was nearly passed out. The men were so fascinated they could barely pay attention to their captives.

Wayne made an attempt to lunge the first punch. Except Bradley blocked it, and slammed him in the stomach. Wayne buckled over, then peered up at the men groaning. He abhorred them seeing his pain. Elandra was sighing with relief. Bradley smirked.

Wayne wasn't having it. Nobody was making him look bad. He lunged again. Bradley blocked it. Another punch was thrown. Bradley blocked that, too. But for the third strike, he was crafty. He kicked, gutting his foot in Bradley's ribs. Bradley winced, clutching his side. A few of the savages cheered. From this, Elandra was not merely speechless. Now tears tumbled from her eyes.

Seeing how upset she was, tore at Bradley's heart. So much so, it lifted him from the soreness in his ribs to the top of Wayne's body. With one walloping leap, he straddled him on the floor. Over and over and over he punched, slapped and pounded until Wayne was nearly unconscious. Blood from him splattered everywhere.

"Get up, you punk!" Bradley demanded. "Come on and fight or let us go. We had a deal."

The terms, however, were not to be met. Instead of merely struggling to his feet, Wayne did something else. Badly shaken from his horrific experience, he managed to nod toward Angel. Yet instead of Angel and another thug helping him to his feet, they kicked him down further. More shocking, they aimed guns on their esteemed boss.

Elandra didn't know where this nightmare was heading. All she saw was the guns, and then the shouting exchanged, Wayne's, Bradley's, Angel's, the men. It all made her close her eyes for a second to pray. If only God could hear her, if her mother could hear, if someone could hear her cries for help. Then suddenly there was the blast. A sound, which hysteria assured her was gunfire. Only when she opened her eyes did she know it was actually a door bursting open. It was followed by Trina's screams of joy, and sights Elandra prayed weren't imagined.

"Get up against the wall," the police commanded Wayne and his partners in crime.

"We were at the window," Richard declared. He was standing around, observing, smiling. "We saw and heard everything."

Bradley hugged him, then quickly came toward Elandra.

"You're all right?" he asked, hugging her.

"Yes, yes." She exhaled into his chest.

"I'm so sorry you had to go through this. I'm sorry about the lewd things I said as well. It was just to distract all of them from you and Trina, so you could get away."

"I know, baby. And if it took that and everything else to get them arrested, I'm glad I went through it." She gazed up, staring in his eyes. What she saw in them, made her kiss him, her arms wrap around him. Elandra never wanted to let go. "I'm so glad you were here for me."

"I wouldn't be anywhere else. I'll always be here for you. Always."

Rights were read. Wayne and the rogues were handcuffed. Elandra, Bradley, Richard and Trina followed them out to the police car. Trina agreed that she would testify. They were also informed about Crystal's evidence against Wayne.

Twenty-three

"How do you like your room?"

Elandra was strolling into Crystal's bedroom, surveying the surroundings before she took a seat.

"It's so pretty," Crystal answered. Digging her hands into the mattress, she was propping up on a pillow. "It's even prettier than the one you had me in last week. It must be nice to have so many rooms you have a choice of which one to sleep in."

Elandra slid a chair close to the bed. "I'm glad you like it. I moved you in here because this one was bigger. And I added the lace spread and canopy because I remembered how you always wanted a canopy bed with a lace spread."

"How could you remember that? I told you that a long time ago."

"It stuck with me. All those little details about you stuck with me."

"The room is beautiful, Lani. I so appreciate you and Bradley letting me stay here."

"Our home is your home."

"Thank you." Crystal perused the elaborate design of the room. "You were always good at decorating a room. You could take a room and really make a person want to be in it. You could make a person want to live in it. You have a talent for that."

"I'm an interior decorator now."

"For real?" Mouth agape, Crystal sat up. "Bradley Davenport helped you get that job?"

"I work with his company. And stop calling him Bradley Davenport. You've been here three weeks and you're still calling him by his last name. He's going to be your brother-in-law for heaven's sake."

"I can't help it, Lani. He's so rich. I've never met anyone who had as much as he does."

"What about Wayne?"

Crystal chuckled dryly. "Wayne was a fraud. He wasn't as rich as people thought. He spent so much on the high life and paying those goons, he was up to his ears in debt. But he had many people do things for him because they thought he was so powerful, and could wreck their lives. He didn't really know about business. He wasn't smart at all. He was nothing like Bradley."

"You're right about that. His was dirty money."

Crystal looked to the side, as if ashamed. "What kind of person does that make me to fall in love with a man like that?"

Elandra reached over the covers, clutching her sister's chin, curving it so that it faced hers. "You were human, Crystal. And I'm sure you didn't know he was into this stuff when you became involved."

"I'm giving up on love. After what Wayne did to me, I couldn't take any more heartbreak. You have no idea."

"But yes I do."

"No, you don't! Your world is beautiful. You have a wonderful man who adores you. Anyone being around you can see how much Bradley loves you. And your heart has never been broken the way mine has. You might think so, with all the experiences you used to tell me about, but I've been in the major leagues."

"I do know what it's like, Crystal."

"You couldn't possibly know."

"Oh but I do. Remember Dan?"

"The guy you were dating? What happened?"

"Nothing except that he devastated me."

"How?"

"I caught him in the office one night with my boss."

"Joyce?"

"They were about to make love."

"Oh I'm sorry, Lani. I know how much you cared about him."

"I didn't just care, Crystal. For some odd reason, I loved him. He didn't treat me good at all, and I loved him. I didn't think I deserved better. And when he dumped me for Joyce, I vowed I would never fall in love again. You see, I was not only devastated over the break-up, I was also pregnant with his child."

"For real?"

"But I lost the baby after he hurt me. I had a miscarriage. So you see, I do know what your pain is like."

"Lani, I'm so sorry. I'm sorry I said you didn't understand."

"It's okay. I wouldn't have if I hadn't gone through that. I would be sitting up here with you trying to tell you how to get on with your life when I didn't have a clue. But I do."

"Tell me then. I'm desperate to feel something again. Sometimes I feel so dead inside. I wonder about my future and it seems so bleak. Like there is nothing to look forward to."

"But there is. There is life, and it can become so beautiful you won't even know what hit you."

"You can say that because you have Bradley."

"But I didn't have him when I came here. All I wanted was to find you. Falling in love was the farthest thing from my mind. But somehow a higher power than myself made our worlds weave together. I fought it to the death. Yet soon I just realized that I not only was so attracted to Bradley physically, but I was in love with his heart and soul as well. He's a good man, and he showed me that in every way possible. After a while, I couldn't deny what I felt inside. I was so in love with him. And he was just as deeply in love with me. He made me feel so good inside, so appreciated, so smart, so beautiful, so needed, so purposeful. He even gave me a reason to get out of the bed in the morning, by showing me that I had something to offer the world. Now I have a talent that I love to use. All the other times, I just had jobs. And I'm good at interior decorating. Damn good.

"He showed me that I had to believe in myself. That I had to think positive. That I was worthy of the best. And I started to feel that way inside, that things would turn out positive if you really hoped and prayed and took action to make sure they would. He's probably the reason that I never stopped looking for you. He kept my spirits up. He gave me love. He gave me understanding. He gave me himself."

"You're so lucky, Elandra. I'd give anything to have a love like that."

"You can have it. Men are going to approach you. You have to weed out the bad, and get to know the good. If someone does something to disrespect, or hurt you, or lessen you, he's not for you. A good man should bring your spirits up. He'll respect you. He'll make you feel as beautiful as a flower. He'll value you and treat you preciously. And you should treat him the same. Don't let the taste of love pass you by. It's a taste so sweet you don't ever want to let it go. You just want to hold it in your hands and savor it forever."

"Hurry up out of that room, you hussy," Daisy teased. Dressed in a soft peach chiffon gown, she divided her attention between powdering her skin before the mirror and glancing at an adjoining door.

"Yeah, hop to it, before Bradley decides to leave," Crystal added, making herself and all the women in the room chuckle. Adorned in a gown with a black velvet top and white satin bottom, she was stunning.

Several of the other women in the room, Bradley's maid, some of Bradley's cousins, his sister, and his mother, drew Daisy and Crystal into deep conversation with wedding disaster stories, hard and easy labors, and men who were good and others downright low-down. Interrupting their chatter in the throes of the tales, the door cracked slowly, widening and widening. When Elandra revealed herself in the doorway, their voices shut off for that instant. Every woman's mouth gaped open.

"You make a dashing groom," Richard complimented Bradley, admiring his white tuxedo with tails.

They were killing time in the anteroom, while a vocalist inspired the crowd with a stirring gospel song in the chapel. Bradley's brothers, friends and cousins had just left to be seated. The time was coming.

Adjusting his bow tie, Bradley strived not to feel nervous. "Thank you for the compliment. Guys like to know that they look all right."

"You do." Richard was grinning. "More than all right. Elandra's not going to believe her eyes."

"And I know I'm not going to believe mine. She's so beautiful. Lord knows, my woman is fine!"

Grinning, Richard stomped one foot. "Amen!"

"When I first saw her though, I was in my funk about women. So of course I noticed her face and body. Who could miss all that? But then I was like, so what—she looks good, but I'll be damned if she'll make me crazy and rob me blind. I yelled at her so loud, she took off and ran down the street so fast she was like lightning."

"Ha, ha, ha." Richard threw his head back laughing.

"But it all changed somehow." His mind trailed off to those days not so long ago. "She just got to me. I started seeing her in a whole new light. I loved the way she cared so much about her sister. That kind of love is rare. And I loved this innocence and honesty about her. And I could sense that her spirit could be so high, but I knew something or someone had darkened it. And when I started getting to know her better, I was right. She started opening up to me. And her spirit was bright and alive, just like a child's, but then again, so much woman."

"Fella, I think you're in love."

Joy radiated all over him. "I think so, too."

"I'm glad you took my advice on this one."

"I can never repay that priceless advice. The taste of love isn't something I want to miss out on. No way I would want to miss out on feeling this."

At that point, the adjoining door which led to the chapel opened. A cousin of Bradley's saluted him. "Aye-aye captain, it's time for sail."

Richard left the room, eager to escort the bride down the aisle. Bradley made a start to follow him, but as he did, he began swallowing. He adjusted his tie again. He played with the cuff links. When finally he stood in the front of the church, he continued fidgeting, adjusting his tie, his cuff links, his jacket, his shirt. All the while, an avalanche of family waited before him.

Unexpectedly then, it hit him. Mentally, he was right there again. It was that day in the church when he stood before the altar . . . and stood before the altar and stood before the altar. No bride glided down the aisle. Before long, he had to think of something to say to friends and family. Reliving it all, a knot formed inside his stomach. It fought its way up through his chest and throughout his throat and even up inside his head, making him dizzy, then came back down again to the back of his mouth. A sickness almost flew out of him. If it weren't for the nudge of calmness the bridal march's melody brought with it, there might have been an embarrassing incident.

The bridesmaids and the maid of honor, Crystal, strode down the aisle, appearing colorful, comparable to flowers in a garden. Bradley felt less sick, but was still fighting that fullness that ached to flee from him. It was only *her* that stopped it all.

Arm in arm with Richard, Elandra was riveted to her groom. Gliding down the aisle, she glowed and sparkled like the fine sequins on her gown. The taffeta and chiffon dress had a sweetheart neckline, with off the shoulder, short, gathered sleeves. Everyone adored the gorgeous fitted gown with the considerable train. It was complemented by her face, soft and exotic, surrounded by millions of loose, dangling curls.

It was her eyes, though, that entranced Bradley, as his eyes entranced her. And when Richard released her at her groom's side, solely the preacher's voice beckoned the dreaminess of this moment to him.

"Family, friends who are gathered here to see this man and this woman become husband and wife, we thank you for sharing this blissful event today. We also would like to share with you the bride and groom's thoughts to each other before I bless them with traditional vows. Elandra, you may start."

She faced Bradley, gently lacing his hands within hers. "I want to thank God for making this day, and most of all you, possible, Bradley Davenport. Thank you God, and Bradley for showing me a way out of the darkness. I admit there were times when I thought God had forgotten about me. When hell inhabited my world, knocking all the light, I just knew God had abandoned me. And to be honest, right at those moments, I abandoned him, too. I thought he was someone else's God. I thought he didn't want me. I thought he said to himself that I wasn't good enough for him.

"But I was wrong. He was with me all along. When I cried, he was listening. When I hurt, he was listening. When I couldn't sleep at night and had to lay in the dark, he was listening. God was listening and he answered my prayer. And that's you, Bradley.

"God not only made a way for me to get my sister back, he brought me love so beautiful it's like magic. It truly is. Real love. True love. It fills me up with so much joy twenty-four hours of the day. Bradley, you are the man I've been waiting all my life for. You are kind, caring, responsible, sensitive, intelligent, funny, and you have such a good heart, and lots of soul. Once I thought you would never exist in my world. Once I thought a man like that would never love someone like me. But now you've shown me that I'm precious and I deserve to be treated that way.

"But I'll never forget that you are precious also and deserve to be treated that way, too. I'll never hurt you, Bradley. Sometimes we may have minor disagreements." She chuckled. "Our little disagreements have even been fun sometimes." Her smile reflected his. "But God knows, I'll never, ever hurt you. I'll always treat you like the precious jewel you are. Because I know deep in my heart and soul how strong our love is. It's magical. I also know that if I searched the whole world over, I'd never, ever find a man as perfect for me as you.

"So again, I thank God for you. I thank him for sending me a man who'll love me, like I've never been loved before. It's still like a dream. But I guess this day confirms that it's real. It's real. Thank you. Thank you for vowing to share with me the love of a lifetime. I won't ever doubt you again, Lord. I know you're with me now. And I know you'll always be with me. Always. And I know you'll always have all my love, Bradley. And I know deep in my heart that I'll always have yours."

The preacher beamed. He tilted his head to Bradley.

Bradley kissed Elandra's hand, before meeting the sparkle shimmering in Elandra's eyes.

"I want to thank God, for his exceptional blessing to me today, and that is you, beautiful lady. A few years ago, I thought I would never get to this point again. I never wanted to get to this point again. I did everything to stay away from this circumstance, to stay away from this feeling I have now. But God had other plans for me. He showed me that I was wrong. He showed me that someone would love me. Love me for who I am. Love everything about me, and think I am one of the most precious gifts on this earth. I needed to feel precious. I know I'm a man, and I'm strong and fearless, but you know that I'm a human and I have needs and desires and emotions. I need love just as powerful and deep as anyone else. And that's what he gave me.

"I want to thank God for sending me you, Elandra. You're just as beautiful on the inside as you are on the outside, and anyone can see that is in abundance. When I get up in the morning and go through my day, there is going to be even more of a purpose to my life. I know that there is someone waiting for me. Someone who would rather be with me than anyone else on the earth. Someone who makes me feel like I'm a gift from God. Someone who I want to do everything for, because it makes me feel so good to see her smile, to feel her overwhelming happiness. Today, I thank you, dear Lord, for giving me this beautiful woman. I know it was you who brought us together. You know what I needed and you sent it to me. Everything is how it should be now. Everything is perfect in my world. For this is the woman of my dreams. And you all are my witnesses, I will love her with my whole heart and soul for the rest of my life. I'll be with her in sickness and health, for richer, for poorer, till death do us part. I'm going to do everything in my power to make Elandra happy. You'll see. You will see. I'm in love with you, Elandra, and I'm going to prove it to you for the rest of my life."

Dear Reader:

I hope you enjoyed the love shared between Elandra and Bradley in *Most of All*. I wanted their passion to touch your heart and bring something beautiful to linger in your thoughts. It's my great wish that this story becomes a movie.

Please feel free to let me know what you thought of *Most of All*, or even my debut novel, *Nightfall*. I would love to hear from you at

PO Box 020648
Brooklyn, New York 11202-0648

May all of you be blessed with the success and prosperity that Bradley and Elandra experienced, but *Most of All*, the love.

About the Author

Louré Bussey is a graduate of Borough of Manhattan Community College. She wrote 56 short stories for romance magazines such as *Bronze Thrills* and *Black Confessions,* before her best selling novel, *Nightfall* was published in 1996. A former secretary and administrative assistant, she is now pursuing a singing/songwriting career, along with writing novels. Her third novel, *Breathless Dreams* will be published in 1998. She lives in Brooklyn.

I thank God for blessing me, making this dream come true. I also want to thank those whose love and support inspired me while writing this book. To my son, Brandon, you're my precious gift. I'm blessed with your love and beautiful presence in my life. To my parents Carrie and William, you nourished me with your love and raised me with strength, which always tells me I can do anything I set my mind to. To my sister, Sharon, you're my best friend, a great supporter, and the most wonderful sister a person could have. To NB, you are a beautiful dream, a true blessing, and heaven-sent to bring joy to my world. To my editor, Monica Harris, I'm so grateful for your belief in me, your tremendous talent and for you bringing Arabesque romances to readers around the world.

Look for these upcoming Arabesque titles:

December 1997

VOWS by Rochelle Alers
TENDER TOUCH by Lynn Emery
MIDNIGHT SKIES by Crystal Barouche
TEMPTATION by Donna Hill

January 1998

WITH THIS KISS by Candice Poarch
NIGHT SECRETS by Doris Johnson
SIMPLY IRRESISTIBLE by Geri Guillaume
A NIGHT TO REMEMBER by Niqui Stanhope

February 1998

HEART OF THE FALCON by Francis Ray
A PRIVATE AFFAIR by Donna Hill
RENDEZVOUS by Bridget Anderson
I DO! A Valentine's Day Collection